THE HEART OF AN AGENT

ALSO BY TRACEY J. LYONS

The Adirondack Pinkertons Series

A Changed Agent (Book 1)

The Women of Surprise Series

A Surprise for Abigail (Book 1)
Lydia's Passion (Book 2)
Making Over Maggie (Book 3)

THE HEART OF AN AGENT

TRACEY J. LYONS

Waterfall
PRESS

Published by Waterfall Press, Grand Haven, MI

www.brilliancepublishing.com

Amazon, the Amazon logo, and Waterfall Press are trademarks of Amazon.com, Inc., or its affiliates.

ISBN-13: 9781542046671
ISBN-10: 154204667X

Cover design by Kirk DouPonce, DogEared Design

Printed in the United States of America

*This book is dedicated to the memory of my aunt
Virginia (Ginny) Davis, who also happened to be my
first-grade teacher. She made me promise not to call her
Aunt Ginny when we were at school.
Mrs. Davis . . . Aunt Ginny, this one's for you.*

Chapter One

Adirondack Mountains
Heartston, New York, 1892

The sun skimmed the horizon in the eastern sky, bathing the far hill-side in a pink morning hue. Lily Handland stood at the window in her bedroom on the second floor of the rooming house, watching for the man. At first, he was nothing but a speck on the horizon. But as he rode into the town, she began to make out his form. He sat tall in the saddle, dressed in black pants, a collared shirt, and a tan jacket that settled just below his thighs. Even though he wore the brim of his hat pulled low on his forehead, she could see the wisps of his straight brown hair. He stopped, as always, outside the wrought iron gate of the cemetery, dismounting and looping the reins three times over the hitching post. And today, as with every other day, he took his hat off before he unlatched the gate.

Gripping the hat in his hands, the man walked into the cemetery with his shoulders hunched and his head hung low. His steps faltered as he drew closer to his destination. Walking along a short row of four headstones, he knelt beside the last one. Lily's fingers tightened around the heavy curtain. The hat fell from his hands, landing on the soft earth. His head dropped back. He turned his face heavenward and cried out. His raw pain shook her to the core.

Lily knew she should look away, but she couldn't. Something kept her there by the window, pulling her to look out for him. She wiped tears from her eyes.

Finally, he picked up his hat and stood at the foot of the grave. She sensed a change in him. Whereas moments ago he'd been crying out in pain, now he stood silent and still. A yellow butterfly circled his head and dipped down to land on his shoulder. He didn't notice. The insect fluttered off to sip from the nectar of a beautiful red flower growing next to the fence. The man took the path back out to the road. He paused next to his horse. And then he looked up.

Their gazes met. Lines of fatigue stretched over his face and bracketed his eyes. She knew sorrow could bring even the strongest person down, but Lily saw something more troubling in this man's expression. His eyes, though reddened from his tears, seemed hollow, lifeless. Her heart broke for him.

He turned away. Untying the reins, he mounted the horse and rode back the way he'd come.

Lily left the window. As she moved about the small room she'd been renting for the past month, her thoughts tumbled through her mind. She worried about the man in the graveyard, wondering who it was he visited every day. She supposed it wasn't her concern. Yet after having watched him for so many days, she felt an odd connection to his plight. Perhaps it would be best if she put him out of her mind and concentrated on the day before her.

Lily's job as a Pinkerton agent had taken her many places, but none were as beautiful as the Adirondack Mountains. People came from far and wide to this sleepy New York town, nestled at the base of the towering high peaks, to fish in the magnificent crystal-clear lakes and to hunt the wild game that roamed the thick surrounding wilderness. Pine trees grew in such abundance that the area supported several lumber camps. The region was also known for the Great Camps that dotted the landscape. She'd heard that the camps carried all the amenities of city hotels, including long porches and rocking chairs where a person could sit and get their fill of the crisp air. Of course, Lily hadn't had time to enjoy any of those things; she'd been too busy pretending to be someone she wasn't.

Today that was all going to change.

She moved away from the window, pausing in front of a medium-sized trunk. She knelt and raised the rounded top. The black dress and bonnet that she'd worn when she'd been posing as a widow lay on top. Beneath that was the emerald-green ball gown that she'd had on the night she'd been tasked with enticing a certain gentleman to hand over the jewels he'd stolen. At the back of the trunk lay her most recent saloon girl finery, the frilly red dress with the black petticoat. They were all disguises of her past. Pushing those garments aside, she reached in, groping around until she felt the sack containing her savings.

She pulled it out and slammed the trunk's lid. Lily stood, thinking how the contents were the key to her future—her new beginning. She placed the cloth sack next to her reticule on the nightstand and crossed the room to the large wardrobe. Opening the doors, she looked at the modest dresses hanging in front of her. She selected her favorite light-blue dress, the one with the three-quarter-length sleeves and lace collar. Lily added a pair of side-laced white kidskin boots to her ensemble. She set the outfit on the bed and went about her morning ablutions.

After she got dressed, she walked back to the mirror to finish getting ready. She took great care in pulling her hair back from her face, and then she reached into a small jewelry pouch and took out a copper hair clip that had belonged to her mother. Lily carefully secured the clip at the back of her head, then ran her fingers gently over the raised scroll design.

Mama, I miss you. I'm thankful you're not here to see what I've done.

Doing a quick spin in front of the mirror, Lily felt refreshed. For the first time in a very long time, she'd be leaving this room without pretense. Her future lay beyond these walls. After carefully placing her money inside the reticule, she left the boardinghouse.

She stepped out into the summer sunshine. The warm air felt good against her skin. Off in the distance she heard children, and turning her head, she saw that they were playing in the school yard. She couldn't help but smile. Stopping at the edge of the walkway, she waited for a buckboard loaded with supplies to pass. Then stepping down, she crossed the street, heading to the Oliver Lumber Company office.

John Oliver, a semiretired Pinkerton agent himself, greeted her at the door. "Good morning, Lily."

She tipped her head back and looked up at her mentor, a man whose massive presence could fill any room. She noticed that his dark hair had started graying at the temples, but his blue eyes were still sharp as he took in her appearance.

"Good morning, John."

Stepping back, he said, "Looks like we're in for another nice summer day."

Lily looked back over her shoulder at the cloudless sky. "Indeed. I could get used to this sort of weather." She turned to follow him back to his office.

"Here, take a seat," he said, removing a pile of old newspapers.

Lily sat.

"So tell me what brings you by?"

Toying with the fringe on her reticule, she searched for a way to broach the matter of her service. After a few uncomfortable moments had passed, during which John watched her with increasing curiosity, she decided to take a direct approach. "I've fulfilled my duty to the Pinkertons, and I've decided to leave the agency. I've already written up my resignation letter."

Steepling his fingers under his chin, he studied her for a few seconds. "You've been a fine agent, Lily. One of the best. I don't think there will be any problems. If you can get me the letter, I'll sign off on it."

"I'd appreciate that." She pulled open the drawstrings of her bag and took out the letter. "I have it right here." She smiled, handing it across the desk.

After a cursory look, he signed the bottom. Setting it aside, he asked, "What are your plans for the future?"

"I think I'd like to stay in Heartston. After I leave your office, I'm going to the bank to open an account." She paused. "I have a fair amount of money saved. What I'd really like to do is have a business of some sort."

"Maybe you could open up an inquiry office."

Lily laughed. "Goodness! After years of chasing down criminals, the last thing I'd want to do is spy on my neighbors. I'm going to stay open-minded. I have a feeling that there will be an opportunity coming my way."

He rose and came around his desk to stand in front of her.

Lily stood. "Thank you for everything you've done for me, John," she said.

"I was only doing my job."

"We both know you did more than that," she replied.

He studied her for a moment, the wrinkles fanning out from his eyes deepened as he frowned. "Lily, I think you need to be prepared for what it takes to return to civilian life."

John Oliver had watched over her especially this past month. And for a long time before that. In the beginning of her career, he'd been in charge of her assignments. Several years ago he'd returned here to his hometown, to his family's lumber company. And then they'd worked this last case together. In some ways Lily owed him her life.

She brushed off his warning. "You were able to settle back into your former life with little trouble."

"I had a life to come back to, whereas you don't. You're going to be starting fresh."

Lily bit her lip, wondering why he was trying to put a damper on her future here. Pulling her shoulders back, she replied, "I'm sure I'll be fine."

He tipped his head, looking at her as if trying to read her mind. "I want you to be happy. You deserve that. But if you get into trouble, you know you can always come to me for help."

"I don't anticipate there being any trouble. Like I said, I'll be fine." She gave him a quick hug and left him to his work.

Once back out on the walkway, she turned left toward the center of the village. She found the bank and entered through a tall set of thick wooden doors. A desk sat in the middle of the room, facing the entry. Behind that was a long narrow counter with two small windows covered in bars. The man behind the counter was bald and middle-aged, and somehow the small spectacles he wore on his round face made him appear childlike. He smiled at her from behind the counter.

"A great, good morning to you, young lady!"

"Good morning to you"—she took a closer look at the name plaque on the front of his station—"Mr. Goodwin."

"What can I do for you?"

Walking up to the counter, Lily set her reticule between them. "I'd like to open a bank account. And would you happen to have some sort of safe box where I can keep some other items?"

He studied her, his sharp eyes taking in every inch of her face. Lily didn't know what he thought he might see in her, but she hoped that her being a woman wouldn't present a problem. She'd been independent for so long now that she didn't know what she'd do if he turned her away.

He came out from behind the counter, stopping in front of her with his hand out. "I'm Seamus Goodwin." He gave Lily's hand a rigorous shake. He must have noticed the question in her eyes, because he added, "My mother was Irish and my father from England."

Gently, she extricated her hand from his. "That's a nice solid lineage, Mr. Goodwin."

He squinted his green eyes at her. "Now might I know your name?"

"I'm Lily Handland." For so long she'd been using other names; it felt good to finally be using her real one. No more keeping secrets, no more pretending to be someone she wasn't. From today forward, Lily was going to be her own person. And opening an account here would be a good start toward securing her future.

Taking hold of her elbow, Mr. Goodwin led her to the desk. "Take a seat and let's see how I can be of service to you."

She sat on the edge of a spindle-back oak chair. She loosened the strings on her reticule until the fabric gaped open. Lily reached in and pulled out the cloth sack containing all her savings from the past five years.

"I need to open an account immediately."

Mr. Goodwin's eyes widened when he saw what she had placed in front of him. "Yes, you do." Regaining his composure, he asked, "I trust you came by this honestly? Because my bank has a good reputation."

Lily stiffened. She'd done a lot of things in the name of justice, but one thing was certain—her virtue remained intact. Using a firm tone, she said, "John Oliver can vouch for me."

"John Oliver, you say? His family was one of the first to settle here in Heartston. Very well, then." He opened the top desk drawer, pulled out a ledger, and opened the black leather binding. "I think it best if I give you your own page."

They spent the better part of the next hour setting up Lily's accounts. She felt relieved that he didn't pry into how she'd come to be in possession of such a large sum of money and bonds. Since she hadn't had a home for the past five years and nothing to invest her monies in, Lily had been carrying her stash around with her from town to town. Not the best decision, to be sure. But now that she'd decided to stay here, it was time to put her hard-earned money in a safe place. The First Bank of Heartston was a perfect spot.

"Mr. Goodwin, I'm also looking to do something with a portion of my savings. I'm hoping you might know if there are any business opportunities that might be fitting for a woman such as myself?"

He scratched his head and then readjusted his spectacles. "I don't know. Maybe I could see if Mrs. Mahoney is looking for someone to put some money into her seamstress shop. Between you and me, the place could use a little sprucing up."

Lily shook her head. "Aside from knowing how to thread a needle to stitch on a button, I don't have much use for sewing, Mr. Goodwin. Perhaps you could think of something else?"

"Well, now, there's the restaurant in the rooming house you're staying at. I know they've been wanting to expand for a few months now."

She shook her head again. There had to be something less domestic for her to be a part of. Lily couldn't help thinking that if the banker knew what she'd done to earn a living, he'd be of a different mind-set when it came to her future.

"Maybe I should simply open a new business," she said, thinking John's earlier suggestion about opening an inquiry office might not be such a bad idea after all.

"Now hold on a minute. I might have something that could be of interest to you." The man shuffled through the ledger and stopped at a spot near the middle. He stabbed his finger on the page. Raising his gaze from the book, he looked at her as if trying to determine her character. "Thing is, I'm not sure how open this particular gentleman would be to having someone help him out. He's a stubborn sort. More so now than ever before."

Lily's curiosity was piqued. She scooted to the edge of the chair. "Tell me about this business."

"It's one of the Great Camps. I'm sure you've noticed how many people arrive here daily. The weekends are the busiest times. The Murphy place used to be busy. Sometimes you couldn't get a reservation there for weeks. Owen Murphy and his wife worked hard to make their place a success. While not the largest camp, it offered all the amenities of the best ones." He paused for a moment, a solemn look on his face. "I'm afraid, after the tragedy, Owen let the business go into decline."

"There was a tragedy?"

"Yes, his wife died."

"Oh." She thought about the man she'd been watching at the cemetery every morning. That had to be Mr. Murphy. After all, Heartston was a small town, and the grief on his face seemed fresh. "That is terrible." She placed her hand over her heart, saying a silent prayer.

"Still, Owen assures me he wants to keep the Great Camp. I've been trying to find a way to help him out. I've managed to keep him afloat for months now. He hasn't returned any of my requests for a meeting."

"And yet, you still want to help him. I can see that, Mr. Goodwin."

"Yes, I do. Owen is a good man who has fallen on hard times." Mr. Goodwin took off his spectacles and rubbed his eyes. Putting them back on, he looked at Lily with a sudden shrewdness that startled her. "Make no mistake, Miss Handland, regardless of how I feel about the owner, I'm still in the business of making money. The fact is, if Owen doesn't listen to reason, I will have to serve him foreclosure papers. Your stopping by here today could be the answer to my prayers."

Lily doubted she was the answer to anyone's prayers. She wasn't proud of some things she'd done over the past few years, even if they were in the name of justice. She imagined there were few who would understand the circumstances that led her to be here today.

Still, she pondered the opportunity that the banker had placed before her. She didn't know anything about running a Great Camp. She imagined the proprietor would need to see to the guest accommodations and provide good meals. She recalled seeing advertisements in the local newspaper telling of parties and activities at those places. So there was that to consider. And did this Mr. Murphy have a staff in place to handle such things? The way Mr. Goodwin described the Murphy Camp gave Lily pause. Maybe it would be too much for her to take on.

And maybe the challenge was just the thing she needed to make a new start. She'd heard many a preacher say that everyone deserved a second chance. She wondered if that applied to someone like her.

"Tell me how you think it best to handle this situation."

"I feel you should go out there and see the place firsthand. Stay a few nights as a guest. Then you can decide if this is something you'd be interested in doing. The Murphy Camp is about an hour's ride outside of Heartston." Pulling out a clean sheet of paper, he drew a simple map and wrote out the directions. He handed her the paper.

She looked the directions over. The trip looked pretty straightforward. "I can rent a buggy and horse from the livery," Lily said, her plan already taking shape in her mind. "I'd like to get out there today, if possible."

"All right." Mr. Goodwin nodded. "You do understand that if you decide to do this, you may not see a return on your investment for quite some time?"

"I do." The thought didn't bother her at all. Lily had already decided she wanted to remain in the Heartston area. Anticipation built inside of her. This could be the new beginning she was looking for!

With the map in hand, she left the bank. She could barely contain her excitement as she made her way back to the rooming house. The heaviness of uncertainty that had surrounded her future for days began to lift.

The direction Lily took back to the boardinghouse brought her right by the cemetery. She slowed her steps as she neared the wrought iron fencing. The black scrollwork swirled in delicate circles on the tall gate, framing the date: "1800." A blue jay, perched atop one of the finials, squawked at her. She glanced at the bird, wondering if it was trying to intimidate her. Little did that bird know she'd been in far more frightening situations. It would take more than a few soulful sounds to scare her off.

Looking over the top of the fence, she studied the place where dozens of townsfolk had been laid to rest over the years. She thought about the man who'd been coming here day after day. His sorrow had been palpable. Because she'd watched him from her window, Lily knew the exact path he'd taken through the maze of headstones. Lifting her head, she could just make out the top of the grave site where he'd knelt. Her curiosity got the best of her. She sent the bird a determined look and pushed open the gate.

As if to say, *I warned you,* the creature fluttered open its wings and launched itself into the air.

A breeze blew through the cemetery, lifting the strands of Lily's hair from her face. When she reached the spot, the air stilled, as though waiting in anticipation to see what she would do next. A twig snapped under her foot as she moved closer. A strange feeling settled in the pit of her stomach, one she couldn't quite define. It wasn't fear, or trepidation. *No.* Something she couldn't quite put her finger on took hold of her. For a moment, Lily felt as if she were trespassing on sacred ground. The closer she came to the grave, the stronger the feeling became, until she thought perhaps she should heed the bird's warning and turn back.

But there was another, stronger pull tugging at her. Even though she suspected what she was going to find, Lily needed to see the name on the headstone. She read the inscription on the marble stone.

REBECCA LOUISE ALDEN MURPHY
BORN MARCH 5, 1869
DIED AUGUST 15, 1890
BELOVED WIFE TO OWEN

Lily stared at the name and then the date of Rebecca's death. Owen Murphy had been in a state of mourning for the better part of two years.

Chapter Two

"Mr. Murphy! Mr. Murphy!"

Owen heard the sharpness in his housekeeper's voice and spun his chair so that his back faced the door. He wanted nothing more than to continue to hide out in his office.

The day had been like every other day. He'd risen, dressed, had breakfast, and then had gone into town to visit his wife's grave. His darling Rebecca, the love of his life, had departed this earth, and every day since her death had been nothing short of an ocean of grief. Some days were better than others, but mostly Owen moved through the day in lifeless motion. While he was still a young man of eight and twenty years, he felt much older. He supposed the combination of his wife's death and his guilt and grief was to blame for his state.

"Owen!" This time her voice sounded from right outside the closed door.

He turned around to face the door. "Mrs. Cuddieback, you may come in."

The housekeeper entered the room in a flurry, her round face flushed with what he assumed was a bit of frustration toward him. She wore a white pinafore over her dark dress, and her hands were fidgeting with the long tie strings that secured it around her matronly figure. Her quick gaze swept through the messy room before finally settling on him.

"Mr. Murphy, I've made up three of the rooms and prepared the muffins for tomorrow's morning meal, just in case."

"Just in case what, Mrs. Cuddieback?" He stared at her. Owen knew he owed this woman a great deal more than just the wage he'd been paying her. Without Alice Cuddieback and her husband, Theodore, this place would have fallen into complete ruin. In the past they'd been able to charge top dollar for a room, but as the business stood now, Owen had been forced to lower the price for a second time.

"Just in case we get some travelers stopping by who might wish to stay here and take in some of the exhilarating mountain air for a few days. I expect now that the blackfly season has passed, business will pick up," she said, referring to the tiny pests that filled the sky with black clouds during the months of spring. The insect's bite was itchy and left behind reddened welts.

But blackfly season had ended weeks ago, and still they hadn't had a single guest at the Murphy Camp. They both knew it was more than blackflies keeping people away.

"You'll need to work on the list I left you earlier this week. Theodore can see to some of it."

Owen glanced from the housekeeper to the top of his desk where the list lay. He didn't see why fixing a garden gate to a garden that no one bothered tending anymore was of such great importance. Added to that was the stone walkway that needed to be reset, a rocking chair on the porch that needed to have one of the back slats replaced, and a broken windowpane in the kitchen. None of this mattered.

Except, it all mattered.

The older woman approached his desk. He could tell from her expression she was sharing his thought. Removing a cloth from the pocket in her pinafore, she swatted it around what empty space could be found on top of the desk. Dust motes flew into the air. "There now, that's a sight better—don't you think?"

He nodded, already weary, though it was only midmorning. Deep in his soul, Owen knew he had to find a way back to the living. A few months after his wife's death, he'd stopped going to church services. The kindness, the sympathetic stares—they were too much. He'd even stopped accepting invitations to lunches and dinners. Being around couples and families, seeing the happiness of others, people who could get up every day knowing their loved ones would be beside them, led him to shutting himself in his office for days after. Once there, he refused to open the curtains or eat a decent meal.

Even the banker in town, Mr. Goodwin, had been pestering him for the past few weeks to come in for a meeting, but Owen had put it off again and again. He knew he was behind on payments and that the banker had been more than generous with him. But the one thing Owen had a mind to do was visit her graveside every day. Instead of showing up for the appointment, he had found himself wandering over to Rebecca's grave, as if his feet had a life of their own.

Today, though, he'd felt a change. He'd knelt beside Rebecca's place in the cold earth, and it had been as if she were reaching out to him from beyond, telling him to let go, begging him to move forward.

Letting go of Rebecca was the last thing he wanted to do. He didn't want her short time in this world to become nothing more than a wistful memory. He could hold on to her for a little bit longer, couldn't he?

"Mr. Murphy . . . Owen. It's past time to move on. If you keep on this way, you'll end up losing everything. Rebecca wouldn't want you to be living like this."

He leveled his gaze on the woman, wondering if she was a mind reader now, too. "Don't you dare tell me what Rebecca would want." Saying her name out loud was like opening an old wound. Owen didn't need to be reminded of his failings. He turned back to face the window. He heard what sounded like a sniffle coming from Mrs. Cuddieback.

He couldn't stand to have her crying. Shutting his eyes, he knew he should apologize for the sharpness of his tone.

"Well then, if that will be all, I will leave you, sir."

"Mrs. Cuddieback?"

"Yes."

"Thank you for seeing to tomorrow's breakfast."

"You're welcome. There is supper set up for you in the kitchen. I'll stay in the main house for a while longer in case we get any guests."

"You are too kind to me; you know that, don't you?" Owen offered up an apology by way of his question.

"I know, Mr. Murphy."

Her confident response brought a small smile to his lips. He heard her footsteps fade, and then the latch of the door closing behind her. Silence descended on him once more.

Lily stepped out of the buggy she'd rented from the livery. Since there didn't seem to be anyone about to help with the horse, she tied the reins off at the hitching post at the bottom of the porch steps. Putting her hands on her hips, she gazed up at a three-story lodge that looked a lot like an enormous log cabin. A faded sign read "Murphy Camp." Each level was bordered by a porch punctuated at regular intervals by screen doors and rocking chairs. A nice place to relax.

The trim around the windows and doors had at one time been painted a bright red, but now the paint looked faded, and here and there Lily could see where it had chipped away. Neglected shrubbery grew wild around the foundation, and tall weeds crowded the rosebushes. She shook her head. This did not bode well. She feared what she might find on the interior of the property.

Reaching behind the buggy seat, she picked up her overnight bag and headed up the steps to the front door.

"Good afternoon!" A voice called out from above her.

Looking up, Lily paused midstep. "Oh, hello."

An older woman stepped outside and joined Lily on the third step. "Welcome to the Murphy Camp. Did you have a reservation?" The woman cast a worried look toward the doorway.

"No. I was out here exploring the woods and came upon your lovely accommodations. Will there be any problem getting a room?" Asking questions when one might already know the answer could be tricky, but Lily suspected she wasn't about to be turned away. After all, the sun was nearly setting, and if she had to go back to town, she'd be traveling alone through the dark woods. She fully intended to have that argument at the ready should she be asked to leave.

"And is there someone who can see to my horse?"

The woman nodded, a broad smile suddenly appearing on her face. "Yes. I can send my husband out."

They entered a good-sized room with a fireplace along the outside wall and some comfortable-looking chairs sitting at an angle in front of it. A settee that had seen better days faced a long set of windows with a serene view of what looked to be a pond or lake at the edge of the vast backyard. She followed the woman to a desk.

"Let me see what rooms are available." The woman made a great pretense of flipping through the first few pages of the ledger. "I can put you in the Franklin Room. It's right at the top of the first flight of stairs—not our most private location, but the room has a beautiful view of the woods and the lake. Now, if I might have your name?"

"I'm Lily Handland, and you are?"

The woman looked flustered. "Oh my goodness, forgive my rudeness. I'm Alice Cuddieback."

"Very nice to meet you, Mrs. Cuddieback."

"How many nights do you think you'll be staying with us?"

Lily supposed she'd be staying for as much time as it took to find out if this was a good investment. Her answer was quick.

"I'll be here for two nights." *That ought to be enough time to decide,* she thought.

The woman told her the price for the room and added Lily's name to the guest book. "Let me show you around down here first," she said. "That way you'll know where to come for all your meals. As you can see, the room we're standing in is where all our guests enter and gather for our afternoon teas."

Lily's nose twitched from a faint mustiness, which she hadn't noticed when she first entered the room. That would need to be seen to if she stayed on. Following Mrs. Cuddieback through a door off to the far corner of the room, she found herself in a dining room. A large china cabinet that housed a collection of white dishes sat close to a large table with enough chairs to seat at least a dozen people. The windows along the back wall overlooked the water and a wooded area.

Mrs. Cuddieback led her through a swinging door to the kitchen, and the most scrumptious scent filled the air. Steam rose from a pot on the back of the stove with a low flame underneath it.

"What is that delicious smell?"

"Oh. That's my midweek stew. I'll be serving it up for dinner later."

"Mrs. Cuddieback, are you expecting any other guests tonight?"

"Um . . . no. You'll have the place all to yourself for your short stay." She gave Lily a forced smile. "We've been slow this week."

"I see." The banker had told her how the Murphy Camp had fallen on hard times, but he'd been kind in his assessment. The place appeared to be empty, save for her and the woman giving her the tour. "Might I ask, is the owner of the place about?"

"Mr. Murphy? He is here, but he's very busy. I'm afraid you won't be able to meet him."

Lily knew when a person was lying. And Alice Cuddieback wasn't very good at it. There was no doubt in her mind that Mr. Murphy had something going on. If Mr. Murphy's behavior at the cemetery was any indication, he was more than likely shut away in a back office somewhere, avoiding his guests. Again, she felt a tug of sympathy on her heart. Taking a breath, she reminded herself that an investment was an investment, not a charity. In a few short weeks, this entire place could be owned by the bank if he didn't take charge. Lily frowned, thinking how sad it would be if this beautiful place was lost.

"That's all right," Lily said. "Perhaps tomorrow I'll run into him."

Mrs. Cuddieback shook her head. "I'm not sure he'll be about then." But then the housekeeper's face brightened. "Come along. I want to show you my favorite room," she said, her voice animated. "This is the great room, where we have our entertainment. There's a grand piano. Do you play, Miss Handland?"

"I'm afraid I don't." Lily followed the woman through another doorway and down a short hall lined with tall cabinets. "What do you keep out here?"

"All sorts of things. Skis and snowshoes, for one. This is also where you'll find the lawn tennis set and horseshoes. We keep the oars and paddles for the boat and canoe down by the lake in a shed. I can take you around outside tomorrow if you'd like."

"Oh, I wouldn't trouble you for that. I may take a walk along the paths after breakfast."

"Yes, that's the best time to be out there. Take care in the afternoon, though. The heat brings out the bees."

"Thank you for the warning."

Lily noticed their trek through the house had brought them almost full circle, back to the room that overlooked the front porch. Three tables dominated much of the space, one set with a checkerboard, another with decks of playing cards, and the last with a stack of periodicals. Books and knickknacks lined the floor-to-ceiling shelves on one wall, and across the room, near a grouping of sofas and chairs draped in sheets was a massive stone fireplace with the head of a brown bear mounted above. A large woven rug covered the center of the room. The grand piano, also covered with a dust cloth, looked as if it hadn't been played in a very long time.

It wasn't hard to imagine what this room would be like filled with guests just back from a hike or a boat ride. Lily pictured the appetizers Mrs. Cuddieback would pass around while the ladies sipped tea and the men enjoyed a bit of a repast. Perhaps someone from the village would be here, playing sonatas on the piano. The game tables would be filled, too. Her mind wandered as she followed the woman past a closed door.

"Wait," Lily said. The sound of her voice halted the woman's pace.

Mrs. Cuddieback turned to look over her shoulder. "Do you have a question?"

"Yes." Pointing to the door, Lily looked at it with curiosity. "What's in there?"

"That room is not open to visitors, I'm afraid."

They hurried past the closed-off room and back out to the spot where they'd begun.

"I'll have a light dinner ready for you in an hour if that suits you?"

"Yes."

"Good. As soon as I get you settled, I'll set a place for you in the dining room." The woman picked up Lily's bag and headed for the staircase.

Rushing over to her, Lily took the bag from her. "There's no need for you to show me to my room. You said it was located at the top of the stairs? I can find it on my own. Please don't go to any more trouble on my behalf."

"It's not any trouble at all." The woman bustled ahead of her. "I'm sure you'll find the room to your liking. I always keep it ready just in case we get an unexpected visitor such as yourself."

Lily handled the bag and followed Mrs. Cuddieback up the stairs. Her accommodations turned out to be better than she'd expected. There was a large four-poster bed and a fireplace flanked by two windows. What she hadn't noticed before was that the porches wrapped around to the back of the building. Opening the porch door, she stepped out into the late afternoon. Sunlight dappled through the trees, leaving mottled shadows on the wooden decking. The view was stunning. Lily spotted several rooflines in the distance, peeking out from beneath the canopy of trees.

"Are those buildings part of this property?"

"They are. In the past we've put families with young children out there."

Lily's gaze trailed along until she saw the lake.

"What kind of birds are those?" she asked, pointing to the black-and-white-spotted birds bobbing up and down in the water.

"They are called loons. Quite lovely, aren't they?"

"Yes."

"I'll leave you to unpack and see you shortly for supper. I'll ring the dinner bell so you'll know when to come down." Mrs. Cuddieback left her alone.

Reluctant to leave the view, Lily stepped back inside the bedroom and took her nightclothes out of her bag. After laying them out on the bed for later, she found a nightstand with a mirror and some necessities. She picked up a hairbrush and ran it through her hair before carefully pinning the long strands back in a simple bun at the nape of her neck. Running her hands along the front of her dress, she wondered about that closed-off room downstairs. What lay inside? Could it be where Mr. Murphy kept to himself? Or was it some sort of room dedicated to the memory of his dead wife?

She thought about going down and seeing if she could access the room, but then quickly decided against the idea. Lily gave herself a mental shake. She should be ashamed, thinking that she could break in to someone's private room. Maybe John Oliver had been right, and she would be wise to put her Pinkerton ways behind her. Lily wondered if she'd ever be able to forget those days. And what if Mrs. Cuddieback caught her? She'd toss her out for sure.

Lily opened the door to the outside and wandered the length of the porch until she came to another door like hers. Trying the handle, she found it locked. She pressed her face up against the glass. Another bedroom, but this one was in great disrepair.

The bed and what looked like a small dresser and a rocking chair were all covered in white dust cloths. Sunlight reflected off a rather large cobweb hanging from a small mantel. This room either hadn't been used in a very long time or was waiting for some sort of renovation. Lily left the door and continued in the same direction until she came to yet another room. She'd hoped for something better, but the cracked panes of glass on this door were a disappointment. Using great care not to knock them loose, she peered in. Her eyes widened in surprise at what she found on the other side.

Pieces of ceiling plaster lay in chunks on the dusty floor. Someone had leaned what looked to be parts of a bed up against one wall. A broken lamp and a rolled-up carpet blocked the hall door. This was far worse than anything she'd expected.

Moving on, she rounded a corner and let out a gasp.

Dipping behind the towering pine trees that covered most of the landscape surrounding the lake, the sun had begun its descent. Loons fluttered their wings and took flight, the lake's surface rippling in their wake. The air stilled. From a distance came the sound of an owl, just as a deer stepped out of the shadows to drink from the water's edge. A moment later, when the deer was joined by a pair of speckled fawns, Lily's breath caught in her throat. Never in all her travels had she seen such beauty. She felt a tug in her soul. It was easy to see why Owen Murphy and his wife had settled here. This place was home.

And in that moment, she realized this picturesque scenery was why people came here—to take in the peace and remarkable pristine beauty that was the Adirondacks. She understood why the banker had fought so hard to help Mr. Murphy. Lily knew, as she watched the last traces of sunlight scatter over the lake's surface, that this business needed to be saved.

The sound of a bell interrupted her thoughts. Lily made her way back to her room and down to the dining room, where she found a single place setting at one end of the long table. The housekeeper entered the room with a tray full of food.

"Mrs. Cuddieback! I can't dine in here all alone. This is too much."

"This is where all our guests eat their supper," she said, setting the tray down next to Lily's plate. "We've been doing it that way for years. There's no sense changing our ways now."

Lily let out a frustrated sigh. "All right. But tomorrow I can take my meals in the great room at one of those smaller tables."

"I'm afraid Mr. Murphy won't like that."

"Well, when I meet him, I'll ask him about the change."

Again Mrs. Cuddieback gave her head a shake at the mention of Lily and the owner meeting.

"I will have a chance to tell him how lovely this property is, won't I?" Lily asked.

Ignoring her question, the woman set down a steaming bowl of stew for Lily. A basket of warm bread and a small plate of churned butter followed. Then she took a pitcher of water from the sideboard and filled a tall glass.

"There is pie on the sideboard for your dessert," she said, setting the glass in front of Lily. "Please help yourself when you're ready."

"Thank you, Mrs. Cuddieback. Won't you join me?" Lily would feel better if she had some company while she ate.

"Oh no! I've got work to do in the kitchen and then I'll be off to my rooms. My husband and I have quarters off to the back of the house, behind the kitchen. We serve breakfast between six and nine in the morning. Guests take their lunch at noon, unless you'd like me to pack a picnic basket. That would require an extra fee be added to your stay.

Should you need anything at all, just ring the bell on your nightstand. I'll hear it."

"I'll be fine, thank you."

"Have a good night."

The woman left her alone to dig in to the stew. Lily must have been hungrier than she thought; in no time at all, she'd finished off the entire bowl. After that, she helped herself to a large piece of apple pie, all the while wondering when the elusive Mr. Murphy would emerge from hiding, and what he would say to her offer.

Chapter Three

Owen sat up in the chair, rubbing the sleep from his eyes. He'd spent yet another night in his office, waking every so often. He rarely slept in the room he'd shared with Rebecca, and his office was as good a place as any to collapse after a long day. Some nights he even managed to make it to the sofa. Not last night, though. He'd been annoyed with Mrs. Cuddieback, even though he knew he owed her and Theodore a great deal. After she'd left him, he'd drifted off.

His stomach grumbled as he turned to the window and pulled aside the heavy curtain. Dawn was just beginning to light the edge of the woods. Owen thought he might get up and go to the kitchen to see what Mrs. Cuddieback had left him for breakfast. Then again, maybe he'd sit and stew a bit longer about the upcoming day.

He heard a floorboard creak above his head. Thinking it was the wind blowing against the house, he turned around to look at the top of his desk for a match. After taking one from the box, he struck it and touched it to the wick of a lamp. A soft glow covered the surface of the desk.

Owen reread the list from last night. He pulled another piece of paper closer to the light so he could read it over. Then he heard the noise again.

"What the devil?" He knew Mrs. Cuddieback wasn't about yet. Except for the two days last year when she'd been stricken with a bad cold, the woman arrived at the kitchen a half hour before six each and every morning. Glancing at the sky, he knew the time to be near five.

The floorboards above his head creaked. There was someone or something up there! Owen got up and headed out the door into the great room. Making his way through the room to the front entry and up the first set of steps, he noticed the door to the Franklin Room was ajar. He tiptoed over and peered around the edge of the door. Someone had been there. The bed was unmade and a small overnight bag rested at the foot of the bed. A light floral scent lingered in the room. Save for that, the room stood empty.

After a quick turn in the hallway, he walked in the direction of the muted creaks and thumps. His pulse rate picked up as he drew closer to the last bedroom on this floor. At one time it had been the room he and Rebecca had shared. When the camp had become more popular and rooms were at a premium, they'd taken up residence on the third level. It had been months since he'd set foot inside that doorway.

He stopped when he saw the shaft of light under the closed door. Owen did not believe in ghosts. At that moment, though, the thought occurred to him that there could be a spirit inside that room. Shivers ran down his spine. He paused outside the door. Holding his breath, he waited.

The light went out. Owen stepped to one side of the door so he could capture whoever would soon cross the threshold. The handle turned. Just as the door opened, he jumped in front of it.

"Ahhh!" a woman screamed.

Owen was so relieved to see an actual person and not an apparition that he darn near fainted.

He grabbed at her arm, pulling her out of the room and into the hallway. "Who are you and what are you doing prowling around here?"

"Let go of me!" She tried to squirm free of his grip.

"Not until you answer me."

She shoved an elbow into his side.

"Ouch!" He released his hold on her and rubbed the spot below his rib cage where her elbow had connected. "I'll ask you again; who are you and why are you in this room?"

The woman stood about half a head shorter than him and was of a slender build. He watched as she pulled the tie on her wrapper tighter around her waist. The morning light slid through the window at the end of the hallway, giving him enough light to see that her hair was long, falling just below her shoulders. Even with the dim lighting, he could see the light red color of it. That gave him pause. Owen didn't think he'd ever seen a red-haired woman before.

She cleared her throat, drawing his attention back to his questions. "I'm a guest here."

Her voice came out sounding soft and confident. He knew the guest book had been empty for days now, so maybe she had wandered in off one of the trails while he'd been brooding in his office.

"When did you arrive?" he asked.

"Late yesterday afternoon."

"I see." He reached behind her and pulled the door closed. "You shouldn't be wandering around in the dark."

"I'm sorry. I thought I'd heard a noise and came to investigate."

He raised an eyebrow, looking down at her and noticing that her eyes were blue with tiny brown flecks. "Don't you think that was a dangerous thing to do?"

"Well . . . I . . ." She stumbled over her words, looking up at him. "Yes. Yes, I guess there could have been something or someone in there who might have wanted to hurt me. But there wasn't. So you see, I'm fine."

She walked down the hallway and paused in front of the door to the Franklin Room. He stared at her back as she stood there waiting with one hand poised over the glass doorknob. He knew he should probably see her safely inside. Instead, Owen stayed transfixed at the opposite end of the hallway. The heady scent of her flowery perfume lingered in the air. Closing his eyes, he inhaled.

The scent tickled his senses, triggering a memory—the day he and Rebecca had first come here. They'd stood at the bottom of the overgrown walkway, hugging in their joy at finding the perfect place to start their new life together. His heart swelled inside his chest. He could feel the softness of his wife's curves nestled in his arms. The snick of the doorknob turning shocked him back to the present.

Rebecca was gone. He looked down the long passageway to where the woman had disappeared into the guest room. He stood alone in the hallway. This was his reality now. He moved down the hall, pausing outside her door to listen. He heard a rustling of what sounded like bedding being moved. He raised his hand to knock and then lowered his arm to his side. He'd best leave her alone. Perhaps he'd see her again at breakfast, where he could apologize for his sharpness.

He went downstairs to the kitchen, where he found a covered cake dish filled with breakfast muffins. He'd have to talk to Mrs. Cuddieback about leaving out such large portions. So wasteful. Carefully removing the glass dome from the plate, he reached for one of the sweets. He took a bite, thinking about the guest. How on earth had she even found the place? And was she traveling alone?

He knitted his brows together, wondering if that were the case. When he'd peeked into her room, he hadn't seen evidence of anyone else. Perhaps someone had dropped her off and then left to go back to town.

Maybe she'd come out on a birding expedition, or she could be an artist, here to draw one of those nature sketches visitors to these parts were so fond of doing. It had been so long since there'd been anyone here other than himself and the Cuddiebacks that Owen didn't know what to make of the situation. He supposed the young woman might want to go for a hike or possibly paddle around the lake. At any rate, Mrs. Cuddieback could see to her needs. The day hadn't even gotten off to a start yet, not counting the run-in with the lady upstairs, and Owen already felt weary. He took what was left of the muffin and went back to his office.

He wasn't there more than ten minutes when a light knock sounded at his door. Thinking it was Mrs. Cuddieback coming to do her morning check on him, he called out, "What lists have you for me today, Mrs. Cuddieback?"

The door opened ever so slightly, admitting the slender woman from upstairs. He sat up with a start. "What the dickens? The dining room is out there." He waved his hand through the air as if that would be enough direction for her.

"I know where the dining room is, sir."

"Then why aren't you in it?"

Leaving the door partway open, she stepped into his room. His inner sanctum. His dungeon. The last thought gave him pause. He sat behind the desk, waiting to see what she was up to. It was highly unorthodox to have a guest come to his office, especially at this hour. And he still couldn't quite get it out of his head that this woman appeared to be unchaperoned.

"I arrived yesterday afternoon. Apparently you were too busy to greet your only guest."

He blinked at her boldness. "I had things to tend to."

"I had to have dinner alone."

"I am sorry about that." He ran a hand through his hair. He couldn't remember the last time he'd gone into town to visit the barber. Making an effort to look presentable, he shifted around in the chair, tucking in his shirt.

"What can I do for you, Miss . . . I'm sorry, I don't know your name."

"My name is Lily Handland. And you're Owen Murphy, owner of this Great Camp by the same name?"

She sauntered around his office, looking at the prints on the far wall. She'd changed out of her nightclothes into a light-blue day gown, and her red hair was tied off in a matching ribbon, the locks skimming the top of her shoulders. Pausing in front of the fireplace, the woman trailed her fingers along the edge of a gilt frame. Owen knew the picture well. It was the last one he'd had taken with his wife. He stood up, walked to the fireplace, and snatched the picture off the mantel.

"I'm sorry." Miss Handland looked up at him with understanding, and perhaps a bit of pity. Well, he didn't need her pity. He still didn't know why she had come to see him.

"Miss Handland, I've a very busy day ahead of me, and I would appreciate it if you could state your business and go on about your day. I'm sure Mrs. Cuddieback is almost ready with your breakfast." As if on cue, the fragrant scent of fresh hotcakes wafted into the room.

She moved by him and stopped to lean against the corner of his desk. "I was going to wait until later to discuss this with you, but I woke this morning with so many ideas floating around in my head."

The last of Owen's patience left him, and his next words came out harsher than he intended. "Discuss what with me?"

She swept her arm in front of her body. "This. All of this." She stopped moving and looked him straight in the eye. "I've seen all I need to see," she said in a firm voice.

He had no idea what she was going on about. "I'm sorry, are you leaving? You only just arrived."

And then she smiled, and her eyes sparked with a light he could only describe as hopeful. That's when Owen felt a shift in the atmosphere.

"No, Mr. Murphy. I'm not leaving. In fact, I think I'll be staying for quite some time. I have a business proposition for you."

Lily had trouble understanding why the man sat there in a darkened room like an undertaker when outside lay one of the most beautiful landscapes she'd ever set eyes upon. She wanted to draw him up out of his chair and make him see the surroundings the way she did—the lush forest and a sky so blue it almost hurt her eyes to look upon it.

Still, Lily knew something about deep emotional pain, and she could almost feel it in every breath he took. Staring into his dark eyes, she saw his anger, and perhaps a bit of wariness. She supposed she deserved a bit of that. After all, she had barged into his inner sanctum and at a very early hour.

Lily drew in a breath, waiting for him to send her packing. She expected as much. But she hoped he might disappoint her and at least hear her out.

"You're a woman. What does a woman know of any business?" He spun his chair to face the window.

She softly expelled the breath she'd been holding. Although she'd been prepared for this to be an issue, she hadn't expected "you're a woman" to be his first line of attack. Her Pinkerton instincts pricked. His being defensive meant that she'd hit a nerve. Lily decided to use a gentler persuasion.

"I know that this was probably at one time a lovely place to come for a respite." She walked over to the long window and drew back the heavy green velvet curtain. "Out there are mountaintops to climb and fresh, clean air to breathe. But you are aware of that."

She looked at him out of the corner of her eye, wondering how he would respond to her next statement. "I imagine you used to get a lot of visitors."

He grunted, gave her a quick glance, and avoided making eye contact. "I still don't see why you're concerned with my business. How did you even come to know about this place?"

Lily knew she had his attention; she had to tread carefully now. Revealing what she knew about his past would be a mistake. And yet she didn't want to fabricate the truth. She was tired of spinning tales. She'd spun so many over the past years that at times she pictured them to be like the balls of yarn her mother used to keep in a basket beside the fireplace . . . waiting to be unraveled. The memory gave her pause. She hadn't thought about the old days in a long time. She turned her full attention to Mr. Murphy.

"I heard about it from a friend in Heartston." That wasn't far from the truth; albeit, Mr. Goodwin was more of an acquaintance than a friend. "I was looking for a place to spend a few days resting, and my friend suggested I come out here."

He gave her a wistful look. "I guess I should be thankful I still have any friends left. But if I'm to understand correctly, after one night at the Murphy Camp, you've decided this place could use your help. I may have been keeping to myself over the past few years, but I'm not daft." He stood. "Tell me what you're really doing here."

Lily straightened her spine. "I'm here looking for an investment opportunity, and my friend suggested you might be interested in partnering with someone."

"That is a preposterous idea!" He looked her over. "Tell me the name of this so-called friend."

She hesitated to give up the banker. Mr. Goodwin had warned her about Mr. Murphy's unwillingness to listen to reason when it came to saving his business. Lily needed to come up with a different way to approach this—and quick—because she had a feeling the man was fixing to toss her out.

"Let me guess; you are really here to *buy* the Murphy Camp. Well, I'll tell you what I've told all the others: the Murphy Camp is not for sale."

"Mr. Murphy. I don't want to buy the camp—I want to partner with you."

He didn't look the least bit convinced. He turned away and walked to the door with a determined stride. "I would like you to leave the premises, immediately."

He opened the door only to find Mrs. Cuddieback standing on the other side, her mouth agape and a full breakfast tray in her hands.

"Mr. Murphy, that is no way to speak to the lady," Mrs. Cuddieback said. "And what's this nonsense about tossing out the only guest we've had in weeks?" She pushed past him and bustled into the room. "I'll not be hearing of it!" She set the tray on the desk with a loud thump.

Taking a step toward the desk, Lily placed her hand over the woman's. "It's fine, Mrs. Cuddieback. I'm afraid I've upset Mr. Murphy. There's no need for him to make any explanations."

"You're not going to be leaving us, are you, Miss Handland?"

Before she could form an answer, a knock sounded at the front door of the lodge. While Mrs. Cuddieback hurried away to admit the visitor, Lily worked at coming up with a way to convince Mr. Murphy to at least consider her offer. She felt deep down in her bones that this was right. With her funds, they could bring this place back to life. And maybe the man who stood before her could find his place again. She knew nothing about mourning the loss of a beloved spouse, but that didn't mean she couldn't understand those feelings.

"Mr. Murphy, if I might try to explain my reasons for being here, again—"

He held up a hand. "Stop! I already know why you're here. You want to take what's mine and my—"

His words were cut off by the arrival of the banker.

"Ah, Owen, I see you and Miss Handland have met and are talking. Good. Good." Mr. Goodwin burst through the doorway, carrying a large brown satchel and smiling at them. "Your housekeeper was kind enough to offer me some coffee and a taste of her freshly baked blueberry muffins. I told her to bring them to me in here. I hope that's all right?"

"Yes. Yes. Forgive my manners. Won't you come in, Mr. Goodwin?" Folding his arms across his chest, he studied his two unwanted guests for a moment and then scowled. His voice rose a notch as he asked, "You two know each other?"

"I met Miss Handland yesterday when she came to my bank looking for an investment. I sent her here, Owen."

Lily shifted her weight from one foot to the other, wanting nothing more than to throttle the banker. She'd been working Mr. Murphy in her own way. Clearly, he needed to be handled gently. Now by blurting out their entire plan, Mr. Goodwin may have overplayed their hand. She expected to be escorted to the door and off the property.

"Why would you do such a thing?" Mr. Murphy asked, his voice rising in anger.

"I've been telling you for months now that you need to do something to shore up your finances. I don't think you want to throw away what you and Rebecca worked so hard for." Mr. Goodwin placed his satchel on the desk and flipped open the latch. "I took the liberty of bringing along some papers, just in case."

"Just in case what?" Mr. Murphy crossed the room in long strides and stopped by the side of the desk.

Lily's head practically spun as she looked from one man to the other, afraid she may have to intervene. Mr. Murphy's face had turned a beet red. Lily feared he might harm the banker.

"In case we can talk some sense into you. Owen, I'm afraid this is your last chance. You either take Miss Handland's money and sign these finance papers, or you refuse"—he paused to tap a finger on the second sheaf of papers—"and I proceed with the foreclosure papers. Take my word for it: I've done everything within my power so it doesn't have to come to that. So, which is it going to be?"

Chapter Four

Owen couldn't form a single thought. His stomach rolled with emotion. How could he give up even a portion of what he and Rebecca had built? This had been their dream . . . their life. And it had died two years ago the day she'd left this earth.

Then he asked himself, why hadn't he sold the place before it had come to this? How could he have let their dream fall into a state of such disrepair?

The answer came quickly. This was the last place he and Rebecca had been together. He couldn't bear the thought of leaving here. He'd clung to what little he had left as if it were his life raft. But to give up even a portion of this to some stranger . . . Owen's hands began to tremble.

He closed his eyes, knowing he needed guidance. He could almost hear Rebecca's voice telling him to pray. He *knew* he should be praying for strength, praying for some sort of divine guidance.

Dear Lord, show me the way. Help me. Please. Those were the only words his troubled mind could form. He could feel the eyes of Miss Handland and Mr. Goodwin upon him.

"Owen, I need your answer now." The banker picked up the straight pen on the desk, dipped it into the inkwell, and held it out to him.

Owen moved with leaden feet. He took the straight pen from Mr. Goodwin, unable to make eye contact with either of them. Bending slightly, he scrawled his signature across the papers that would seal his fate. He wanted to take the papers and burn them in the fireplace. He was losing his wife all over again. Leaving the straight pen on the desk, he then spun on his heel and left the room.

He hurried through the house, pushing open the door at the far end of the entry hall. Once outside, he took in a lungful of crisp air and blew it out on a shaky breath. A family of gray squirrels skittered along the branch of a pine tree, launching themselves onto the roof. They scampered overhead. Owen knew he should be worried about their nesting in the eaves. But his thoughts were not on preparing for the fall or winter ahead.

"Mr. Owen?"

Mrs. Cuddieback's concerned voice sounded behind him.

Shoving his hands into his pants pockets, he waited for her to join him. "There are going to be some changes happening," he said with resignation.

She stood alongside him, smelling like freshly baked bread and goodness. He supposed he could use a little of both today.

"Change could be a good thing; don't you think?"

He shrugged. "I'm not ready."

"You have no other choice. I've watched this place fall to ruin. Owen, I understand your pain, but it's time to move forward. No one is telling you to forget Rebecca. Maybe you need to think of this as a way to honor her memory."

"Do you know what I did?" He didn't wait for her response. "Today I entered into an agreement with one Miss Lily Handland. A woman."

"At this point, I don't think it matters if you are partnering with a man or a woman. The fact is this place can now be saved."

He looked down at the angel who had stayed here even when he couldn't afford to pay her or her husband a decent wage. For the first time, it occurred to him that more lives than just his had been hanging in the balance.

"I did what had to be done." The words sounded mighty, yet Owen wondered how long it would be before he felt good about the decision. If one wanted to call it that. Mr. Goodwin had given him an ultimatum. He'd had no choice except to take the offer.

He looked around at the land that belonged to him, thinking that God had truly left his mark here. The tall pines stood proud against the blue sky, the grove stretching on for hundreds of acres. Owen and Rebecca had come upon this property when it was nothing more than a run-down farmhouse stuck in the middle of the wilderness. In five years they'd managed to clear a road big enough for a sturdy wagon to come in with no trouble at all. They'd refurbished all the rooms in the main house, starting with cleaning out the old squirrel nests and scrubbing the dirt off the walls. Owen had built bed frames using tree limbs he'd found on the property. They'd even managed to make three of the smaller cottages livable by adding beds and small private indoor dining areas.

They'd done most of the work with their own hands, along with the help of a few bank loans. It had been a long time since one of those wagons had delivered guests to the house. And due to his neglect, most of the guest rooms were in need of renovations. Some of the repairs were minor, but a few of the rooms had suffered serious water damage during one of the storms that had blown through in the spring. Owen knew full well he should be thanking the banker for bringing that woman here.

As soon as that thought entered his mind, an image of his wife followed—her face pale as she lay on their bed, breathing in her last breath. He closed his eyes, as if he could shut out that image. In its place came the image of Lily Handland picking up his wife's favorite vase, the one that sat on the piano in the great room, as if she owned it. He opened his eyes, knowing he couldn't bear to part with one inch of what had been touched by his wife.

He'd no idea what to expect from his new *partner*—a partner he knew nothing about beyond the banker's hastily formed opinion of her reliability. For all they knew, she could be here to pick him clean. But Owen didn't think that was true. Why on earth would anyone in their right mind, most particularly this woman, want to come here, to the middle of nowhere, to start a new life?

Owen wanted nothing more than to go back to hiding out in his office. But once again Mrs. Cuddieback interrupted his thoughts.

"My husband wanted to know if you'd be coming to look at the vegetable garden. We're having a problem with some woodchucks getting in under the fencing," she said, referring to the large, voracious brown pests that liked to get into the chicken coops to steal the eggs and ravage the plants in the garden. "I can't help him fix the hole they've dug. Would you have some time later today?"

He couldn't very well leave the project to the caretakers to deal with on their own. "Tell Theodore to give me half an hour. Then I'll come out to help."

Leaving her on the porch, he trudged back into the house, ready to set some rules for the officious young woman who'd just bought a piece of his soul. Entering his office, he stopped midstep.

"What do you think you're doing?" he asked, a low growl erupting from his throat.

Miss Handland had made herself at home behind his desk. She'd been busy stacking papers in neat little piles.

"I'm sorting out this stuff. Gracious me, Mr. Murphy! Some of this correspondence has been sitting here for months. Why, you never even opened half of them." She picked up a square envelope and opened the flap, pulling out a single white sheet of stationery. "This woman wanted to know if she could bring her family here for two weeks."

Owen wanted nothing more than to make her disappear. He opened his mouth, fully prepared to respond to her indignation, but then snapped it closed. From the determined look on her face, he knew there would be no stopping her onslaught of words.

Miss Handland looked over the top of the envelope at him. "That was exactly one year ago, Mr. Murphy. And here!" This time she plucked a cream-colored note card from the pile. "This couple wanted to stay here for a weekend after their wedding nuptials this past spring." She rose from the desk and walked around to stand before him.

Owen realized he hadn't cared about the mail for a long time. Just another part of his downfall, he supposed. But what did she want him to do now? Certainly not answer all these requests. He wouldn't do it. If she wanted to be part owner, this could be her first task.

"I think you should see to the correspondence, Miss Handland," he told her on his way to take his seat back.

She stepped in front of him, blocking his path. "I can do that, but only if you agree not to spend all your time in here."

"I don't know what you're talking about." He managed to side-step her.

She followed right on his heels like a tenacious hound on a hunt. "I'm talking about you never leaving this room. Not even to sleep."

"I like to retire here at the end of the day." He looked down at her. "And how do you know I never leave this room?"

She ignored his question. No doubt the housekeeper had already been telling her tales about him.

"You do more than retire here, Mr. Murphy. I think you've been sleeping here. Either in this chair or"—she turned to point at the worn-out sofa where a woolen blanket lay balled up in one corner—"over there. It's not proper for the owner of a prestigious Great Camp to sleep in the office."

Owen's temper snapped. "I'll lay my head wherever I see fit, Miss Handland!"

The nerve of the woman! She didn't even blink at his outburst. They remained at a silent impasse for several lengthy minutes. He thought she would budge when he sank back down into *his* chair and began tossing some of the unopened mail into the wastebasket underneath the desk. But she looked only more determined and perhaps just a tad bit angry. Her blue eyes narrowed as she stared him down.

He continued to clear out some more of the paperwork. Most of it he hadn't even looked at. Mrs. Cuddieback added them to his desk every few days as her husband brought them back from the post office in Heartston.

For some strange reason, Owen almost took delight in goading the young woman before him. Almost. He paused in midmotion, the next stack of papers tipping precariously close to the edge of the oak desk. For the first time in a long while, he realized he was feeling something other than the overwhelming sense of loss that he'd become so used to.

He didn't quite know what to make of this. Feeling a bit out of his element, he pushed the papers back onto the desk. "I have to go help Mr. Cuddieback with a pest issue."

Lily watched him leave. Then she returned to the desk, picked up the basket where he'd tossed all the papers, and placed it squarely on the desk. For the next half hour, she took out each piece of paper and sorted it into the piles she had started before Mr. Murphy's tantrum. She would deal with the correspondence first. She reached behind her for the chair. Pulling it closer, she sat. She would need clean sheets of stationery to write on.

After a few minutes of rummaging, the only thing she could find were torn pieces of paper, so she went to find Mrs. Cuddieback. Perhaps she would know where to find the supply. She found the woman in the kitchen preparing the midday meal.

"Mrs. Cuddieback, I can't seem to find any stationery. Might you happen to know where it's kept?"

The woman looked up at her with a befuddled expression. Setting down the wooden whisk she'd been using to beat some batter, she carefully wiped her hands on a dish towel. "I'm not sure there is any. Did you look on the desk?"

Lily laughed. "You've seen Mr. Murphy's desk. I've only started to clean off the top. The man hasn't looked at the mail in months. I'm going to answer every one of those letters. But I need some paper."

The woman came around from behind the counter to take Lily by the arm, gently guiding her out of the kitchen and back into the office. "I know there has to be something here you can use. Miss Rebecca had Mr. Peck at the print shop design some beautiful letterhead when they first opened the camp. There has to be some left."

Together they searched the desk drawers and looked on the bookshelves lining the walls.

"I try to get into his office once a week or so to dust, but Mr. Owen can be stubborn when it comes to letting me in here."

"If I have my way, this will become the office once more, and you can come and go as you please." Lily smiled at her. "The man needs to go back to his bedroom to sleep."

Mrs. Cuddieback stopped rifling through the books. "I agree with you. Not only does he need to get out of this room, but he needs to get out of this house. The only reason he goes into the village is to visit Rebecca's graveside."

Lily remembered watching him from her room and wondered if he were planning on going there today. If they couldn't find the stationery, she would have him pick up something at the mercantile, though she imagined doing the errand would not sit well with him. Well, today was a new day for the Murphy Camp.

"Oh! Look!" The housekeeper held up a letter-sized box. "This was stuck in amongst this stack of old newspapers. This room is in worse condition than I thought. Perhaps I should help you in here."

She brought the box to Lily and set it on the desk. They both held their breath as Lily blew the dust off the top. After the cloud settled, she opened the box. Gently lifting out the first sheet, Lily took a closer look at the letterhead and with a start, put it down. She couldn't use this.

Along the top was a sketch of the main house. Running her fingers along the crisp top, Lily admired the simple block lettering. "Murphy Great Camp. Proprietors, Owen and Rebecca Murphy." Below that was a simple image of a pine bough. Rebecca had gone to great lengths to design a simple but beautifully embossed stationery.

Lily put the paper back in the box. Her heart ached for Owen. She imagined the couple had had wonderful plans for their future. And death took that away from them.

"Perhaps I should go into Heartston to pick up some new stationery."

Mrs. Cuddieback came to look over her shoulder. "I remember the day Rebecca brought this home. She was so excited to have something with their name on it to make the business official." She sighed. "Her passing was such a tragic loss."

Lily turned to look at the woman. There were so many questions she wanted to ask. And she'd learned a long time ago that a household's staff were privy to more than the people they were serving ever realized. Surely, Mrs. Cuddieback would share what she knew.

"Might I ask, if you're going to town today, could you do me the favor of doing a little shopping for me?" Mrs. Cuddieback asked.

Lily nodded. "I'd be happy to help you out." Lily needed an ally, and if doing small favors for this woman could get her what she needed, then she had no problem picking up a few things.

"I have a list started. Let me run to the kitchen to get it for you," she said. The woman hurried off.

Lily set the box of stationery next to the letters. She went out into the entryway to wait for the housekeeper, who came out from the kitchen a few minutes later with the list.

"There you go." She smiled broadly at Lily. "It's not on the list, but if you could stop off at the bakery to pick up some of Miss Amy's cinnamon rolls, I'd be grateful. Let me go find my husband and see if he can bring your carriage around."

While she waited, Lily went over to the large mirror that hung on the wall in the entry. She patted her hair into place and adjusted her white collar, smoothing the edges over the blue material of her dress. Examining her image now, she realized she'd almost forgotten what it was like to appear normal. Dressing the part had become habit for her. It wasn't that long ago she'd been masquerading as a saloon girl. For a moment, she was that woman again, the one wearing the garish red dress and black stockings with her hair piled high on top of her head, her lips painted bright red. Blinking away the image, Lily stared at her reflection, realizing she still didn't know what her life was supposed to be like now.

Today she had stood in the office of one of the Great Camps, a businesswoman, making her own way. Controlling her own future. The thought brought a small smile to her lips. She turned at the sound of the office door opening. A very distraught Owen Murphy stood on the threshold.

She rushed over to him. "Mr. Murphy, what's wrong?"

He sputtered as his face turned a deep shade of red. The vein running along his forehead bulged. He held a trembling hand out to her. Gripped between his whitened fingers were sheets of the stationery.

"Where did you find this?" His voice was low.

Lily reached out to him and laid a hand on his arm. He pulled away from her as if he'd been burned.

"Mrs. Cuddieback found the box on the shelf," she answered, keeping her voice quiet.

"Please . . . tell me you did not answer those letters using this?" He stumbled against the wall. Using his free hand, he grabbed for purchase.

Lily reached out to steady the man, but again he shrugged her off. She'd never witnessed such raw emotion. It had never been her intent to hurt him in any way. She hurried to explain. "I didn't use the stationery. I had planned on going into town to buy some new." She moved to stand before him. "I know this is special."

He took in a deep breath. Lily felt terrible. This was all her fault. "Mr. Murphy, I'm so sorry. I never meant to—"

"You never meant to what? Come here and take away what is mine?"

She shook her head. "No. I don't want to take anything away from you." At a loss for what to do next, she wrung her hands. In all her attempts to make things better here at the Murphy Camp, she'd only managed to make things worse.

Chapter Five

"As soon as Mr. Cuddieback brings my carriage around, I'll be heading off to Heartston."

Her voice seemed to come from far away as Owen fought to gain control. He had to stop reacting to every little thing this woman did. He folded the paper in half and then in half again and stuck it in his pants pocket.

Then he raised his eyes to look at Miss Handland. Her face was pale, her expression grim as she studied him.

"I'm sorry I reacted so poorly," he offered in a weak voice.

"No. No. I was the one who was wrong. The next time I need something, I'll come find you. I had no right to go off searching your things without you present."

He stood taller, squaring his shoulders. He had to start coming to terms with what his future was going to look like. "You are going into the village?"

She nodded.

"Perhaps I shall tag along."

Of course, he didn't really want to go to town, nor did he need anything. He wasn't even sure why he said he'd go. The front door opened and his caretaker stood there, looking from Miss Handland to Owen as if sorry he'd interrupted them.

"Miss Handland, your carriage is at the ready."

"Mr. Murphy, will you be joining me?"

Owen looked down at his pants and boots. They were caked with dirt from helping secure the garden fence. He was in no condition to accompany her into the village. On second thought, he decided to stay and work on some more of the projects that needed to be done around the property.

"No. You go on. I'll stay here."

Lily said her good-byes and followed Mr. Cuddieback out to the carriage. "I don't know how long I'll be gone. Your wife gave me a list of things to pick up for her. Do you need anything?" Lily asked, settling into the seat.

"Nope. But thanks for offering." He handed her the reins, a kind smile lighting up his face.

She'd only bumped into Theodore Cuddieback a few times, but his gentle demeanor and the twinkle in his brown eyes had put her immediately at ease. He spent most of his time dressed in denim coveralls that hung from his lanky frame. The grass stains alone were a testament to his hard work around the Murphy Camp. Mr. Murphy should consider himself fortunate to have such loyal help.

"Well then, I'll be off." Lily snapped the reins against the front of the carriage, and the horse took off at a slow gait.

The trip down the mountain road took a bit longer than she anticipated. It had slipped her mind that she was now an hour or so outside the village. She traveled along the narrow roadway through the tall pines, which reached so high she had to tip her head back to see the tops of them. *Land sakes,* she thought, *this truly is God's country.* The beautiful blue and white wildflowers dotting the roadside and the red-breasted robins searching for food along the edges of the woods reminded her again why folks traveled from far away to come here.

The road turned a corner and came to an intersection. Tacked against a large tree trunk was a wooden sign that pointed the way to Heartston. Lily nudged the horse onto the wider road. A light breeze floated through the pines, and the trees creaked as they swayed. A squirrel skittered out from the underbrush onto the hard-packed road, and she pulled in the reins, slowing the horse so the small animal could pass. A moment later, a brown-and-white-speckled fawn poked its nose out from behind a wild berry bush where it had been feeding. Lily smiled, enjoying the scenery. The coolness of the heavily shaded woods was a welcome relief to the growing heat of the day.

Soon enough the sounds of voices and the clatter of wagon wheels filtered through the trees. One turn in the road, and Heartston seemed to spring to life right out of the valley. She spotted the church steeple first. Then the buildings of Main Street came into view: the bakery, the bank, and of course, the one-room log schoolhouse. The small town had everything a person could need.

She drove out of the woods into the bright sunlight. Going straight past the stable and the train depot, she came to a stop in front of the mercantile. She picked up her reticule off the seat and climbed down, taking care to firmly tie the reins to the hitching rail.

She gave the horse a pat on the neck. "I'll be back soon."

Taking care not to trip, Lily picked up her skirt, stepped onto the boardwalk that ran the length of Main Street, and headed straight for the mercantile.

With the exception of the saloon, it was the largest building on the street. Lily slowed to look at the display flanking the doorway. She pulled open her reticule and took out the list, scanning it to make sure Mrs. Cuddieback didn't need a new broom. Keeping the list in her hand, Lily entered the store and stopped. This was the first time she'd had a chance to linger here. When she'd been working for the Pinkertons, she'd been careful not to engage with anyone other than her contacts. Excitement building inside her, Lily took in the rows of sewing notions with bolts of fabric resting on a long shelf.

A pretty blue cloth caught her eye. Blue was her favorite color, and she hadn't had a new dress in a long time. The wardrobe she'd brought with her to Heartston was simple and a bit out of fashion. She wandered over to the shelf and touched the fabric, feeling the coolness of it against her fingertips. It would be so nice to have a brand-new dress.

"I have a pattern book you can look through if you'd like. This one would make a lovely gown."

Lily turned to look at the young woman who'd come to offer help. Her curly brown hair, tied off in a yellow ribbon, tumbled down her back. She wore a simple black dress with a white pinafore over it. The young woman smiled kindly at Lily.

"Thank you. I'm afraid I don't know how to sew."

"Well then, you need to be introduced to Mrs. Fenton. She's our seamstress. She makes lovely gowns and even simple dresses. As a matter of fact, I believe she's making the wedding gown for our schoolteacher, Elsie Mitchell. The wedding won't be until October, but making something that special takes time." The girl took a breath and then introduced herself. "I'm Patricia. I can help you find anything you might need."

"It's a pleasure to meet you, Patricia. I'm Lily." Lily let go of the fabric and gave her full attention to the shopgirl. Will and Elsie had set their wedding date? She was happy for them.

Things had turned out well for Elsie Mitchell and her betrothed, William Benton. The reason Lily had found herself in Heartston to begin with was because of William. His last Pinkerton case had been to capture a bond thief, who had turned out to be Elsie's former fiancé.

William had arrived here with two young children in tow, and Elsie had helped care for them while he solved the case. Somehow, in the middle of all that, they had fallen in love.

Lily was glad Will had finally gotten his happily-ever-after. Elsie, who knew Lily was a Pinkerton agent, would probably be a bit cautious around her for a while, but Lily was hopeful that in time the school-teacher would grow to trust her. Perhaps one day they could become good friends.

"Do you know Miss Mitchell and Mr. Benton?" Patricia asked.

"I . . ." She hesitated with her response. What was there to say? Yes, she knew them quite well. She'd helped save Elsie from her former betrothed when he'd come to Heartston in search of his stolen railroad bonds and had kidnapped Elsie, holding her at gunpoint until Will had saved her. *No.* Lily couldn't very well say any of those things.

Lily took a moment to remind herself of the promise she'd made to herself. She was done pretending she was someone and something she was not. Taking part ownership of the Murphy Camp was supposed to be her new start in life.

Looking down at the young girl, whose smile could light up any room, Lily didn't want to lie. "I do know who Miss Mitchell and Mr. Benton are."

"Yes, poor Miss Mitchell has had quite a go of it. She was held at gunpoint by her former fiancé . . . a terrible man . . . but Mr. Benton rescued her"—the girl gave a quick shrug—"and now they are going to be married. Isn't that wonderful?"

"Yes, it is." Lily offered up a smile, truly feeling happiness for the couple. She hadn't seen either Will or Elsie since the near catastrophe. Perhaps after she got settled at the Murphy Camp, she would see if Elsie wanted to come for a visit. In the meantime, the day was moving along, and she had errands to run.

"Could you help me with my list?" She offered the paper she held to the girl, who gave the list a cursory look and headed off down the center aisle.

"Most everything you need is on this side of the store," she said. "I also heard that Miss Mitchell and Mr. Benton are going to officially adopt Mr. Benton's twin niece and nephew."

Lily followed along, holding out her arms as the girl stacked them full. "Oh, that's wonderful news!" she said, happy to hear that the four of them were officially becoming a family. Resting her chin on a particularly bulky bag of flour, Lily struggled to keep the pile of items from toppling to the floor and managed to say, "I need one more item."

The girl stopped midstep and spun around. "Oh my!" she said, seeing Lily's distress. "I'm so sorry. Here, let's set it all up on the counter." Patricia took half of what Lily had been holding and dumped the pile near the cash register. "There. Now that's better." Setting her hands on her hips, she looked kindly at Lily. "What else did you need?"

"I need some stationery if you have it."

The girl tapped her chin with the tip of her finger. "We do have some paper. I'm not sure if it's what you're looking for, though. Mr. Moore ordered a bunch of paper for Miss Mitchell during the school year. I think it has lines on it, though."

Patricia hurried behind the counter, slipping through the curtained-off area that Lily assumed was some sort of stockroom. She heard voices in the back. A few minutes later Patricia returned, carrying a brown paper package.

She set it on the counter, reached for a pair of scissors, and cut the thin twine that held the wrapper in place. "Let's see if this will work for you." She pushed aside the wrapper, revealing cream-colored paper that, low and behold, was unlined.

"That will be perfect. I don't think I'll need the entire package. Can you sell me half of that?"

"Let me check." While Patricia ran off to check with the person in the back, Lily turned to take a closer look at the merchandise in the store.

There were all sorts of household supplies. Pots and pans, along with shelves filled with work shirts and neatly folded denim pants, lined the middle of the store. On the opposite side were the canned foods, sacks of flour, and small bins of hard candy. Lily spotted some dishes in an open crate that would look nice in the dining room. She wondered if Mr. Murphy had an account here.

"Patricia," she called out. "I need to speak to the owner of the store."

Within minutes both the shopgirl and the owner appeared from the back. "This is Francis Moore."

The tall, rail-thin man stepped forward to shake her hand. He may have appeared weak, but the strength of his grip surprised her.

"Hello, I'm Lily Handland. I'm wondering if you could tell me if Owen Murphy has an account with you. I'll be working with him up at the Murphy Camp, and after seeing all the wonderful things you have here, I think there might be some items I'd like to get for the camp."

Mr. Moore retreated behind the counter and stooped to retrieve a ledger hidden underneath. Lily waited while he paged through it.

"Patricia, would you mind going in the back and bringing out some of the new teas?" he asked.

The girl nodded and went off.

"I don't like to discuss my patrons with the staff." He squinted at her through his dusty spectacles. "You say you work at the Murphy Camp? Last I knew they were closed."

"We will be opening again very soon."

He raised his bushy gray eyebrows in disbelief. "This is the first I'm hearing of this."

"Yes. Well, it happened a short time ago. I'm going to be partnering with him on getting the place ready for a grand reopening." The words were out of her mouth before Lily could stop them. She knew Mr. Murphy would be upset if he'd heard her. She suspected it wouldn't be long before the rest of the town became aware of this change.

The man stood behind the counter, looking confounded. "I'll be needing Owen's confirmation of this before I can reopen his accounts. You see, I had to close them a few months ago due to nonpayment."

This bit of news caused Lily some concern. She shifted her weight from one foot to the other. If Owen had debts, they had to be paid before they reopened. She couldn't abide keeping the creditors waiting while spending money on improvements.

"How much does he owe you?" she asked, hoping that it wouldn't amount to more than she could handle.

Mr. Moore pushed his spectacles up higher on the bridge of his nose. "Ten dollars would bring the account up to date."

Lily thought about what she had over at the bank. If she left here, withdrew the money, and brought it back to the mercantile, they'd be set.

"I'll be back in half an hour," she said.

"But what about your things?"

"I'll pay for those when I get back."

Lily hurried out of the shop and crossed the street to the bank. She found Mr. Goodwin behind the teller's window and explained what she needed. Before long, he had a stack of crisp bills for her. She made it back to the mercantile in under half an hour.

"Mr. Moore! I'm back!" Lily rushed to the front of the store and made quick work of settling the old account and opening a new one to pay for the items she needed today. She'd figure out a way to inform Mr. Murphy of this development on the ride home. If her instincts were right, he'd be none too pleased with her interfering in his business affairs. Well, this was what partners did for each other.

"It was a pleasure doing business with you, Miss Handland." Mr. Moore gave her a sly wink. "You be sure to tell Owen I said hello. And we miss him."

"I will."

Taking her packages, she headed back to the carriage and loaded it up. She had one foot on the carriage step when she remembered she needed to go to the bakery. Leaving the things where she'd put them, Lily made her way along the wooden walkway that stretched in front of the shops to the bakery. Off in the distance she could see the high peaks of the mountain range above the tree line. She couldn't resist tipping her face skyward, savoring the warmth of the sun on her cheekbones and eyelids. It was refreshing, this freedom to simply roam where her heart desired.

Opening her eyes, she looked down the roadway and saw the church. The white clapboard shone in the sunlight. The doors were open, and she felt a sudden draw to the building, as if those doors were a beacon. As her gaze followed the white spire up from the peak of the roofline, Lily's heart swelled with unexpected emotion. She almost couldn't remember the last time she'd stepped foot inside a church. Since she'd been here in Heartston, she'd been more or less confined to the saloon or her rented room. Staying in disguise had meant keeping to herself.

She walked to the church steps and rested her hand on the railing. The emotion swelled inside her again, and she let the Holy Spirit pull her inside the coolness of the building. She blinked as her eyes adjusted to the dim light. Looking about, she realized she was alone. She found a pew near the back and sank down onto the worn wooden seat.

Running her fingers along the rounded edge, she imagined all the people who had sat there over the years. Finally resting her hands in her lap, she folded her fingers together and bowed her head in prayer.

"Dear Lord, thank you for giving me this fresh start. Please help me to be patient and kind to Mr. Murphy. Thank you for guiding my life. Amen."

She gave the simple church one last look, rose, and left through the same doors that had called to her. As she crossed the street, she passed two women walking slowly in the other direction, their heads close together as they exchanged a bit of lively conversation. One of the women glanced her way and smiled at her. Lily smiled back. The women continued walking, their laughter drifting after her as she walked toward the bakery.

Lily felt a tug in her heart. She'd never had a true friend, someone to confide in or simply have a cup of tea with. She looked around at the other villagers chatting in groups or carrying on their day's business, thinking maybe now she could make friends and a place to call home.

All of that could be waiting for her, right here in Heartston.

She crossed the street in front of the bakery. Oh, the sweet, wonderfully enticing smells that greeted her even before she crossed the threshold were like a warm elixir for the soul. Lily smiled as she approached the counter where dozens of cookies, rolls, and little cakes were lined up on trays like bakery sentinels. A young woman stood behind the counter, wiping her hands on a flour-covered apron.

"Good afternoon. Welcome to the Heartston Bakery. I'm Amy Montgomery. How can I help you?"

"I need to purchase some cinnamon rolls."

The young woman, who looked close to being the same age as Lily, smiled back at her. "My most popular item. I swear I could keep this shop open even if that's all I baked."

"I'm picking them up for a friend."

"How many do you think you'll need? I only have a few left. These are baked first thing in the morning. You're lucky. Usually they're gone before noontime."

"Three should do it." Lily watched Amy pick up a pair of tongs and put three of the largest cinnamon rolls she'd ever seen into a brown paper bag.

"That will be fifteen cents."

The young woman's smile reached clear up to her sky-blue eyes, and Lily couldn't help but wonder what it might be like to have a new friend, someone she could confide in, or simply share a piece of cinnamon roll with. "I've heard good things about your bakery, Miss Montgomery."

The young lady blushed. "That's very nice of you to say. And please, call me Amy."

"Amy, it is, then. And I'm Lily Handland."

"It's a pleasure to meet you, Lily."

"You, too. I'm in town running some errands, and your shop is the last stop on my list."

"It's a lovely day to be out and about," Amy said, brushing some crumbs off the counter into her cupped hand.

Lily felt as if a ray of sunshine had poked through a dark cloud. She had missed having casual conversation with another woman. "Yes, it is."

Almost forgetting she hadn't paid for the cinnamon rolls, Lily quickly reached into her small reticule, counted out the proper amount, and handed Amy the coins. "Thank you so much," she said, taking the bag from her. Then as she turned around, she bumped right into Elsie Mitchell.

"I'm so sorry."

Elsie looked at Lily and then blinked as she recognized her.

"Lily!" Elsie gave her a quick hug. "I didn't expect to see you here."

Lily suspected that Elsie had believed her long gone, now that her mission in Heartston was over. "Elsie, I heard the news about your wedding and the children."

"Yes. Will and I are going to be married in October. Of course, he wanted to get married right away, but I've waited a long time for my wedding. I want the day to be perfect."

"I'm sure it will be."

"What keeps you here in town?" Elsie asked.

"I'm going to be living out at the Murphy Great Camp. I'm part owner now."

"You're working with Owen?" Elsie seemed surprised by this. Her expression turned grave as she said, "It was terrible when his wife died. I haven't seen him in a very long time."

"He's been keeping to himself. But I'm hoping to change that. Would you have a minute to talk?" Lily asked.

"Amy, I'll be back in a few minutes." Taking Lily by the arm, Elsie led her outside. "I can't believe you decided to stay in Heartston."

"I did. I am. I know this is hard for you, considering everything that happened. And I have a big favor to ask. I know you'll understand. Elsie, no one can know about what I did before."

Elsie stood on the walkway, looking at Lily as if seeing her in a new light. "I'm not sure I do understand, Lily."

"I haven't told anyone about my Pinkerton days. And I don't intend to."

"Aren't you worried that Owen might find out you were a Pinkerton agent? I'm not the only one who saw you when you were working with Will."

A shiver of doubt ran along her spine. She knew she'd been careful. "Those people only saw me in the saloon. I don't even look the same."

"What about John Oliver?"

Lily wasn't the only one who knew that the owner of the lumber-yard had once worked as a lead Pinkerton agent. He was the one who'd headed the investigation into Elsie's fiancé—the same investigation that had brought Lily here.

"John is aware of my situation, and he agrees it would be best to keep my past just that . . . the past."

Lily's gut instincts were telling her that Elsie might struggle with this deceit. She could only hope that her loyalty to her future husband—and her gratitude for the role Lily had played in her safe return—would influence her answer today. It was, after all, the only solution that made sense.

"I think you deserve a fresh start. I owe you so much for helping me and the children. All right, I'll do as you ask."

Lily hugged her. "Thank you so much."

Elsie frowned. "But, Lily, secrets like this have a way of coming back to haunt us. So be careful."

"I promise." Relieved that Elsie was on her side, Lily said, "There was one more thing I wanted to ask you. Now that I'm helping Mr. Murphy get his business up and running again, I'd like to host a tea to celebrate your engagement. What do you think?"

"That would be wonderful! I haven't been out that way in so long."

"You could invite your friends."

"And I can help you get the word out about the Murphy Camp. I'm glad we ran into each other today, Lily."

"Me, too."

Elsie glanced over her shoulder at the bakery. "I really have to get going. I promised the children I'd bring them a special dessert."

"I have to get back to the camp. You let me know what date works for you for the tea."

"What do you think about three weeks from Saturday?"

"That would be terrific. Don't worry about anything. Mrs. Cuddieback and I will arrange for the food and tea. You bring your friends at four o'clock."

"I'll be in touch with a final head count beforehand. Thank you for going to all this trouble for me," Elsie said, her face breaking into a bright smile.

Lily grinned. "It's a good way for me to show people what the Murphy Camp is going to be like."

Elsie went back to the bakery, and Lily stepped up into the carriage to begin her return trip to the Murphy Camp, with her shopping list fulfilled and the tempting cinnamon buns nestled next to her on the seat. She had the ride back to figure out the best way to tell Mr. Murphy about all that had transpired during her short visit to Heartston.

Surprisingly, that was not where her thoughts took her. As her wagon rumbled over the uneven roads and the sounds of the town faded into the background behind her, Lily began to fret over Elsie's warning. Now, more than ever, she wanted to move on with her life—to not only find a home but also build friendships. There was no doubt in Lily's mind that Elsie knew firsthand how painful secrets could be, especially when it was a loved one keeping them. Though she knew her . . . *friend* . . . was only trying to look out for her happiness, Lily knew she had to keep a close guard on her past.

She clutched the leather reins between her fingers, frowning as this new dilemma took hold of her confidence. The truth could take away everything she'd already gained in such a short time span. Her plan to start a new life hadn't seemed this complicated when she'd developed it during those long, lonely days in her room on the second floor of Heartston's boardinghouse. She realized now just how naive she'd been with her thinking. Starting a new life wasn't going to be as easy as putting disguises away in a trunk.

The Murphy Camp came into sight around the bend. With a deep breath, Lily pushed down the doubts she'd been experiencing and spurred the horse into a trot. She would find a way to make all of this work.

Chapter Six

Owen sat behind his desk, staring at all the neat piles of papers and books put there by his new partner. He still wasn't convinced agreeing to this ludicrous idea had been the right thing to do. After giving it a bit more thought, he had to admit it was nice not to have the banker sending him constant notices—although that inconvenience appeared to have been replaced by Miss Handland's many demands on his time. Yesterday she'd asked him to think about which cabins he wanted to refurbish. They hadn't even started on the house.

And now this mess of paperwork. He took in the sight, shaking his head. This had been his doing. If Owen had been vigilant with the mail, the stacks wouldn't have built up.

Taking a sheet off the first pile, he looked it over and tossed it into the wastebasket. The next one was a request to hold a group hike here. He squinted, looking at the date. Last year. He tossed it into the wastebasket. He glanced at it a few times and took it back out. He might be able to have Miss Handland send a note inviting the group back when the camp reopened.

He stayed at his desk for the rest of the afternoon and into the night, culling through piles of paperwork. Mrs. Cuddieback came and went several times, bringing him a sandwich for dinner and several cups of tea. He rubbed his tired eyes. Swiveling his chair around, he stared out the window at the sky, which was slowly turning pink. It was usually this time of day when Rebecca would come in to get him, and they would walk hand in hand down the bridal path to the lake. He'd assumed they would have decades together. They'd planned on having a family. And then she'd been taken from him.

He swiveled his chair back to his desk, looking down at the spot where the framed image of his wife sat. Since her death, it had been on the fireplace mantel, but he'd moved it here a few weeks ago after he'd seen Miss Handland holding it.

The picture was one of the few things he owned that carried Rebecca's image. She stood beneath the oak tree in front of the church. Rebecca had loved going to church. Not only that, but she adored serving the Lord, and in so many capacities. Even though they didn't have children, she'd been in charge of the little ones' choir. She spent Saturday afternoons rehearsing with them for the next day's services. He remembered how she smiled every time they sang, the joy she wore as she listened to those tiny voices singing the simple hymns.

Owen had tried going back to the church after her death. He'd sat in their pew, the third one from the back on the right side of the church. But instead of feeling comforted by his neighbors and friends, he'd felt lost and alone. Not what the Lord he'd known would have wanted, to be sure. After that day, Owen had stayed home on Sundays. He'd turned down invitation after invitation for Sunday dinners.

In the short amount of time Rebecca had been on this earth, she'd done so much good. She'd been in charge of bringing food to the shut-ins who lived on the outskirts of Heartston, and he knew she added little extras to their baskets. Books, some special teas. Every last one of those people had come out to bid her good-bye and had stood alongside him in the cemetery. Rebecca had been filled with kindness. Owen doubted he would ever meet another woman like her, nor would there be one who could fill her place in his heart.

Darkness fell. Owen lit the lamp and continued going through the paperwork. He paused, his hand hovering over a box he recognized. It contained the stationery Rebecca had designed. He left it there, moving on to the next thing on the desk, a stack of booklets. They'd had them made when they first opened the camp to guests. "A good way to get the word out about the place," Rebecca had said. She'd made sure everyone had gone home with one to share with a friend.

He blew out a breath, the memories overwhelming him. Carefully, he added the pamphlets to the stationery box. He'd have Mrs. Cuddieback put them somewhere else. He needed this misery to end, and yet he didn't know how to make that happen.

Fearing what the next stack of papers might hold, he moved the lamp to the last pile, where he found a handwritten note.

> *Dear Mr. Murphy,*
> *I know this task was not an easy one for you. You should be proud of all you have accomplished. Your efforts bring us one step closer to the grand reopening of the Murphy Great Camp.*
> *"For I know the plans I have for you," declares the Lord, "plans to prosper you and not to harm you, plans to give you hope and a future." (Jeremiah 29:11)*
> *Don't despair, Mr. Murphy. —L. H.*

Owen had to admit her choice of Bible verse was interesting, and the words almost brought a smile to his face. But his truth of late had nothing to do with hope and a future. He read the scripture once more, trying to feel a spark of the optimism that had once burned in him. He put the note down and sat back, staring at it, wondering if he'd ever feel whole again.

He glanced from the note to the box of Rebecca's stationery, its empty pages a cruel taunt. He needed to move on with his life *and* hold on to what had been. How could he do that when Lily Handland seemed so set on breathing new life into everything around him? He ran his finger over the edge of the box one more time. Then, opening it, he rifled beneath the brochures until his fingers found a sheet of the old stationery. Lifting it out, he brought it to his face, inhaling, hoping to find the sweet rosewater scent of his wife there.

Instead, his senses were overrun with a musty smell.

This brought a bitter chuckle from him. Putting the paper back, he ran his finger along the edge of Miss Handland's note. He hesitated and then brought the paper to his nose. He smelled fresh lemons and something else that eluded him. He tossed the note into the wastebasket. Exhaustion seeped into his muscles, filling him with a familiar lethargy. He stood, ready for bed. His feet guided him to the sofa. Owen lay down, tugging the blanket over him. He slung his arm across his forehead and lay there listening to the house settle for the night. The words from the scripture flitted through his brain. He drifted off to sleep, the musty scent of Rebecca's stationery tugging at the edges of his mind.

Owen awoke as the sound of something hitting the floor with a loud bang penetrated his subconscious.

"What?"

He blinked against the brilliant sunlight pouring into the room. As his eyes adjusted to the light, he made out the form of Miss Handland standing over him. He wanted to turn back over on his side and continue with the sweet dream he'd been having. But alas, the images of the woman who'd preoccupied his slumber were already receding into his memory. Owen rolled onto his side, hoping to grab a few more minutes of sleep, but it seemed his visitor had other plans.

"*Mr. Murphy.* I thought you and I had an understanding." The woman stood, bending slightly at the waist, picking up the stack of books she'd dropped next to his head. She wagged a finger in front of his nose. "No more sleeping in the office."

He pushed himself up on an elbow and looked her square in the eye. "I worked late into the night, and *my* sofa was convenient."

She put her nose in the air and sniffed at his excuse. Owen bit back a smile. Working with this woman had turned out to be quite the challenge for him. What he needed more than anything was a strong cup of Alice Cuddieback's coffee . . . not to be sparring with his *partner* at this early hour.

"What time is it?" he asked, pushing himself into a sitting position.

"It's seven thirty," she snapped.

Running a hand through his hair, he wondered what had her in a snit already. "I'm going to the kitchen for some breakfast. Would you care to join me?"

"I've already had mine." She folded her arms across her chest, frowning at him.

After two weeks of having her underfoot, he recognized the signs: she had something on her mind that might not sit well with him. Whatever she was hiding from him today must be very important, because she kept averting her gaze from his.

"Miss Handland, why don't you accompany me to the kitchen anyway, and you can tell me what is bothering you this fine day." He stood and started for the door, but she darted in front of him.

"Wait! You can't go to the kitchen just yet."

Now what was this all about? She looked as if she were teetering on the edge of hysteria. Owen didn't have time for this nonsense. He'd plenty to do today, and dealing with her antics was not on his list, but his curiosity got the best of him. "And why can't I go to the kitchen?"

"Um . . . because."

"'Because' is not an answer, Miss Handland," he said, his ire rising. The last thing he needed or wanted was to have another go-round with a woman who was proving to be a stubborn thorn in his side.

Pushing past her, he strode down the hallway into the kitchen. The sight that greeted him almost caused him to completely lose control.

This time *he* was the one who stopped *her* in the doorway. He put his hands on his hips, drawing himself up to his full height of nearly six feet. Yes, Miss Handland deserved a little intimidation. He'd allowed her to rearrange the office and agreed to new landscaping around the main house. But this was too much!

Owen stared down at her and then looked over his shoulder at the crates lining the kitchen floor. He knew there were no coffers for any kind of extras.

"Would you care to tell me what is in those boxes?" He could feel the growl coming from his throat and couldn't stop it. He knew Miss Handland was behind this. Yet another thing she'd seen to without discussing it with him first.

She laid a hand on his forearm. He brushed it off.

"I didn't expect these things to be delivered yet."

"Exactly what things are you speaking of? Because I don't remember our discussing an order of any kind. You keep telling me we need to be careful with the budget. How is this"—he paused to swing his arm behind him—"being careful?"

"Now let me explain." She stepped around him. "When I was in the village a few weeks ago, I saw these dishes in the mercantile and thought we could use them for less formal events."

He raised his eyebrows. Hearing about "less formal events" was again news to him. He wondered when she found the time to plan events. And just what kind of event was she thinking about?

"Mrs. Cuddieback! I need my coffee."

"I've got your cup all poured and ready just the way you like it," Mrs. Cuddieback said, her back to him as she stirred a large copper pot on the stove. "One sugar cube and a healthy pour of cream. I fixed porridge for breakfast. Can I scoop you out a bowl?"

"Yes. Please. And thank you." Owen found the much-needed coffee at his place at the table. He picked up the thick white porcelain mug, taking a healthy gulp before turning to face Miss Handland. He eyed her over the rim of his cup.

"You were supposed to clear all purchases with me."

She ran her hands along the front of her plain brown dress, taking an extraordinarily long time to smooth out some nonexistent wrinkles. Today she wore her hair tied back with a blue ribbon. He tried not to notice how pretty she looked.

"I'm waiting."

"They are dishes to be used for teas. A pretty floral pattern that I thought would be a nice addition to the great room. I'm planning on using them for the tea party we're having next Saturday."

He sputtered at her last statement. *A tea party?* "When did you decide to have a tea party?" It was ludicrous, having a fancy event like that at a place usually limited to day hikes and hunting excursions.

"I ran into the schoolteacher Elsie Mitchell a few weeks back, the day I went into the village to shop for Mrs. Cuddieback."

Owen remembered the day well. It had been the day she'd unearthed the stationery. He continued to stare at her.

"Elsie—Miss Mitchell, I mean—is to be wed in October. I thought it would be nice to host a tea for her and her friends."

"I see." He didn't really see this at all. The house wasn't ready to host anyone yet, let alone a party of women. He set his mug down on the table and busied himself with dressing his porridge with dried fruit and a drizzle of maple syrup.

"I did get the dishes at a really good price."

"How did you pay for them?" Owen asked, remembering the debt he still owed the store owner.

He watched her out of the corner of one eye. She seemed to be fixated on her dress again. Owen had been meaning to go into town and pay off the bill. The amount, while not astronomical, when added to his debt at the bank, had seemed insurmountable. Now that Miss Handland had signed on to be his partner and, in doing so, had given money to the business, his intent had been to pay off all his outstanding loans. Except he hadn't found the time to go into the village. Now he wondered how she'd managed this. More importantly, why were they having this discussion only now?

"Miss Handland, answer my question. How did you pay for the dishes?"

"I paid for them in cash, after I saw to the old bills."

He squeezed his eyes shut. "Who told you to pay off my debt?"

"No one. I did it of my own accord. You see, I was there and the shop owner told me the amount on your account. I didn't see the harm in settling up while I was right there. It's what a business partner does, Mr. Murphy." Her voice took on a hard edge as she stepped closer to him.

The walls of the kitchen closed in on him. Owen struggled to even his breathing. He became aware of the fact that Mrs. Cuddieback had discreetly left the room. He couldn't stand to let this woman—this person whom, for the most part, he didn't even know—run his business.

The set of her jaw told him she wasn't ready to apologize. He watched as she squared her shoulders as if to engage him in battle. And battle they would.

"Why didn't you consult with me?"

Ever so slowly, she tilted her head and narrowed her eyes. "I'm sorry. I should have, but like I said, I was there and the bank was nearby. I told Mr. Goodwin what I needed, and he gave me the money from the business account to pay off the store debt."

Pride goeth before a fall, and his was taking a tumble. Regardless of the circumstances, she should never have taken it upon herself to fix his troubles. "The debt was mine and mine alone," he said, working at keeping his voice calm.

He felt a flush creeping over his cheeks and prayed she didn't notice. The whole town would know she'd canceled his debt. The flush deepened, and Owen wanted nothing more than to shut himself away in his dark office and stay there for the next week.

"When you signed those papers, your debts became ours. Like it or not, Mr. Murphy, we are partners."

He fisted his hands against his sides, clenching and unclenching them while he worked at remaining calm and businesslike. "When exactly did you purchase these dishes?"

"I bought them the last time I was in Heartston. And before you say another word, I can assure you it was not an impulse. We will use these for years to come. Once the women see what a fine place this is for teas, they will come back in droves. I promise you."

"There's no guarantee of that happening!" he shouted, the last of his patience snapping. "I can't abide by you going off and doing things on your own. It simply won't work."

"Mr. Murphy, it has taken me nearly half a month to get you to clean off the top of your desk. How on earth am I supposed to get things done when you insist on either not answering my inquiries when I bring up these things or ignoring my requests?" She pointed a finger at him. "You brought this on yourself."

"Maybe I don't think we need to change. Maybe I like this place the way it is. The way my—" He stopped speaking. He'd been about to mention Rebecca's name. Deciding that arguing would get them nowhere, Owen said, "Fine, have your tea. But the next time you decide you need to make a purchase, you will speak to me about it first. Agreed?"

She nodded. "Agreed. Oh, and one more tiny thing." She pressed her lips together for a moment, as if considering her next words. "There will be a wagon arriving with some food supplies."

Before he could call her out, she pushed ahead. "We needed some specialty items for the—"

He raised a hand to stop her. "I know, I know, for the tea party."

"Yes. Exactly. Mr. Murphy, I'm sorry I caused you distress."

"If you would confide these things to me beforehand, perhaps that would help to lessen our disagreements." He'd never met a more impulsive person. Miss Handland seemed to simply plow ahead in life. Well, he wasn't like that. He preferred things to remain the same.

He watched as she set the kettle on the back burner, struck a match against the side of the stove, and lit a fire under the kettle.

"I'm going to have some tea. Would you care to join me with your coffee?" She smiled at him, one of those bright smiles that beckoned him like a warm summer's day. Why did she always have to be so happy?

"No," he grumbled. "I usually prefer to have my first cup in silence."

She raised one of her pale eyebrows.

"Thank you for offering," he said, trying to be kinder.

She busied herself with fixing her teacup while waiting on the water. He knew he should be feeling better about having her here, but he couldn't shake the feeling that this woman would never be more than a constant intrusion on his once secluded life.

Steam began to rise from the kettle, followed by a shrill whistling sound. Grabbing hold of it with a pot holder, Miss Handland poured the boiling water into the teapot she'd set up.

He needed to make changes, he thought as he sipped his coffee. He had to start letting go of the past. Perhaps the time had come to begin again. He shook his head, feeling his stomach muscles clench. *No.* He wasn't ready.

She set the kettle back on the burner, turning off the heat. He could smell the light lemony scent of the tea leaves, which reminded him of the note she'd left him on his desk.

For I know the plans I have for you . . . plans to prosper you and not to harm you, plans to give you hope and a future. He thought about the words, wondering why she'd chosen that particular Bible verse.

Grabbing his mug off the table, he joined her alongside the stove. He reached behind her, took the coffeepot from the far back burner, and refilled his cup. He glanced down and found her looking up at him with a questioning gaze.

"About that Bible verse," he finally said.

Her eyes widened. "The Bible verse?"

"The one you wrote on the bottom of your note."

He saw the clarity dawn on her. Lily tipped her head, narrowing her eyes ever so slightly. And then the corners of her delicate mouth turned upward. He grew impatient. "Well?"

"I thought you could use a little inspiration. Plans for hope and a future. Everyone needs to have those things, Mr. Murphy. Even you."

He took a sip from the mug, pondering her words. Any further discussion would have to wait because it seemed her wagon of supplies had arrived.

Chapter Seven

Lily stood in the great room, studying her list. Today being Friday, she had one day left to get everything done for the tea party. The menu that Mrs. Cuddieback had come up with sounded divine. There would be tea cakes with fresh strawberry filling, topped with a light cream frosting, and cucumber and lettuce sandwiches—crusts off—cut corner to corner. After giving the warmth of the season fair consideration, they'd decided on lemonade and cool tea for beverages. Tucking the list in the pocket of the apron she'd borrowed from the housekeeper, Lily surveyed the room.

The new dishes were still sitting in the crate. After Mrs. Cuddieback had washed and dried them, Owen—*Mr. Murphy*—had brought them here yesterday and put them on the floor in front of one of the round tables. Lily walked over to the crate, took the lid off, and placed it on the floor. Carefully, she picked up a teacup, admiring the pretty rose pattern. The place setting was for forty. Not that Mr. Murphy had cared to ask, but Lily had managed to get a good deal on the set because the lady who had ordered them had moved back to the city and didn't want them after all. Lily could hardly wait to see the expression on Elsie's face when she saw how pretty the room would look with the tea set and simple decorations she had planned.

Putting the cup back, Lily stood and took account of the stack of linens Mrs. Cuddieback had found hidden away in one of the large storage cabinets out in the hallway. Now Lily began to separate them, gently unfolding and smoothing them out, one on top of each of the tables. They were planning on a dozen guests. She'd decided to give the ladies plenty of room, putting four each at three of the smaller tables. Three larger ones had been added to serve the food and beverages from.

After placing the last tablecloth, she stepped back, admiring her handiwork. The room looked more festive already. But she had more than just a few white tablecloths and the dishes planned for the decorations.

Earlier that day and at her request, Mr. Cuddieback had set a round wicker basket and garden shears by the door to the front porch. Lily picked them up on her way out, inhaling the pine-scented air. *What a lovely day to be here in the mountains,* she thought. Pulling the door closed behind her, Lily headed off to the gardens.

She'd noticed the flowers when she'd been looking out her bedroom window. There were so many pretty ones blooming right beneath her nose. Saving money by using nature's provisions should make her partner quite happy. Humming a few notes from her favorite hymn, "Amazing Grace," Lily took her time walking the pathway that led to the back of the property. She paused to cut a bunch of Queen Anne's lace. The wildflower grew in abundance here. The delicate head at the top of the long, thin stalk had a lacy appearance.

After she cut enough to fill five vases, Lily continued along the path toward the garden. She swatted at a bee buzzing around her head. The soft sound of the pine boughs brushing against each other drifted on the gentle summer breeze as she walked through the forest. Around a small bend the garden came into view. There, bent over in one of the rows, was Mr. Murphy.

She wondered where he'd gone off to this morning. They were supposed to have a meeting to discuss the tea party. With him being a man and all, she imagined tea parties didn't hold much interest for him. Even so, he'd made it abundantly clear he didn't like being left in the dark, and she wasn't about to be the cause of another fight.

"Hello!" she called out, scaring a flock of wrens up off the ground.

He looked up from his spot, tipping back his broad-brimmed hat. "Good day to you, Miss Handland."

Entering the garden through the gate of the white picket fence, she picked up her skirt and stepped over a row of beans. The vegetable plants were flourishing. Mrs. Cuddieback's husband was down a few rows, picking cucumbers for the sandwiches.

"Hello, Mr. Cuddieback," she said.

"Miss Handland, you're looking mighty fine today."

Now this man knew how to charm a lady. Lily was keenly aware of the dust smudges on the front of her apron and the sad state of her hair, which had started to come apart from the halfhearted attempt of a bun she'd managed early that morning. Coming to a stop by the men, she noted their baskets filled with vegetables. "It looks like you've both been busy."

"My wife told us to get out here and pick all the cucumbers we could find. She's come up with a new recipe for tomorrow."

"Ah. I can't wait to taste it." She looked from Mr. Cuddieback to Mr. Murphy, noticing the latter had kept his hands busy picking tomatoes. "Mr. Murphy, I went to find you this morning for our meeting, but you were nowhere to be found."

"That's because there is plenty of work to be done for your tea party." Pushing the brim of his hat back, he looked up at her. "Is there something you need to tell me?"

"Not particularly. Thank you for bringing the dishes into the great room."

"You're welcome."

"The guests should be arriving by four in the afternoon. I'd like there to be a small fire in the hearth."

He gave her a funny look and then laughed.

"Is there a problem with that?"

"It will still be mighty warm at that time of the day. I don't think your lady friends will like perspiring beneath their finery."

He did have a point. She thought for a moment and came up with a new idea. "All right. What about some extra candles for the mantel?"

"I think there is a box in the storage closet. When I'm finished here, I'll find them for you."

Mr. Cuddieback finished his harvesting and stood, picking up the basket practically overflowing with cucumbers. "I have to get back inside; the Mrs. and I will be heading off to the village. Seems she's come up with another one of her lists. I'll get the candles and put them in the great room for you, miss."

"That's so kind of you, thank you." Lily looked over to find that Mr. Murphy had gone back to picking the tomatoes. He didn't even look up as Mr. Cuddieback prepared to leave. Did the man even realize how fortunate he was that this couple had stayed with him all this time?

She imagined that good help in these parts was hard to come by. That thought brought to mind the issue of extra hands: the Murphy Camp would soon need to hire more employees. Even with the devotion and hard work of the Cuddiebacks, Lily knew they wouldn't be able to handle all the work when the guest rooms were full. If Lily got her way, the grand reopening would be happening by Thanksgiving, before the winter weather set in. And she had her sights set on having the camp done up properly for the holidays. What better time to show off the new improvements than Christmas, when people were already in good spirits? Of course, she hadn't broached either of those matters with Mr. Murphy. As soon as their tea was over, she would inform him of her plans.

She watched Mr. Cuddieback walk up the path before she returned her attention to her partner. The man seemed intent on getting every last tomato plant picked clean. Lily jostled the basket on her hip, thinking she'd best get on with her project, too. The day would be gone before she knew it.

Some pretty blue flowers growing along the edge of the garden caught her attention. Lily cut a bunch, adding them to the basket. Then she said good-bye to Mr. Murphy and headed back out to the spot where she'd seen some tiny clusters of pink roses growing along a trellis.

On closer inspection Lily saw that the only thing holding the trellis in place was some roping attached to four stakes. The plant stood a few feet away from the vegetable garden, along the side of the trail, and looked to be about six feet high. The green leafy branches were covered in hundreds of pink blooms. She cut along the bottom of the plant where the stalky branches started to spread upwards. But the best ones were at the very top of the bush. Lily reached up, grabbing hold of a thorny branch and pulling it down. After snipping a few delicate stems and using the tips of the shears as holders, she dropped each pink rose in the basket. Taking stock of the flowers, she realized she'd need a lot more of the blooms to make the arrangements the way she wanted.

Phew! It had gotten warm. She plucked at the front of her dress, pulling the damp fabric away from her skin. Then she wiped the back of her hand across her brow. She should have thought to bring out a container of lemonade to help soothe her parched throat. Placing her hands on her hips, she tipped her head back to look up at the last bunch of roses at the top. Those were beauties. Their delicate, pink-toned petals swayed in the summer breeze. And she had to have them. The only problem was not that they were high on the plant, but that they were surrounded by one of the thorniest branches she'd ever seen.

Where there's a will, there's a way, she thought. Lily positioned herself in the middle of the tall bush. Standing on tiptoe, she stretched her arm as high as she could. Careful not to prick her fingers, she grasped the branch and tugged.

The bush gave way.

Lily let out a scream as the rosebush pulled away from the trellis. She tumbled onto her back with the plant firmly in place over her. She became aware of pain in her arms and hands. She knew better than to try to move quickly. Her hair had come loose from its bun and strands of it were stuck in among the roses. Slowly, she turned her head but stopped as soon as she felt a tug on her scalp.

Oh dear, she'd gotten herself into a bit of a pickle.

"Help! Mr. Murphy! Help!" Parts of her arms and hands stung from where the thorns had scratched her.

"Miss Handland! Are you all right?" His voice came from the other side of the bush.

She felt the branches moving away from her legs but then let out a yelp when they didn't let go of her hair.

She felt his hand on the top of her head.

"Lie still so I can get these little thorns out of your hair."

While he worked at pulling the pesky branches off her, Lily was able to sit up halfway. Leaning back on her elbows, she peered down the length of her body. Broken twigs and torn flower petals lay strewn around her. A little branch filled with blooms poked out her apron pocket. As she reached for them, she tried to stifle a small groan—her hands were stinging from what felt like dozens of tiny cuts. She felt the long strands of hair sticking against her wet neck and realized she must be presenting quite the sight to Mr. Murphy, who now sat back on his haunches, staring at her with a big grin on his face.

"This isn't funny." She huffed.

"No, it is not." Tucking his chin in, he regained a modicum of composure.

Lily could see he was trying hard not to laugh. "The least you could do is offer me a hand up."

His shadow fell over her as he stood and held out his hand. Lily took it, surprised by his tender grip. "Ow." Once she was on her feet, she shook out her fingers, trying to release a bit of the pain left by the rosebush.

"Come on. Let's get you into the house so we can take a look at those hands." He placed a hand underneath her elbow and started to walk her up the path.

"Wait! I need the basket of flowers. Can you get them for me, please?" Looking quite put upon by her request, he didn't move. She offered him a weak smile and a coquettish "Pretty, please?"

Sighing loudly, he turned back down the path, picked up the basket, and brought it to her.

When she looked inside, she realized the roses were missing. "I need the roses. Would you mind terribly going back for them?"

This time he replied, "If you insist."

"I do," she said, ever so softy.

She brushed her skirt off, watching him through hooded eyes as he tromped over the path to the spot where the flowers lay in bunches on the ground where she'd fallen. After picking them up, he tossed them into the basket.

She bit her lip to keep from admonishing him. Those blooms were delicate. Once again he returned with the basket. He held it out to her.

She took hold of the handle, letting the basket dangle from her hand.

"Are you okay to walk on your own?"

"Of course I am." As soon as those words left her mouth, she managed to stumble over a rock. "Oh!"

Mr. Murphy grabbed hold of her arm, steadying her balance. "Perhaps you should avoid this section of the property, Miss Handland. There seems to be a lot of peril out here for you."

"Don't be silly. I'm perfectly fine," she said, though she was relieved when they made it back to the house the rest of the way unscathed.

"Let's go to the kitchen sink so you can wash up your hands."

On the way to the room, they passed one of the hall mirrors. Lily gasped when she caught sight of her reflection. Her hair was pointing every which way, the ends adorned with leaves and twigs. Stepping closer, she saw pine needles sticking out on one side. She'd be needing more than her hands washed.

Shaking her head in disbelief at how quickly the day had gone awry, Lily followed Mr. Murphy. She set the flower basket on the worktable as he stood at the sink, pumping water into a basin.

"Would you like me to heat the water for you?"

"No."

Once the basin filled, he gathered a towel and some soap, making short work of washing the garden soil off his hands and deftly drying them on the towel. "Come over here and let me take a closer look at your injuries."

Lily let him take her hands in his. Gently, he looked at the tops before turning them palms up. Her right hand had two tiny thorns in the palm. For something so small, they sure did hurt. She tried to pull her hand away, but he held it in a tender grip.

He tugged her over to the window for better lighting. Goose bumps rose along her arms, and the strangest flutter built in her stomach. The feeling caught her off guard, and she started to pull away. As he looked down into her eyes, she stopped resisting, noticing the tawny flecks around his irises. His gaze stayed on her eyes for a few moments and slowly moved down her face and back to her hands.

He cleared his throat. "Wash your hands while I get the medical kit."

She turned her back to him and put her hands in the cool water. She picked up the bar of soap, turning it in her hands. From behind her came the sound of him rummaging around in the small anteroom. She didn't want to think about her reaction to his touch. Instead, she concentrated on getting the thorns out of her right hand.

Owen stepped out of the pantry. Walking over to Miss Handland, his first thought was that she'd made quite a mess of herself. His second thought: she still looked very pretty, even with her hair sticking out every which way and dirt smudging her dress. He set the metal box containing bandages and other medicinal supplies on the counter next to the sink and took out a small jar of salve.

"Let me see your hands. We'll take care of the left one first. Then I'll see about getting those prickers out of your other hand." Opening the jar, he grimaced as the bitter smell of herbs mixed with lanolin floated out. He rubbed a hand beneath his nose. "This stuff might smell bad, but trust me—it works."

Miss Handland peered over his shoulder. "That smells like the earth."

"I'm not sure what all is in here. If you are ever in need of this again, we keep it on the second shelf to the right in the pantry."

"Hopefully, this will be the only time."

Taking her hand in his, Owen forced himself to concentrate on the treatment and not on how soft her skin felt beneath the hard calluses of his fingertips. He swallowed. This was the first time he'd had contact with a woman since Rebecca. His hand trembled. He couldn't tell if Miss Handland noticed. She seemed to be concentrating on the motion of his fingers as he rubbed the salve onto her skin, but he noticed the tinge of a blush riding high on her cheekbones. He released her hand. She leaned back against the edge of the sink.

He rummaged around in the metal box until he found some tweezers and stepped around her to wash them in the sink. Turning back, he reached for her other wounded hand.

"This might hurt a bit," he said.

Owen worked as swiftly as he could. He found the first thorn and pinched the tweezers around the edge, giving a tug. It came out smoothly. He rubbed his thumb over the spot. He heard her intake of breath. Owen couldn't look at her. He worked at staying focused.

Locating the second thorn, he noticed there appeared to be some redness around that area. This one surely would cause a bit of pain.

Miss Handland must have been thinking the same thing, because she said, "Go ahead. Pull that out."

Once again, he pinched the tweezers around the tip of the thorn. He felt her pull back. Owen stepped closer, repositioning his free hand so he had a better grasp on hers. She sucked in her breath. He dug in. The thorn didn't budge.

"Miss Handland, I'm afraid I'm going to have to cut the top layer of skin to remove this. Sometimes, like with a splinter, you could leave it in and let it work its own way out. In this case, I don't think that would be a good idea. The area is already reddened. I'd hate to see you develop an infection."

She winced. "Mr. Murphy, I have a dozen guests arriving tomorrow afternoon. I'm only halfway through my list for today. So please take it out the best way you know how."

Owen found a sharp knife and a tin of matches. He lit a match, pulling the tip of the knife through the flame, heating it enough to sanitize the instrument. Very carefully he placed her hand palm side up on the flat surface of the counter. Miss Handland stiffened against his side. Owen tried to ignore the feel of her body so close to his. He made short work of exposing the thorn and pulling it out.

The area bled a little, and he dabbed a bit of the salve there before wrapping her hand in a white cloth bandage. She took stock of his handiwork, dabbing at the corner of her eye. Had she been brought to tears? Owen thought he'd been gentle.

He put his hand underneath her chin, tipping her head up so he could see into her eyes. "You were very brave." He smiled at her. Before he could stop himself, he started to pull some of the pine needles from her hair. "Your hand should be fine. You know to keep it clean." His voice came out sounding gravelly. Owen realized, too late, his touching her hair was a mistake.

"Yes. Thank you," she said, brushing his hand aside.

He began to clean up the sink area as she pulled the rest of her hair free of the bun, running her fingers through the strands, picking up pieces of twigs and pine needles along the way.

She looked down at the bunch of yard debris in her hands. "What a mess. I'm going to go up to my room and clean up." She tossed the twigs and leaves into the bin and walked across the room, pausing in the doorway as if she'd forgotten something. "Thank you for helping me. And . . ." There was a hesitancy in her voice as she turned to face him again. "Would you mind terribly if I started calling you by your first name? We are business partners after all. You can call me Lily if you'd like."

Owen shuffled from one foot to the other. Thoughts of Rebecca filtered through his mind. He couldn't remember a time in his adult life, before her passing, when she hadn't been in his life. They'd met as teenagers at a church dance. They had been smitten with each other from the first glance. After a few years of courting, they'd married. But ever since Miss Handland had arrived, Owen had been struggling to hang on to those memories. Miss Handland was always bustling about the lodge, leaving the scent of her perfume in her wake. He needed to keep Rebecca close to his heart. In order to do so, he had to keep *this* woman at arm's length.

"Miss Handland, you may call me Owen."

"Thank you, Owen. And please call me by my first name."

He gave a slight shake of his head. He saw the dawning realization in her eyes that he wasn't ready to do so.

"I understand." She turned and left him alone with his thoughts.

Chapter Eight

The day of the tea party dawned with a bit of a drizzle. Standing in front of a big window in the great room, Lily looked out beyond the porch, praying the sun would poke through the clouds soon. Beyond the tree line, the gray clouds were edged in blue—the end of the rainstorm, she hoped. Heavy footfalls sounded behind her, and she turned away from the window to find Mr. Murphy. *Owen,* she reminded herself. The man did not look happy.

"Good morning, Owen."

"Miss Handland, I've been informed by the housekeeper that you're in need of more flowers?" He gave her a stern look. "There are flowers on every tabletop in this room. How could you be in need of any more?"

What he said was true, but because Lily had added a small arrangement to each table, she had none left to decorate the piano. And she needed some there because she'd arranged at the last minute for a young lady to come play during the tea as a surprise for Elsie.

She took a step toward Owen. "I only need a few more of the roses. I saw another bush outside the back porch." Since the little run-in she'd had with the nasty bushes yesterday, Lily had no intention of setting foot near them today. "It would only take you a minute to cut them for me."

He frowned at her. She didn't have time to parley with him. "Please, Owen. I have so much to do before the guests arrive. I have to help get the food plated and bring all the refreshments in here. And the girl I hired to play will be here any minute to practice."

The color drained from his face. Lily's eyes widened. Fearing he might faint, she rushed to his side. "Owen?"

He gestured one hand to the right. "You . . . hired someone to play this piano?"

What on earth could be wrong with her inviting a pianist to the tea? "Yes. I thought the guests, our guests, might enjoy a bit of music playing in the background while they mingle. I didn't think there would be a problem."

"How could you do this without discussing it with me first?"

"I didn't think you'd mind."

"I do mind!" he bellowed.

She took a step back. Why was he so angry? She'd been working for days on this party, and she'd thought Owen had been fine with all the arrangements. The music had been a last-minute addition, but she'd planned on paying the accompanist out of her own savings as a gift to Elsie.

She tried to explain. "Owen, this is my gift to Elsie. There's no need for you to worry about the cost."

"It's not the cost, Miss Handland. This . . ." He seemed to be grasping for composure. "My wife was the last person to play here."

Lily's heart sank. "I'm sorry. I didn't know." Even though she wanted to, Lily couldn't take her actions back. How could she know such things when Owen never spoke of his wife?

She took a tentative step closer to him, hoping to make him understand that it hadn't been her intent to cause him pain. "Owen, you never talk about Rebecca. I had no idea using the piano would be so painful for you."

"She was my wife. She died much too young, leaving me here. Alone. There is nothing more you need to know."

The color in his face began to return, but Lily couldn't move past the haunted look in his eyes . . . the same look she'd seen when he'd come to the cemetery. Having witnessed much loss in her own life, she imagined the pain of losing a spouse was of the worst kind. She longed to tell him everything would be all right, but she wasn't sure how to convince him that he had to have faith, that there might be a bigger plan for him. Owen started to back away from her.

Lily had to think fast, or the day would be ruined. She'd actually thought they'd been getting on better. Maybe she'd read too much into his kindness yesterday. She tried to think of something she could do to make this right, but it was too late to get a message to the young lady she'd hired. More than likely, she was already on her way from Heartston.

"I can't stay here." Owen pushed his way out of the room, bumping into Mrs. Cuddieback on his way out, nearly knocking a tray filled with freshly washed plates out of her hands.

Lily raced across the room to rescue the poor woman.

Mrs. Cuddieback handed the tray off to Lily. "Miss Lily, there had better be a good reason for that man nearly knocking me off my feet! And with only a short time left before our guests arrive. I don't have time to be cleaning up broken glass."

"You did a good job of holding on to the tray and averting a crisis. I apologize for Owen's behavior. I'm afraid it's all my fault. I've done something."

"I hear you calling him by his given name. Does this mean you two are getting along?"

"After today, I'm not sure. You see, I hired a young lady to come play the piano during the tea. It's my gift to Elsie."

The woman's eyebrows shot up. She pressed her lips together as if she were trying to form her thoughts before speaking. "You should have asked about the piano beforehand," she said in a gentle voice.

"I didn't know it would be a problem," Lily said, trying hard to make her case. "No one here ever speaks of Rebecca."

The housekeeper began taking the dishes off the tray and setting them on the large round table where the sandwiches would be. "Owen has had a difficult time since Rebecca's death. Since you arrived, I thought he was moving forward."

"I'm sorry." Lily knew the words sounded hollow.

There were constant reminders of the woman throughout the house—the stationery in the office, a certain feminine touch she'd noticed in the way the room was organized, and now the piano. Lily's job right now was to concentrate on this afternoon's event. If the women were happy with the tea, then they'd be more apt to spread the word to their friends about the Murphy Great Camp. She imagined that making this place successful again would be a good way to honor Rebecca Murphy's memory.

"I'm going to bring in the pitchers of tea. I found a refreshing recipe that called for lavender and honey, both of which we have here on the property."

"That sounds lovely. Thank you, Mrs. Cuddieback, for being so understanding about Owen's and my disagreement."

The housekeeper left the room, leaving Lily to finish adding in the last-minute special touches. It appeared that Owen was not coming back with the flowers, so Lily improvised by taking a few out of the vases and mixing them together in the one on the piano. Stepping back, she looked around the room, admiring her handiwork. On the mantel were white candlesticks set in the crystal holders she'd found in the back-hall storage closet. White linen cloths covered the tables, and the flower arrangements sat in the middle of each one. The pink roses along with the white Queen Anne's lace looked delicate—perfect for a bride-to-be's celebration.

Looking at the clock on the mantel, she realized she had to get herself ready before the guests arrived. She hurried out of the room and headed upstairs to her bedroom, where she freshened up and changed out of her dark-colored work dress into a yellow day gown. Standing in front of the full-length mirror, she repinned her hair into a bun at the nape of her neck and tugged the neckline of her dress into place. Her hand stilled alongside her face as she paused to think about the risk she could be taking by inviting these women here today.

For a moment, she worried that someone might recognize her from the saloon. Giving herself a mental shake, she realized how ridiculous the thought was. These women would never have been seen in the saloon, and Lily had been careful never to go about town, in or out of her disguise. For the most part, she'd been busy with the last case, and she'd spent the little free time she had left alone in her rented room.

She gave herself one last look in the mirror. No one would remember her, she told herself again, turning away and heading downstairs to help with the finishing touches.

Joining Mrs. Cuddieback in the kitchen, Lily helped her arrange the sandwiches on a beautiful cut glass platter.

"These look scrumptious," she declared, smelling freshly cut cucumbers and lemon-dill sauce sandwiched between the slices of sourdough bread.

"This is a family recipe, but I added a little something special for Miss Mitchell's tea." The woman beamed in delight. "Even if things got off on a bad footing with you and Owen, I'm glad you convinced him to open the camp for this event."

"Me, too."

The door knocker thumped against the front door, so Lily left the sandwiches and hurried down the hallway to answer it. She found the young pianist standing on the doorstep. From the look of the smile beaming out from beneath her bonnet, the girl was no more than nineteen or twenty years old. The pianist removed her bonnet, revealing round cornflower-blue eyes and straight blonde hair that hung to her waist. A blue satin ribbon tied around her head held her hair off her face.

The young lady stuck out her hand. "Miss Handland, I'm Myra Smith. It's a pleasure to meet you."

Lily shook her hand, holding the door wide so she could enter the foyer. Peering around her petite frame, she saw the sun breaking through the clouds. "Looks like the weather is going to cooperate for us today. I hope you didn't get rained on."

"No. The rain stopped soon after I left Heartston. I'm lucky to have an enclosed carriage."

Lily saw that Mr. Cuddieback had come around to tend to the horse and buggy. She hoped Owen might be with him, but he was nowhere in sight. Closing the door, she escorted Myra to the great room and led her to the piano.

Myra ran her hand lightly along the ivory keys. "My, this is a lovely piece. Do you mind if I warm up?"

"Please sit." Lily stepped back so Myra could pull the bench out.

Soon the room was filled with the sound of music. Lily had gotten so used to the tinny saloon piano that she'd almost forgotten how nice a tuned instrument could sound. She didn't know the name of the song that Myra played, although she did recognize the tune as one she'd heard during church services. Leaving the woman to play, Lily went back to the kitchen.

There was still no sign of Owen. She found his absence disturbing. Lily had a feeling that any headway they'd made over the past weeks had taken a few steps backward. There'd be more time to dwell on that later, but right now the food and drinks needed attention.

She picked up one of the platters piled high with the cucumber treats and took it into the great room. Once she'd found a place for the sandwiches on the far side of the buffet table, she retraced her steps and grabbed one of the two pitchers off the worktable. This one was filled with a divine lavender-honey lemonade; they had another filled to the brim with a special herbed tea blend. Mrs. Cuddieback had assured her both drinks used to be the most requested beverages during the camp's previous heyday.

Again, Lily imagined how this camp could be brought back to life. If she had her way, her planned makeover would happen in a few short months. Today was a new beginning for the Murphy Great Camp. She only hoped Owen would come back and join her to see what possibilities lay ahead.

"Miss Handland, if I might make a suggestion?"

"Yes." Lily paused, raising an eyebrow, picking up a bit of a tone in the housekeeper's voice.

"Add some kid gloves to your wardrobe." She pointed at Lily's hands.

Following her gaze, she saw the red welts left behind by yesterday's mishap. Of course, she'd intended to cover them and had simply forgotten to grab the gloves from the drawer in the closet. "Thank you for reminding me. If you're set here, I'll run along and get them before our guests arrive."

The door knocker sounded as she made her way back down the staircase. Pausing on the second step from the bottom, Lily ran a nervous hand down the front of her dress, smoothing out nonexistent wrinkles. Then she took a deep, fortifying breath and blew it out.

She answered the door to find Elsie Mitchell on the porch, smiling warmly, a pretty white parasol clutched in her hand. Behind her stood a dozen women, all chattering excitedly, which made it difficult for Lily to make out a word Elsie was saying.

In the middle of the group she recognized Amy from the bakery and gave her a welcoming smile.

"This place is as pretty as I remember it," said a tall, thin older woman with dark hair.

A shorter blonde woman stepped forward, untying her peach-colored bonnet. "The drive through the woods was stunning! There were deer and birds. The flowers looked so dewy after the rain."

Another lady came at Lily, wagging a blue parasol in front of her. "The sun came out just as we boarded the wagon. But if you expect to keep your skin from reddening, then this"—she snapped it closed—"is a must!"

Finally able to extract Elsie from the group, Lily took hold of her arm and gently pulled her through the doorway and into a warm embrace.

"It's good to see you again!" Lily said, unable to keep the excitement out of her voice. She really wanted to have a lasting friendship with Elsie. Even though they'd been through a lot together over the past year—with much of their experiences mired in subterfuge—Lily hoped they could move beyond those dark times into brighter ones.

"Lily," Elsie said, kissing her on the cheek. "We're so lucky the weather cleared. It made the trip out here a pretty ride. It's been a long time since I've been out this way. Amy and I have always talked about coming out to one of these camps for tea."

Lily's smile widened. "Now you get to have your very own in honor of your upcoming nuptials." Stepping back, she swept the door open, inviting everyone inside. Elsie stood nearby, introducing each woman in turn as they passed through the doorway. Lily couldn't even begin to keep all their names straight. She squeezed Amy's hand as she walked by.

"Thank you for having us," Amy said, pausing by Lily with a bright smile.

"You're welcome. I hope you enjoy our tea service."

"I'm sure I will." Amy followed the last of the ladies into the great room.

As Lily moved to close the front door, she noticed a wagonette parked in the yard. The large conveyance had springs and a long back where two green velvet–covered benches faced each other. The group must have all ridden out here together. Liking the idea of being able to transport large groups of people back and forth from the village—and in such comfort—Lily made a mental note to look into getting one for the camp.

A man stood with his back to her, tending to the horses. Lily assumed he was a hired driver. Closing the door against the humid air left behind by the summer rain, she made her way into the great room.

Clapping her hands together, she had to shout to be heard above the din of female voices. "Ladies! Ladies! If I could have your attention for one moment."

They settled, and Lily welcomed them. "I'd like to thank you all for accepting Elsie's invitation to come all the way out here to celebrate her engagement. The staff and I have been hard at work putting together some special treats for this afternoon's tea."

The women of Heartston, dressed in their Sunday best and scattered about the great room, watched her with rapt attention. Lily felt so proud of this moment, it was hard for her to keep those feelings inside and remain professional.

"We have some delicious cucumber sandwiches and some lemon iced tea cakes. To quench your thirst, the pitchers on the refreshment table are filled with your choice of honey-lavender lemonade or herbed iced tea."

Trying not to appear too pretentious, she glided across the room, coming to a stop behind the table and spreading her arms wide. "Please come help yourselves. And then find a seat. I have a special treat in store for you."

The chatter grew louder as the women rounded their plates. Lily filled the cut glass cups with tea and lemonade, catching snippets of conversations. The woman with the blue parasol talked to the shorter blonde about a trip she and her husband were planning to New York City. Someone else wanted to know if Amy could make up some cookies for an upcoming birthday party.

Lily marveled at the easy comradery these women shared. She'd never had any friends; poverty had left her and her mother concentrating on survival, and the transient lifestyle of being a Pinkerton agent had kept her on the move, making it hard to connect with anyone. She kept a smile on her face, watching them, giving a kind nod here and there, when inside she fought the deep pull of envy. Now that her days with the Pinkertons were over, Lily wanted *this* more than anything in the world.

Amy approached her with an empty glass.

"What can I get for you?" Lily asked.

"I'll take some lemonade, please. Any chance you could share this recipe?"

Lily winked at her. "Unfortunately, it belongs to the Murphy Camp. I couldn't possibly divulge the secret ingredients." Then an idea came to her. If she could add some allure to this event, maybe it would entice the women to return as paying guests. Of course, the recipe belonged to Mrs. Cuddieback, which meant at some point Lily had to discuss keeping this a secret.

Handing Amy back a full glass, Lily realized most everyone had found a place to sit. Elsie took the chair with the ribbons dangling from the sides. The pianist was seated with her fingers poised over the keys. The time had come to give Elsie her gift.

"Ladies, again, welcome. I'd like to say a few words to our bride-to-be. I've heard that Elsie Mitchell is one of the finest schoolteachers Heartston has ever had. I know she is beloved by many." She paused as the women applauded, doubtful about the rest of her speech. She couldn't be certain what any of the women knew about the circumstances that had brought the happy couple together.

"The path that led Elsie and William Benton to each other has been filled with challenges." She heard the murmurs and saw several of the women nodding. Her good spirits stumbled, leaving Lily uncertain as to whether she'd crossed a line. She looked to Elsie for assurance. Elsie gave her a warm smile.

Lily took a breath and continued. "And through it all, and with their faith in God, their faith in family, and their faith in love, the two of them have remained steadfast and steady." Walking to Elsie, Lily bent and laid a hand on her shoulder. "My gift to you is a special performance by Heartston's very own, Myra Smith."

Myra's fingers trailed over the piano's ivory keys as she began playing a lovely soulful tune. Lily stepped away from Elsie's table to allow everyone a good view of the pianist. She glanced around the room, satisfied. All the guests were smiling and seemed to be enjoying the refreshments, as well as Myra's performance. It thrilled her to no end that all their hard work had paid off. Once again, she reminded herself how lucky she was to have made her way to Heartston and to the Murphy Camp.

Careful not to disturb anyone, she wandered back to the refreshment table. The lemonade needed refilling, and one of the tea cake platters was running low. Taking the pitcher and plate with her, she left quietly. She passed by Mrs. Cuddieback, who had been standing in the doorway, enjoying the music.

"You stay here. I can handle this," Lily told her. The poor woman had worked tirelessly all week long; she deserved a respite.

Heading into the kitchen, she noticed a man standing with his back to her, looking out the window over the sink. "Excuse me, may I help you?"

He turned, and she found herself looking into the dark eyes of her former Pinkerton partner, William Benton.

"Will!" She couldn't keep the surprise from her voice. His tall form and broad shoulders blocked some of the sunlight streaming in through the windowpanes. He swept his black felt wide-brimmed hat off his head.

"Lily. I know you're surprised to see me." His voice sounded as gravelly as she remembered it.

"Those words would be an understatement," she said, holding her head high as she moved past him, wondering how she could have been so naive as to think she wouldn't see Will again. Of course she was going to run into him at some point. *But why did it have to be today of all days?*

"What are you doing here?" he demanded in a quiet voice.

Putting the plate and pitcher on the worktable, she spun around to face him. "I could ask you the same question, Will," she said, folding her arms across her chest. The minute the words left her mouth, she knew how foolish they sounded. Will was Elsie's fiancé; it made perfect sense for him to be here.

"I escorted Elsie and her friends. Lily, I thought you'd left town. You could have knocked me over with a feather when Elsie informed me that you were staying here at Owen Murphy's camp. And that you were hosting a tea for her."

She pursed her lips, reining in her temper. "I'm not staying here, Will. I'm a partner in this business."

"You can't be here."

A knot formed in the pit of her stomach. His blunt words took more than a bit of the shine off the day, and for a split second, she felt the shame of her past creeping in. She tipped her head back a notch. "Why can't I be here?"

After the last case had been closed, Will had stayed on in Heartston. Why did he think it should be different for her?

He took a step toward her with his arms wide. "Lily, does Owen know who you really are?"

"He knows I'm Lily Handland. Because that's who I am."

Will narrowed his eyes and lowered his voice, glancing over his shoulder to be sure no one could overhear them. "Does he know that you were a Pinkerton agent? How does he think you know Elsie?"

"Will! This is nonsense." She tried to shrug off his hurtful remarks. "He hasn't asked me about my past."

Will sighed. "Don't you think he's eventually going to want to know about you? About where you come from? How you came to be wealthy enough to invest in his business?"

"You make it sound like I should be ashamed of my time with the Pinkertons." Lily wasn't sure what bothered her more, the fact that he was suggesting she didn't deserve a new beginning to her life or that somehow Will thought he could have a new life here and she couldn't. "You really don't think I belong here." Her voice came out small, and she realized he'd hurt her deeper than she'd thought possible. What did he want her to do, disappear into the night?

He shook his head. Poking a finger at her, he warned, "I said no such thing. You are treading on very thin ice, Lily."

"I know." She admitted. "I can't tell him about the things I've done. You of all people should understand that. I'm not even sure what he thinks about me, but I do know he was a broken man when I came here. These past few weeks I've seen a subtle change in him. For the better. He seems interested in the business."

"Owen is one of Elsie's friends, Lily, and because of that, I consider him a friend of mine. Elsie tells me he suffered a tremendous loss when Rebecca died. He's kept himself closed off from the world for far too long. If you can make him involved in living again, then you have my blessings. But you need to tell him the truth before things go too far."

Before things go too far. Did Will think there was something other than a business relationship between her and Owen? "There is nothing going on between Owen and myself," she said in a soft voice. "We are partners. That's all."

He narrowed his gaze, studying her for a moment. "You can keep telling yourself that, Lily, but I'm not buying any of it."

Will wasn't convinced of her motives. And it didn't matter, because she needed to get back to the party. Her guests would be wondering what was keeping her.

"If we're finished here, I need to go back out there." She turned her back to him, busied herself with refilling the plate and the pitcher, and noticed her hands were trembling. Pausing, she took a moment to compose herself. She turned around to tell Will she could handle the situation with her new partner only to find that Owen had returned.

"Owen!" She gripped the platter to keep it from falling onto the floor. It seemed this was her day for surprises.

Chapter Nine

"Miss Handland? Will?"

He looked back and forth between the two of them. *What was going on?* He could sense a tension between the two of them, and he'd obviously interrupted what appeared to be an important conversation.

"Hey, Owen. It's good to see you." Will moved toward him, blocking Owen's view of his curiously flustered partner. Will stuck out his hand and Owen shook it.

"Will. I didn't expect to find you at the camp today." Owen remembered hearing that the man was a former Pinkerton who'd come to Heartston to find a thief. Somehow he'd ended up saving Elsie and falling in love with her in the process. Owen had also heard that Will was working with John Oliver at the local lumberyard.

"Elsie decided at the last minute to rent one of those large, fancy wagons from the livery. I offered to drive them out here. Have you ever ridden for any amount of time with a dozen women?" he asked, grimacing.

"Can't say as I have," Owen answered, casting a glance in Miss Handland's direction. He could see her now, standing at the worktable where she appeared to be busy rearranging the cakes on the platter and avoiding eye contact with him.

"Let me tell you their chattering was enough to scare a flock of geese out of the swamp water. Between their carrying on and the geese squawking, it was all I could do to keep the horses from spooking."

"I'll try not to get myself involved in anything like that."

"Elsie tells me you're going to be opening the camp again. I'm glad to hear that, Owen."

Again, Owen tried to catch Miss Handland's eye. This time she out and out avoided meeting his gaze. "I didn't realize that you and Miss Handland knew each other," he said. Thinking through his own words, Owen realized he had no idea who Miss Handland's friends were, other than Elsie Mitchell.

"You know how it is in a small town; eventually everyone knows everyone," Will said, glancing at Miss Handland.

Owen shrugged. He had a point. "Sure." That still didn't explain the ongoing tension in the room. He didn't think it had anything to do with the argument he'd had with Miss Handland earlier, either. No, there was definitely something amiss here.

He'd come in to talk about the way he'd reacted earlier. After he'd left her in the great room, he'd taken a long walk around the property, passing by the small cabins situated on a knoll above the pond. After taking a closer look at them, he thought Miss Handland had been right in suggesting they work on renovating them. Maybe he'd even move into one of them while they worked on the house. He couldn't go back to the bedroom he'd shared with his wife.

In the time it took him to walk along the same path that the deer used when coming to drink at the pond, Owen had come to a conclusion. Either he was all in for the changes being made at the Murphy Camp, or he could simply hand the keys over to his partner, lock, stock, and barrel. And that's why he'd come to the kitchen—to find her and tell her what he intended to do.

"Lily! Oh, there you are." Mrs. Cuddieback came bustling into the room, looking flustered. "The ladies are inquiring about more refreshments." Clapping her hands, she declared, "It seems my tea cakes were a big hit. And to think I added them at the very last minute. Miss Amy wants that recipe and the one for the lemonade for her bakery. But I think we'll keep those for ourselves." She winked.

"I have the cakes and lemonade right here." Without looking at Owen, Lily picked up the platter and let Mrs. Cuddieback take the lemonade. The ladies left the room.

Miss Handland's voice drifted down the hallway. "I agree. We need to keep those secret ingredients to ourselves. Little things like that will make people want to come here to the Murphy Camp."

Their voices faded. Owen became aware of Will studying him. He walked over to the table, took a sandwich off the remaining plate, and popped the whole thing into his mouth. This was what those women were calling sandwiches? Why, they were nothing more than scraps to him. Delectable scraps.

He looked over his shoulder, offering one to Will. "You want to try one? They might be tiny, but they sure are good."

Will shook his head. "Thanks. But I'm saving my appetite for dinner." He pushed away from the edge of the sink. "I guess I'll wait outside for the ladies."

Owen felt like a cad. He was being a terrible host. "I think there might be some sarsaparilla in the pantry. Would you like me to grab you a glass?"

"That sounds good."

After Owen found the bottle, he poured out two mugs full and led Will out onto the back porch. Mr. Cuddieback made sarsaparilla monthly, using the roots from a plant he grew out in the garden. Owen didn't know what all was in the concoction, but it sure took the edge off a hot day. He waited while Will settled in one of the rockers and then handed off the bottle, his mind still working on his next conversation with Miss Handland. Owen didn't feel much like sitting still. He sipped from the mug as he paced along the path of the railing, barely tasting the frothy goodness of the drink.

"Owen. You want to tell me what's got you so worked up?"

"Nope."

He felt sure that Will was a good man. After all, the schoolteacher seemed smitten enough with him to agree to marry him. But Owen didn't know him at all, and he'd never been one to spill his guts. As he raised his mug to his lips again, it occurred to him that wasn't entirely true. He'd shared darn near everything with Rebecca.

Owen put his drink on the flat top of the railing, working at keeping his lower lip from trembling. Some days he missed her so much his emotions felt like a wound that never healed, all raw and open. He knew he needed to change his life. Prayer had been his only attempt to dissolve the pain. Some days that worked. Today he felt as if he were in the middle of a tug-of-war. On one side stood his past with Rebecca. The other end of the rope held a future—maybe not one as bright as he'd have liked, but it looked a lot better than where he'd been standing for the past two years.

"I've let this place get run-down. I've been holed up here for so long I think any friends I might have had before"—he swallowed down his emotions—"before my wife died have forgotten me. I got angry with Miss Handland before, over the piano." He spoke with his back to Will, staring out over the rolling lawn to a spot at the top of the tree line that edged the property. He picked his mug up again, mostly to keep his hands busy. Not sure why he'd confided in a person he barely knew, Owen waited for him to say something.

The rocker creaked under Will's weight. "First of all, this place is looking good. Then again, I didn't see it before, so I've nothing to compare it to. Second, I don't think your friends have abandoned you. My best guess: they've been worrying about you and are unsure of how to proceed."

Owen turned and put his back up against the porch railing, facing Will. Listening. Ready to take some advice.

"As for Miss Handland, well, there isn't much advice I can give you on that one. You can talk to her and apologize. She seems like she might be of a forgiving nature."

"I thought you said you didn't know her all that well." Owen saw something flicker in Will's eyes. The man glanced over his shoulder before his gaze shifted back to Owen. Draining the rest of his drink, Will stood. "I don't know her that well. Just a feeling I got is all."

The sound of women's laughter filtered down the hallway and out onto the porch. "Sounds like they're having a good time," Owen commented. Not liking the sediment left behind by the root used to make the drink, he tossed the last dregs of his sarsaparilla over the side of the porch.

He recognized Miss Handland's voice.

"How about one more song from Myra before you leave?"

Her question was followed by cheers and applause. Owen fisted his hands. That piano had been his gift to Rebecca on their third wedding anniversary. He should have given it away.

Then he heard a voice he didn't know. "How about something we can sing to?"

The strains of "Bringing in the Sheaves" filled the house.

Bringing in the sheaves, bringing in the sheaves,
We shall come rejoicing, bringing in the sheaves

The ladies did a wonderful job of harmonizing on the refrain. Closing his eyes, Owen let the music wash over him. This song had been one of Rebecca's favorites. He wanted to run down the hallway and tell them to stop. In the next instant, he wanted the music to continue so he could find some peace. He felt a strong hand grip his shoulder and opened his eyes to find Will standing before him.

"Owen, trust me when I tell you the best way to get rid of your pain is to give it up to the Lord."

He bowed his head. "I'm trying."

"Take it one day at a time, my friend."

Raising his gaze to meet Will's, Owen clapped him on the back. "Thank you."

"Welcome. Now what do you say we go join the ladies."

He nudged his head to the side. "Let's walk around the porch. That way you can enjoy more of the view before we head inside."

They entered the great room through the double glass doors. The women were standing in a big circle with their heads bowed in prayer. Owen and Will stood quietly on the threshold, waiting for them to finish. He heard their "amen" and came inside.

Upon seeing her betrothed, Elsie rushed across the room into his arms. "Will!" She kissed him on the cheek. "I hope you and Owen had a good visit."

"We did." Putting an arm around her, he leaned in to drop a kiss on the top of her head. "We need to start back. It's going to be dark soon."

"Yes. Let's get home." Beaming from head to toe, she came over to Owen, taking both of his hands in hers. She gave them a gentle squeeze. "Thank you so much for letting us spend the afternoon here. Lily is doing a wonderful job of bringing the camp back to life. You are a lucky man to have her for a business partner." Elsie released his hands.

Owen's gaze flickered over to Miss Handland, who was busy ushering the ladies out the door into the hallway. She turned her head toward him. Their gazes met. He nodded, hoping she knew he meant it as a gesture of thanks. She paused with her hand on the piano player's forearm, tipping her head to one side, the corners of her mouth turned up ever so slightly. The young lady said something Owen couldn't make out and Lily laughed.

He didn't think he'd ever heard her laugh before. The sound she made reminded him of sunlight and joy.

As he walked with Will and Elsie to the hallway to meet up with the rest of the group, a woman he recognized from church approached him.

"Mr. Murphy, we had a wonderful afternoon. I'm going to tell all my friends to come out here for an afternoon tea."

"That's very kind of you, thank you." Over the top of the woman's head, he caught sight of Miss Handland holding the door open. From the satisfied look on her face, he could tell she'd overheard the remark.

In a bustle of bonnets and hugs, the ladies left the house, leaving Owen and Lily alone in the quiet hallway. She breezed past him.

"Hey, where are you going in such a hurry?" he asked.

"I should help with the cleanup."

She tried to continue to the kitchen, but he caught hold of her wrist. "Please come into the office with me. I have something to tell you."

Wariness fluttered over her face. "All right. But instead of talking in the office, can we go into the great room? I don't want to leave the mess for Mrs. Cuddieback."

"I suppose we can talk while we work." He released her wrist and let her go ahead of him.

Once inside the great room, he took a closer look at the transformation. He'd been so caught up in his anger that he hadn't noticed how pretty the tables were done up, and even with the empty dishes and crumbs on the tablecloths, the place still appeared a darn sight better than when he'd shut Murphy Camp down and covered all the furniture in dust cloths.

A flash of color caught his eye. She'd placed the flowers on top of the piano. Rebecca's piano.

He gestured toward a chair that had been placed at an angle facing the windows. "You look like you could use a rest."

She nibbled at her lower lip. "I'll take a break, but for only a few minutes. I really do have a lot of work left, Owen."

He clasped his hands behind him, rocking back on his heels. "I understand."

Owen watched as she smoothed out the back of her skirts and then sat in the chair with a sigh. She placed her hands in her lap, linking her fingers together, and looked up at him. When he didn't speak right away, she arched one of her pale eyebrows, curious, he supposed, for an explanation. Silence descended.

He gritted his teeth. Unclenching his jaw, he glanced over at the clock on the mantel and noticed it was nearing six o'clock. He'd lost a bit of that confidence he found earlier. Maybe this wasn't a good time to have his say. Unclasping his hands, he made a great show of adjusting his shirt.

"Owen," she said in a stern voice.

"I'm sorry. I'm afraid I'm a bit nervous."

"About what?"

"Look, I know things haven't been easy for us. I haven't been the most cooperative person to get along with. As you know, I've been through a great deal over the past few years."

"I know that."

He moved on heavy feet over to the middle of the room where the piano sat. He imagined Rebecca sitting on the red velvet pad that covered the bench. She'd be dressed in her favorite blue satin gown, the one with the white lace collar. Her long curly hair would be loose, flowing down to just below her shoulders. He imagined her slender fingers poised over the keys. She'd loved to play. He extended his arm, running his fingers ever so lightly over the ivory and black keys.

"This belonged to my wife. I purchased it as a surprise for our third wedding anniversary." He rubbed his chest, trying to soothe the sudden ache, remembering how she'd cried tears of joy. He moved his hand along the shiny top, feeling the coolness of the wood beneath his fingertips, thinking about that day and how she'd played a full one-hour concert, just for him.

"I shouldn't have yelled at you earlier. Rebecca would have been disappointed in me for treating you the way I have these past weeks." He waited for her to respond. Silence greeted him. Rolling his eyes heavenward, he prayed he'd find better words to express his apology.

"I'm sorry I've been so hard on you," he finally managed.

He heard the rustling of her gown. Turning, he saw that she had moved out of the chair and now stood with her hands resting along the back of it.

"I'm sorry, too. I'm afraid I tend to get carried away when I get excited about something. I shouldn't have pushed to host a tea so soon. And if I had known about the piano, I would have asked permission first. That was insensitive of me."

He smiled at her. "The tea turned out to be a huge success."

"Yes. I think we had a wonderful afternoon. Elsie and her friends had a grand time. A lot of them were asking when the next one will be." She ran her tongue over her lower lip. "Owen, I'd like you to consider hosting a weekly afternoon tea. I was thinking we could start offering them in two weeks' time. We could begin with Saturday afternoons and then maybe add in Sunday dinners."

Owen felt the panic rising inside of him. He didn't want to rush into anything, but Miss Handland seemed set, once again, on pushing forward with her ideas. He focused on thinking about what Rebecca would want him to do.

"Now, Owen. Before you turn me down, listen to my reasoning. If we start holding events like these, we can charge a fair amount for people to come out for our teas and dinners. Maybe Myra would want to play on a regular basis. This way we can begin to build our accounts so we can use that money to keep the day-to-day operations running. In addition, we have to find a way to pay Theodore and Alice Cuddieback for their services. That couple is truly a godsend, and I don't want to lose them."

Alice bustled into the room, carrying an empty serving tray, and slapped it on top of one of the tables. Placing a hand on her ample hip, she declared, "Theodore and I are not leaving here. We consider this our home. Although it would be nice to have a salary, in case we need it for a rainy day." Having said her piece, she began filling the tray with dirty dishes and soiled napkins.

"All right. Miss Handland and I will discuss salaries tomorrow," he said to Mrs. Cuddieback. He turned to Lily again. "Put that on your agenda for our morning meeting."

"I will," Lily said as she balled up a dirty tablecloth and started a pile on the floor next to her.

"Tomorrow is the Lord's Day," Mrs. Cuddieback reminded them. "The only meeting you should be attending is the church one."

Owen paused. He hadn't intended on going to church just yet. "I meant the meeting on Monday."

"The mister and I have extra room in our carriage if the two of you would like to join us." Mrs. Cuddieback stood at the buffet table, looking back and forth between Owen and Lily. "We'll be ready to leave at eight on the dot. I won't be tolerating tardiness on the Lord's Day."

Owen didn't say a word. Lily, on the other hand, accepted the invitation. The ladies seemed to be waiting on him to respond. Chewing the idea over, he thought he might be able to manage a day in the village. "I'll be ready."

Hoping to distract the two of them from thinking any more about tomorrow, he changed the subject. "Miss Handland, there's one more thing you should know."

Chapter Ten

Lily paused in her work, watching Owen warily, not knowing what to expect. He could certainly be a hard man to read.

"And what might that be?" she asked. She had decided that using a bit more caution when dealing with him might make their working together a bit easier.

"I'm going to be sleeping in one of the cabins. Earlier, after I left you, I went for a walk to think things through, and I came upon the row of guest cabins. I think I found one that isn't in need of a lot of work. The roof is in good shape, and there's a single bed inside. It will suit my needs perfectly."

"I don't want you to move out of the main house on my account," she said, although she felt relieved he didn't appear to be too upset by his decision.

"I'm not. For days now, you've been encouraging me to stop sleeping in the office. This seems like a good enough solution."

"But . . . what about the . . ." She exchanged a quick look with Mrs. Cuddieback, who was still gathering up dishes. Lily wanted to know why he didn't use the bedroom at the far end of the upstairs hall—the same one that had remained locked since the morning he'd caught her coming out of it. Mrs. Cuddieback gave her the slightest of head shakes before focusing again on her work.

The expression on Owen's face tightened as his shoulders stiffened. She recognized the signs of his withdrawing from the conversation. It was hopeless to continue with this topic.

He held up a hand, stopping her from any further argument. "I've made up my mind."

"All right. As you wish."

"For now, though, I can stay here and help you clean up . . . handle the heavy lifting." He rushed to the older woman's side, offering aid. "Here, let me take the tray into the kitchen." He took it out of her hands.

Wiping her hands down her apron, she thanked him. "It's right kind of you to stay and help out. And if you need me to gather up some fresh bedding for you, let me know."

"You are a godsend, to be sure, Mrs. Cuddieback." Owen seemed to relax a bit more as he carried the tray from the room.

With the three of them working together, the cleanup was finished in no time. Alone in the room, Lily folded the short lid over the piano keys. After finding the dust cloth in the corner closet, she shook it out over the top. The white sheet billowed out, settling like a soft cloud over the instrument. Pausing in her work, she imagined an early evening much like this one, with dusk falling around the house, coating the mountains in soft rose-colored hues. Owen and his wife might have relaxed here at the end of the day for a bit of music. Knowing it wouldn't be wise to continue with those thoughts, she blew out the remaining candles and left the room.

She found Owen and Mrs. Cuddieback in the kitchen engaged in a lively conversation about the henhouse, of all things.

"I think the entire coop needs to be rebuilt," the older woman proclaimed, wagging a finger at him from the other side of the room.

Owen's face had taken on a reddish hue. Lily couldn't help thinking that this didn't bode well for the woman.

"You can't be serious," he countered. "Your husband and I were out there yesterday, and the coop looks to be in perfect order."

"The hens are not laying as they should be. Clearly, they are not happy." She swatted her hands in the air. "They need more light in there. Put in another opening."

"If we put in another opening, then we risk more animals getting in to harm them. Or have you forgotten what damage the skunks did a few months back?"

"I have not." Narrowing her eyes, she stared him down. "I suppose you could be right, but at least tell me you'll go look at the coop. If we are going to be entertaining guests here, then I'll need more eggs for my recipes."

"I will add it to my list." Owen frowned. "The list that seems to be never ending."

Lily walked over to the sink, where she picked up a towel and began drying the plates that had been washed, rinsed, and set in a wooden rack on the counter. Since she didn't know anything about raising chickens, she thought it best to steer clear of that conversation. From behind her she heard Mrs. Cuddieback's tired-sounding sigh.

Still holding a cup in her hand, Lily paused in the drying. "Owen and I can finish up here. You should go on and find your husband."

Untying her apron, the stout woman's eyes crinkled up as she smiled her thanks. "I'm going to do just that." Nodding in the direction of the stove, she said, "There's a leftover casserole on the back burner."

"Have you eaten?" Lily didn't want to send her off without any supper.

"I've already taken some supper out to our rooms. You and Mr. Owen can carry on without us."

"Have a good night," Lily said. "I'll see you in the morning."

The woman was halfway out the door when she stopped and turned back around to look at the two of them. "Today was a good day for the Murphy Camp." Her gaze passed over to Owen. "You should be proud of what our Miss Handland accomplished. I'll see you in the morning for church." Blowing out a breath, she bade them good night, leaving Lily alone with Owen.

He joined her at the sink. For a few minutes, they stood shoulder to shoulder in silence, drying the remainder of the dishes. She handed him the last teacup. The thin china looked small and delicate in his large, work-worn hands. Lily tried not to think about yesterday, when he'd helped her get the rose thorn out of her hand. Most of the welts had faded a bit, although the wound she'd received from the deepest thorn still ached a little.

"Your hands seem to have healed nicely," he observed, as if reading her mind.

"I rubbed a bit of the salve on them this morning and wore a pair of kid gloves to cover them." Lily let out a small laugh. "I imagine seeing my red welts would have been quite a fright to some of the ladies."

"I think they would have understood," he said, hanging the damp towel on one of the wooden dowels attached to the wall.

A light breeze ruffled her skirts. Turning her face in the direction from which it had come, Lily closed her eyes, taking delight in the coolness of the air as it hit her warm skin. Earlier the weather had gone from rain to humidity, and now they were being blessed with the coolness of a beautiful Adirondack summer's evening.

Owen's deep voice broke into her meditation. "Would you like to fix some plates and eat outside on the back porch?"

She opened her eyes to find him standing so close to her that the tiny beads of perspiration along his dark brow line were visible. He'd rolled his shirtsleeves up above his elbows, showing off strong forearms covered in a light smattering of curly hair. Her gaze traveled across his broad shoulders, up to the rough stubble along his cheeks and chin, and finally rested on his dark eyes.

He appeared to be studying her, too. Lily fought the urge to check her hair. She knew what a sight she must be. After all, the day had been long with preparation, presentation, and now cleaning up. Her hair had come loose from the bun she'd tied it off in hours ago, and her dress had water spots on it from the wet dishes.

And from the feel of the heat on her cheekbones, she suspected her face was sporting red splotches.

"Miss Handland?" He cocked an eyebrow. "Did you hear me?"

Her attention snapped back to his inquiry. "Yes. I'd love to have our supper out on the porch." Making quick work of hanging her towel next to his on a dowel, she helped him plate their meal.

When he took the lid off the pot on the back burner, Lily groaned in delight. She took a moment to savor the delicious scents emanating from the pot where pieces of venison lay nestled in a thick gravy, along with what looked to be turnips and carrots.

"Whatever that woman desires," she said, "she can have. Trust me when I tell you, her talents as a cook will keep people coming back here."

Owen leaned in, waving his hand over the open pot so he could take in the savory scents. Nodding in agreement, he finished adding the stew to the plates. "I'll take these out, if you want to grab us a drink. Oh, and the forks and spoons are over in a drawer in the pantry. You can grab those, too."

Moving over to the worktable, she filled two tall glasses with the last of the lavender-honey lemonade. Then she grabbed the eating utensils and picked up two cloth napkins. "I'm right behind you."

Finally joining him at a small round table that overlooked the backyard, she set their drinks down on the table. Smoothing the back of her skirt, she sat on the rattan chair that Owen held out for her.

She allowed him to push the chair in underneath her. "Thank you."

Out here the air seemed even cooler. Lily understood why people traveled so far to stay at places like this. Even in Heartston the air could be stuffy. She remembered being on assignments in Albany and New York City, where the streets were teeming with people. She didn't miss the long lines of wagons and horses plodding through the crowded streets. On days like this one, there would be no relief from the heat.

Owen shoveled a spoonful of the stew into his mouth, chewing with a gusto she'd never seen. She dug in to her plate, taking a much more manageable, smaller spoonful than his, and savored the flavors of the meal. Once again she wondered how something so simple could taste like it had come out of a fancy restaurant. Maybe one day Mrs. Cuddieback would teach her some of her secrets.

"When Rebecca and I first came here, this porch was in shambles. I had to cut a piece of tree limb and hoist it up underneath to hold up the very spot where we're sitting."

Lily tried not to glance over the edge. The footing felt strong enough under them now.

"My wife purchased all the furniture in the house. She had it brought here in big wagonloads. It took about a month to get everything delivered. The rains that year caused flooding that took out part of the road. That set us back an entire spring while we waited for the road to dry out."

Lily blinked in surprise. This was the most she'd heard Owen ever say about his wife. The best thing to do would be to let him have his say, even though she wanted nothing more than to ask him a thousand questions. How did they come to own this place? Were they both from this area? Did Owen ever want to remarry and start a family? And what on earth did one do out here in the middle of winter?

She felt certain that that season would be filled with little sunlight, frigid mornings, and lots of snow. Just thinking about the change in seasons gave her the shivers.

"But rather than sitting around, lamenting about the delays," Owen said, "Rebecca worked on putting together a special play for the children in her church school classes. She devised an entire program with music and simple things the children could do. They worked on it all summer long and then gave us a special program that fall."

He grimaced, as if in physical pain. "She loved the Lord with all her heart," he said in a soft voice. "Her faith was infallible. Rebecca . . . was perfect in every way. I don't think she'd be too happy with me right now." He pulled the napkin up to his mouth and wiped it clean. He swallowed. "She'd have been pleased to have someone using the piano."

Lily stared at him in stunned silence. This burst of conversation was so unlike the man she knew that she wasn't sure how to proceed. Of all the words he'd said about his wife, one thing stuck out; he thought his wife to be perfect in every way. Lily's insides twisted. What would he think if he found out the truth about Lily?

"Do I have some food stuck on my face, Miss Handland?"

She shook her head.

"You are staring at me. I thought perhaps I'd missed something with my napkin."

"I . . ."

"Go on."

"I didn't expect to be having this conversation with you."

"Ah. I don't normally discuss my wife, but you seem to need to know more about her."

"Knowing things does make my job easier." She paused, debating whether she should venture into dangerous territory. "Like the incident with the piano," she finally said. "If I had known the pain it would cause you, I would have hired a harpist."

He scooped up the last of his stew, leaned back in the chair, and patted his full stomach. "That's water under the bridge. I'll try to be more forthcoming with you, on one condition: you return the favor.

After all, I don't know anything about you other than the fact that you seem to have a knack for running this business."

Lily busied herself by taking a long, slow sip from her glass of lemonade. She took her time tasting the subtle hint of lavender, letting the sweetness of the honey tickle the sides of her tongue. When she was finished, she set the glass down, licking her lips. Thoughts of Will—and his secrets—came to mind. His double life had nearly put an end to his relationship with Elsie.

Her situation was different. She and Owen were merely business partners. Still, he deserved to know more about her. But what could she tell him without revealing too much about her past? Lily's intuition whispered to her that Owen Murphy might not be able to accept the truth about the things she'd done. Imagining his wife on a pedestal wouldn't make accepting Lily's past any easier for him.

In Lily's mind the woman must have been near angelic. How could Lily even begin to compete with her memory? Nevertheless, she had to tell Owen something about herself, other than what little he already knew, which amounted to nothing more than the fact that she'd been living in Heartston and Mr. Goodwin had sent her here to help him save his business.

Toying with the napkin, she rubbed the fabric between her fingertips while gathering her thoughts.

"Tell you what." He leaned in close. "I've told you"—he made a great show of counting on his fingers—"three things about my life here. It's your turn to tell me three things about yours." Satisfied with his request, he sat back in his chair.

Lily blinked. This felt like a test. In fact, she had the distinct feeling he had backed her into a proverbial corner. Being backed into a corner is what had gotten her involved with the Pinkertons to begin with.

Her palms began to sweat as she tried to imagine what Owen would think of her last assignment for the Pinkertons. Even after knowing him only a short time, she could tell his values were somewhat stricter than hers.

Words from the Bible verse, Deuteronomy 8:2 echoed in her mind.

Remember how the Lord your God led you all the way in the wilderness these forty years, to humble and test you in order to know what was in your heart . . .

What could she tell Owen without revealing a truth that he would never understand? She felt certain that this man had been in love with a woman who had been darn near perfect. Lily was far from that. But she deserved a second chance. Didn't everyone? She doubted the man seated across the table from her would think that way. Her instincts, the very ones that had kept her safe for the past few years, were telling her she had to be careful where Owen Murphy was concerned if she wanted any hope of securing a future here.

Just as she opened her mouth, about to say that she came from the city, a ruckus started up from inside the house.

Chapter Eleven

Miss Handland sprang from her seat and headed for the kitchen, and Owen hurried after her. Close on her heels, he rushed through the kitchen, hoping to head her off. There could be an animal rummaging through the downstairs. It wouldn't be the first time he'd had something like that happen. Two years ago a mama bear and her cubs had broken through a window in his office. It had taken him and the Cuddiebacks some creative maneuvering with a broom handle and a bit of leftover roast beef to coax them out of the house.

Charging through the door leading into the center hall, he bumped into Lily, who had stopped just on the other side. Laying his hand on her forearm, his mouth fell open as he stared at the sight that greeted them. Owen let out a quiet groan. He almost wished the noise had come from the bears.

"Owen! There you are! Get over here and give your aunt a hug," Desdemona Franklin Murphy demanded, holding out her fleshy arms.

His aunt looked impeccable in her wide-brimmed hat and light-weight traveling dress. The blue of the fabric matched the color of her eyes. Uncle Rudolph looked his usual disheveled self, his windswept hair sticking up in the back and the shoulders and sleeves of his brown tweed suit covered with dust. There was mud on the toes of his knee-high boots.

Releasing his hold on Lily's arm, Owen skirted around her and made his way to the front of the hall. Aunt Desdemona stepped out of the circle where she and Uncle Rudolph had dropped their pile of luggage, coming toward him with her arms spread wide. Before he knew it, he was enveloped in a perfumed haze. The netting covering her hat got caught up in his hair. He made an attempt to bat the itchy fabric out of the way.

"Owen. How we've missed you."

Finally able to free himself from both the netting and his aunt's enthusiastic embrace, he managed to say, "Uncle Rudolph, Aunt Desdemona, I didn't expect you."

"Oh my. Didn't you get our letter?"

Owen cast a quick questioning glance over his shoulder to where Miss Handland stood, her mouth slightly agape. He imagined seeing his flamboyant aunt and uncle had surprised her just as much as their sudden appearance had him. She shook her head, indicating she hadn't seen their correspondence. It must have gotten lost in the recent shuffle of events.

"How did you get here?" he asked, turning his attention back to them.

Uncle Rudolph took a wadded-up handkerchief out of his coat pocket and swiped it over his face. "We hired a driver and carriage from the livery in town. He dropped us off and turned right back around so he could get out of the wilderness before dark."

"We're on our way to join the voyage to Europe. We plan on leaving in two weeks' time, out of New York Harbor," Aunt Desdemona said, her hands still firmly planted on Owen's arms. He felt her give them a squeeze very much like she was evaluating whether he'd been eating enough. "I thought we'd have a visit with our dear nephew before departing," she said with a smile.

"Well, there's no problem. I'm sure we can find a room for you."

"We could go to our old room at the top of the stairs." Uncle Rudolph nodded toward the hallway and bent over to pick up one of the bags.

"I'm afraid that room is occupied."

Since the camp had first opened, Desdemona and Rudolph had always stayed in what had now become Miss Handland's room. Owen had a sinking feeling that they were not going to like the idea of being sent to another part of the main house.

Uncle Rudolph set the bag down at his feet. "No worries, Owen. Dee and I can rest our weary heads anywhere."

His aunt pulled a fan out of her reticule, snapped it open, and began to fan her face at a furious pace. "Speak for yourself, Rudolph. You know I love the view from that room."

Miss Handland spoke from behind him. "If it's for one or two nights, I could move my things to another room."

Owen raised his hand; he wasn't about to disrupt the household any more than was necessary. "They can use the room across the hall from yours, Miss Handland."

Aunt Desdemona stopped fanning and craned her neck, looking around Owen. "And who might this be?"

"This is Lily Handland. Miss Handland, my aunt and uncle, Desdemona and Rudolph Murphy."

"A pleasure to meet you both." Miss Handland stepped around him offering her hand. "I'd be happy to help you settle into your new room."

"I'm sorry, who are you again?" his aunt asked.

"She's my new business partner," Owen replied, knowing it would be better to simply get that bit of news out of the way from the start.

"Business partner? Since when do you require a partner, Owen?" Aunt Desdemona waved the fan in front of his face.

"Have you eaten yet? I can fix you something," Miss Handland said in what Owen assumed was an attempt at distracting the couple.

Her ploy didn't work. One glance at his uncle's rigid pose told Owen that his declaration had upset them.

"If you needed funds, we would have been more than happy to have helped you out, Owen," Uncle Rudolph said, the volume of his voice rising. "I can't help feeling a bit affronted that you didn't discuss your decision with us first."

"This is something that came up suddenly," Owen said.

There was no need to tell them the truth: due to his incompetence, he'd been hours away from losing his business. While he loved his aunt and uncle, he did not want to be indebted to them. And had the two of them known about his dire situation, it was quite possible they would have moved in here permanently. Dealing with a stranger had been a decidedly better choice. Desdemona and Rudolph Murphy could be a bit overbearing.

Desdemona snapped her fan closed, tapping it against her husband's left forearm. "Now, now, Rudolph, there's no need to yell at Owen. He's been through enough already." Desdemona's attention shifted from her husband to Miss Handland. She narrowed her eyes and gave Miss Handland a slow head-to-toe appraisal.

"I'd like to take the young woman up on her offer of something to eat."

Owen knew when his aunt was preparing for an inquisition. Something told him that his business partner would be up to the challenge.

"Our cook made some delicious venison stew earlier," Miss Handland commented in a breezy tone. "I'm sure you'll find it to your liking."

"Why don't I help you with our repast while Owen and my husband take our bags upstairs?" his aunt offered in a nice-as-pie tone.

Owen wasn't fooled. He cocked an eyebrow, giving Miss Handland one last chance to back out. When she gave him a slight nod, he picked up a set of monogrammed leather travel bags.

"That would be lovely," Miss Handland said with a smile as she escorted Owen's aunt from the hallway, leaving the two men alone.

"How'd you manage to get a pretty woman for a business partner?" Uncle Rudolph asked as he hefted a large floral-print valise up the staircase.

Owen ignored his question. He walked into the large bedroom facing the front of the property and set the bags at the foot of a four-poster bed. He lit a wall sconce and scanned the room. There was a dresser on the far wall, a small writing desk with a wicker chair, and a wardrobe cabinet. The furniture did need a dusting, but other than that, the room was usable. Tomorrow he'd have Mrs. Cuddieback come in to do a cleaning, but for tonight, its condition would have to suffice.

He swiped his hand along the comforter, smoothing out the faded fabric. He made an effort to shake out and plump the feather pillows before placing them back at the head of the mattress. Hopefully, his aunt would be too tired from her travels to notice the place was less than spotless.

His uncle sat in the wicker chair, letting out a wheezy breath. He ran his hand over his face and then looked through the shadows at Owen, fixing his gaze on him. "You could have come to me for money."

"I know. The situation was . . ." Owen trailed off, not wanting to get into his troubles tonight.

"The situation was what?"

"Dire."

"So you partnered up with the first pretty, rich young woman who came along? That's not like you."

"It wasn't like that." Owen felt like he and Miss Handland were getting onto some firm footing; he didn't want any outside interference causing any hiccups. "Look. Let's get you and Aunt Desdemona settled in for the night."

"Ah. Sidestepping me, are you?" His uncle grinned at him.

"I needed help. I didn't have any other choice."

"I understand."

"Do you think you could talk to Aunt Desdemona? I could tell she wasn't pleased with this."

"I can try." He pointed a finger at Owen. "You know your aunt, though. Once she gets a bee in her bonnet about something, there's no telling where she'll get off to."

Lily busied herself with the venison stew while keeping a watchful eye on Owen's aunt, who stood at the counter beside her, observing her every move.

"That stew smells delectable," Desdemona Murphy commented in a haughty tone. "I daresay it may be as good as the meal we had at Ogdon's Public House a few months ago."

Lily knew the woman was referring to one of the premier restaurants in Albany. She hadn't had the chance to eat there, but had heard of its stellar reputation among the wealthy.

"We are very lucky to have Mrs. Cuddieback and her husband here at the camp."

"*We* you say? This is my nephew's camp. His and Rebecca's. I don't care how much money you gave him—that will never change. You'd do well to remember that, Miss Handland."

Lily swallowed. She'd hoped for at least five minutes to prepare for the onslaught from Desdemona. Apparently, she'd misjudged her . . . though not by much. The glances the woman had been sending her husband and Owen had been enough to put Lily's senses on high alert.

Setting the ladle down on a small dish next to the pot, Lily moved around the woman to fetch some bowls and utensils from the pantry. When she came back with those items, she noticed that the woman had taken off her hat. She stood at the sink, pumping the handle of the waterspout.

"I daresay it's not as cool here as I expected it might be." The stream of water splashed into the cast-iron sink.

Quickly setting the dishes on the counter, Lily rushed to give the flushed woman a fresh dish towel to dampen with the cool water.

Mrs. Murphy accepted the offering with a little flourish. After running the towel through the water, she wrung it out and gently dabbed it across her forehead and cheekbones. "That's better," she said, setting the towel in the sink and turning back to scrutinize Lily once more.

"Mrs. Murphy, I can assure you that it's not my intent to do Owen . . ." His first name slipped easily from her lips. Seeing the piercing stare coming from the older woman, Lily quickly amended her words. "It isn't my intent to do *Mr. Murphy* any harm. I'm simply helping him get this wonderful Great Camp up and running once again."

"You do know he loved his wife. She was so angelic. I, for one, think he should have come to his family during his time of trouble. As it was, months had passed before we learned of Rebecca's death."

This news came as a surprise to Lily. She started to ladle the stew into the bowls while she thought about the reasons Owen might have had for not telling his family about his wife's passing. Setting the first full bowl on the counter, Lily could only imagine that his despair over losing her had been too great.

"As soon as we heard, we sent off a telegram telling Owen we'd be here for him to help him through his grief. Before we could board the train in New York City, he sent a telegram back telling us not to come."

The woman wiped a tear from her eye. "The hardest thing I've ever done was to stay away. But we did get here for a visit a few months afterward. I couldn't go on our European journey without seeing Owen first. And now we come by almost yearly."

"Would you and your husband like to dine outside?"

"Gracious, no! I prefer not to have bugs in my food, Miss Handland. I hope you don't plan on making it a habit to offer alfresco dining to your guests. I daresay they'd run back to the city."

She was about to tell the woman that the reason people came to the Great Camps was to escape the confines of the city and relax in the outdoors. Instead, she pasted a smile on her face. "Why don't I bring a supper tray up to your room?"

Owen's aunt puckered up her mouth, looking like she'd sucked on a wedge of lemon. "The day is almost gone. I suppose dinner in our room would be fine."

"Why don't you go on up and get settled while I finish preparing your tray?"

"Yes. I'll go join my husband and Owen."

After gathering her hat, the woman left the kitchen. Lily heard the creak of the third step as Desdemona made her way up the staircase. Lily blew out a tired breath. It had been a long day with the tea, and now they had unexpected guests. Still, she set to work, adding two glasses of iced tea and a dessert plate of leftover tea cakes to the tray. She made sure to have the utensils and napkins before leaving the room.

Careful not to spill any of the food or beverages, Lily made her way upstairs. The door to their bedroom stood open, and the sound of their voices spilled out into the hallway.

"Dee, Owen told you the room will be cleaned tomorrow," Rudolph said.

"I suppose I can wait. But what are we going to do about that woman? I can't abide by her living here with Owen. That's not proper," Desdemona volleyed back.

"Aunt Desdemona, we are not living together. I'll be moving out to one of the cabins by week's end, and Miss Handland will stay in a room right across from yours. So there will be no impropriety. In addition, the Cuddiebacks live in their quarters on the other side of this house."

"Dinner is served," Lily announced, joining them in the bedroom.

She cast Owen a worried glance as she set the tray on the small desk. The look he gave her in return could only be described as one of pure panic.

"I think Miss Handland and I will leave you to your dinner. We had an event here earlier, and I'm sure you both are tired from your travels. I'll see you tomorrow."

Owen caught hold of her elbow and directed her from the room. Lily pulled their guests' bedroom door closed.

"You were rather brusque, don't you think?" she said in a low voice.

"Did you want to be a part of her inquisition?" He ran a hand through his hair.

She bit back a laugh. "No. And it has been a rather long day." The fatigue had managed to creep up on her, leaving her feeling more than ready to settle into her own room for the night.

Lily walked across the hall to her bedroom. Laying a hand on the doorknob, she turned to look back at Owen, who hadn't moved from his spot in the hallway.

"Will you be joining us for church in the morning?" Lily asked. She hadn't forgotten Mrs. Cuddieback's invitation.

"I'm not sure it will be a good thing to leave my aunt and uncle alone."

She might have been mistaken, but Lily thought she saw a bit of trepidation in Owen when she'd mentioned going to church. His eyes had taken on a distant look, as if he were remembering something. She hoped he would come. It would do him good to see his friends.

"Perhaps they'll join us. Good night, Owen." Lily left it at that.

"Good night, Miss Handland."

Chapter Twelve

Owen woke to the sound of birds chirping and the scratching of a small animal running across the tin roof of the cabin. Rather than facing down the question sure to come if Aunt Desdemona discovered him sleeping on the sofa in his office, he'd decided, after he left them last night, to go out to one of the cabins instead. He'd been planning on moving out there anyway. No harm in sooner rather than later. He rubbed a hand over his face, feeling several days' growth of beard stubble, and remembered that today was Sunday.

Rebecca had loved seeing him dressed for church, and he'd always made the effort to look presentable for her. He swung his legs over the stiff cot. Pushing aside the rough woolen blanket he'd found crumpled in one corner of the cabin the night before, he realized he couldn't remember the last time he'd had a decent shave, let alone put on church clothes. Of course, that was a bit of a lie. The last time had been the day Owen had buried his wife.

He bowed his head against the onslaught of emotions and pain that came every time he thought about that day. Bowing his head, he prayed for the strength he would need to get through being in Heartston. When his housekeeper had suggested that Miss Handland and he attend church services, she knew how long it had been since Owen had set foot in that building.

"Dear Lord. Blessed be this new day." The words his wife had always prayed came back to him with no trouble. "Please help me to get through this time. Be with me as I struggle with this pain." His soft-spoken words filled the silence.

Raising his head, Owen knew the time had come for him to put one foot in front of the other and move forward a few more steps. One more step to rebuilding his life without Rebecca. Maybe he could do this. He rose from the bed and walked across the small cabin to the outside door. Opening it, he stepped into the dawn of a new day. Closing the cabin door behind him, he made his way along the wide path back to the main house.

Once inside, he skirted the kitchen, where he could hear Mrs. Cuddieback working on breakfast, walked down the back hallway past the supply closets, cut through the great room, and quietly made his way up the stairs. Once at the top, he realized that, save for the ticktock sound of the grandfather clock keeping time in the entry, the second floor of the house was quiet.

Owen walked down the long hallway past three more guest rooms until he reached the last room on the left. Curling his hand around the cold brass doorknob, he let himself in.

The room looked much the same as he'd left it all those months ago, save for the white sheets covering some of the furniture. He went to the large pine wardrobe that sat against the far wall. The door squeaked on its hinges as he opened it. In the dimness of the morning light, he could make out the Sunday clothes he'd left hanging there.

Then he smelled the faintest scent of roses. He paused with his hands on the door, half expecting Rebecca to appear. He blinked, and then plunged ahead, taking out the dark jacket and white dress shirt. A pair of tall black boots stood like sentinels at the bottom of the wardrobe. He grabbed those, too.

He dressed quickly, before he could change his mind. Sitting on the edge of the bed, Owen shoved his feet into the boots and then stood. The boots were practically brand-new. He wiggled his toes, trying to work out the stiffness in the leather.

Approaching his old nightstand, Owen opened the drawer and took out his shaving kit. Then he went back downstairs to the kitchen to find a washbasin, rolling his shoulders against the starchiness of the shirt.

Mrs. Cuddieback paused in her stirring of the porridge pot. "Looks like you've decided to join us for church services."

He found an empty metal bowl in one of the cabinets and filled it with some of the hot water from the kettle on the back of the stove. "I guess it's high time I made my way back into the fold."

"I'm pleased to hear you say those words, Mr. Owen." The woman beamed at him.

"Oh, before I forget. We have guests."

"We do?"

"Yup. Aunt Desdemona and Uncle Rudolph arrived last night while Miss Handland and I were having our supper out on the back porch."

Mrs. Cuddieback made a face.

He grinned, remembering how the women were always at odds with one another. "I understand. If it makes you feel any better, I suspect her attentions will be on Miss Handland this time."

Owen picked up the basin of water and headed out the back door to wash and shave. When he was finished, he tossed the water out and brought the basin back inside. He wasn't at all surprised to find Miss Handland standing at the stove, helping to dish out bowls of porridge.

"Good morning," he said, noticing she wore a dress he'd never seen before. The yellow fabric had tiny blue flowers running throughout, and the three-quarter-length sleeves ended at her elbows. She had her long hair pulled back in a bun at the nape of her neck.

Miss Handland raised her head a bit and smiled. "Good morning, Owen. I trust you slept well."

Considering this had been his first night in the cabin, he'd slept fairly well. He wasn't sure how she was going to react to his bit of news.

"I slept out in one of the cabins."

Her pale eyebrows shot up. She set the bowl she'd been filling on a round serving tray. "I didn't think you were going to be out there until later this week."

"I know that's what I said last night, but my moving out there seemed like the right thing to do under the circumstances."

"I understand."

Taking the tray off the counter, he said, "I've no doubt you do."

"I overheard your aunt last night. I know she isn't happy about our living arrangements."

"Well then, everyone will be pleased."

He allowed her to walk ahead of him into the dining room, where a coffee service had been set up on the sideboard. Placing the tray on the table, he helped her set the porridge out. Then he poured himself a cup of coffee.

"Would you like some?" he asked.

She shook her head. "No, thank you. I don't know your aunt and uncle's morning schedule, so I thought we could wait on preparing their meal."

"I'm sure that will be fine. If I remember correctly, Aunt Desdemona likes to be up a bit later in the morning, and she is not a fan of porridge."

Miss Handland frowned. "Well then, I suppose I can have Mrs. Cuddieback prepare her something more to her liking."

They both looked on in surprise as Owen's aunt swept into the dining room. "That won't be necessary!"

Lily thought Desdemona Murphy's lovely day gown was a bit overdone for church. The dress was of a deep lilac color and had a cinched waistline with sheer organza sleeves that covered the older woman's arms to her wrists. The neckline dipped a bit lower than might be deemed appropriate for singing hymns and bowing one's head in prayer.

"Good morning, everyone. Rudolph will be down momentarily. Is that coffee I smell?"

"Yes. Would you care for a cup?" Owen asked.

Pulling a chair out, the woman plunked herself down. "That would be divine, Owen. Three lumps of sugar and a generous dollop of cream, please."

While she waited for Owen to bring her the coffee, Desdemona scrutinized Lily. A near expert at reading people, Lily held her gaze steady as she waited for the woman to offer her thoughts, because Mrs. Murphy certainly had something to say.

"Owen, if you don't mind, I'd like a bowl of this porridge," Desdemona said.

"I'll go fetch some for you." Owen left the room.

Desdemona waited until Owen was out of earshot before turning her sharp gaze on Lily. "Are you planning on attending church?"

"Yes. We're going with the Cuddiebacks."

"Rebecca and Owen were faithful churchgoers. She was involved with the children's religious schooling."

"I'm aware of that."

The woman squinted as she narrowed her gaze on Lily. "Let me get one thing straight," she said, lowering her voice. "I don't care how you came to be here, but you will not be the woman to replace Rebecca."

It seemed that Desdemona Murphy was not wasting any time getting to the point.

She pointed a finger at Lily. "I won't have you taking what is Owen's, either. It will do you no good to be getting any thoughts in your head about owning the Murphy Camp."

Lily sat in silence, realizing nothing she could say could persuade Desdemona's way of thinking. It was never Lily's intent to take what wasn't hers. She'd come here to start a new life. Looking across the table at this shrewd woman, Lily knew Desdemona would never understand that. She was saved from further attack by Owen's return to the dining room.

He stopped in the doorway with a bowl in hand, obviously noticing the women's standoff. "Is everything all right in here?"

"Fine, darling. Miss Handland and I were just becoming better acquainted." The woman had the audacity to look pleased with herself. '

Lily pushed her chair back from the table and stood. She wasn't about to fall into this woman's trap. Owen deserved better. She gave a polite nod to Desdemona before she turned to Owen. "I'm going to finish getting ready for church. I'll meet you out front when it's time to leave."

They ended up taking two carriages to the village: Lily rode with the Cuddiebacks, while Owen followed with his aunt and uncle. The churchyard was full of buggies, and townsfolk were milling about in front of the steps leading up to the sanctuary. A few people waved to Owen as a group of young children played a game of tag around a big oak tree at the side of the building. Elsie Mitchell, who'd been talking to Amy in the small rose garden next to the entrance, caught Lily's eye and made her way over to where Lily was standing on the outskirts of the crowd, watching Will and John Oliver. The two men were at the edge of the lawn talking, and a little boy and girl ran in circles around

Will's legs. As he laughed at their antics, Lily smiled, glad to see him so happy.

John spotted her and nodded. Keeping his gaze on her, he said something to Will and started to walk in her direction. Lily felt a sudden stab of panic. She couldn't speak to him. Owen didn't know she knew the owner of the lumber company. If he happened to see her with him, he might want to know how Lily knew the man.

Acting quickly, Lily turned and met Elsie halfway as she came toward her.

"Good morning, Lily," Elsie said, embracing her.

Grateful to see her friend, Lily hugged her back. "Elsie, I'm so happy to see you! I hope you enjoyed the tea party."

"You did a lovely job making my day special. Everyone chattered all the way home about the refreshments and how beautiful the Murphy Camp is. I think you're going to see a lot of reservations coming in."

The sooner that happened, the sooner she could prove to Owen that her ideas had merit. Maybe then his aunt would see she had only her nephew's best interests at heart. The sound of the church bell tolling filled the yard. The service was about to begin. Desdemona Murphy looped her arm through her husband's, leaned close to say something to Owen, and shot Lily a look over her shoulder that clearly said she should keep to herself.

The trio followed Alice and Theodore up the stairs, where Owen paused to say something to his aunt. She seemed to be discontented with whatever he'd said, because she shook her head, casting another scathing look in Lily's direction. Hoping to avoid any more conflict, Lily mixed in with a group of latecomers who were going up the steps. She caught sight of Will Benton joining Elsie.

Putting her head down, she entered the church, almost plowing into Owen, who had stopped just inside the doorway.

"I thought you might like to join us," he said, taking hold of her elbow.

She shook her head. The last thing she wanted to do was to sit next to his aunt for the next hour. When she tried to pull away, Owen simply ushered her to a spot in the last pew. Looking around, she didn't see his family, but she finally spotted them two pews in front of them. Feeling a bit relieved, and somewhat more assured that she might be able to enjoy the church service, she slid across the hard surface, finding herself sitting next to an elderly gentleman.

One good look at him and her heart nearly stopped.

Even though he wore his hair shorter and slicked back, she recognized the man from her time working incognito at the local saloon.

She shifted away from him, bumping up against Owen. Praying the man did not recognize her, Lily pulled a Bible from the holder at the back of the pew in front of them. She flipped the leather-bound book open and kept her head low, pretending to be busy reading the scripture.

The minister's voice boomed from the pulpit in the front of the church. "Good morning! Good morning! And welcome. Let us begin with a prayer."

Amid the sounds of feet shuffling and dresses rustling, the congregation rose.

"Lord, thank you for blessing us with another beautiful Adirondack morning. Thank you for bringing our community together. Bless the people joining us today as we keep those no longer with us in our hearts and prayers."

Beside her, Lily felt Owen stiffen. Casting a sidelong glance at him, she could see his mouth pull into a tight line and the color drain from his face, and she knew he had to be thinking about his wife. She started to reach her hand out to lay it on his arm, but caught herself.

On the right side of the pulpit was an upright piano. Lily focused on the thin young woman with long blonde hair who sat straight-backed on the bench with her fingers poised over the keys. The minister gave the pianist a nod, and she started playing the accompaniment to the opening hymn, "Blest Be the Ties That Bind." Soon the congregation joined in.

For a brief moment, all the stress of what Lily had been doing for the past few years melted away. She felt her heart and soul lift with each verse of the song. The words were a balm to all the fear and pain she'd ever experienced. Hope sprang from deep inside of her. She'd finally found a peaceful haven.

A cool breeze ran along her arm. She turned to find an empty space where Owen had been.

Chapter Thirteen

Owen hurried down the steps, stopping at the last one. Grasping the handrail, he paused to catch his breath. Behind him the last strains of another one of Rebecca's favorite hymns ended.

Owen had tried to stay, had tried to push her out of his mind, but every note and every word of the lyrics brought back his pain. He'd wanted this day to be different. When he'd put on his Sunday best that morning, he'd thought standing among his friends in the church sanctuary would make him feel whole again.

A ridiculous thought, considering that now he felt as if his heart were being wrenched out of his chest, yet again. He stumbled off the step, the heat of the morning sun heavy on his face as he walked away from the churchyard. He should have stayed home.

Within minutes Owen found himself standing outside the cemetery. He hadn't been there for weeks, not since the day Lily Handland had appeared on his doorstep.

Owen wanted to blame his absence on all the new duties foisted upon him by that woman, but he knew that was a lie. He'd finally been doing what others had been encouraging him to do for a long time—building a life without his love. Perhaps he'd been too eager to start fresh.

He put his hand on the latch. The steel felt cold to his touch. He slid his thumb underneath it, ready to flip it up. Just as he was about to open the gate, a pretty male bluebird landed right in front of him on the railing. The head and back of the bird were of a stunning brilliant royal blue, and his breast feathers were a warm red-brown color. These birds normally nested at the edge of the woods. He had no idea what had drawn the creature here today. Owen closed his eyes. When he opened them, the bird was still there. The tiny creature began to chirp, a pure, joyful sound. He stared at the bird, willing it to fly away. He wasn't in the mood to enjoy nature's blessings.

But darned if that little bird didn't take to singing even harder. The tiny mouth opened wider as the delicate notes poured from its throat. Owen took his hand off the gate, and his gaze followed the wrought iron fence line all the way to the back of the cemetery and to the oak tree beneath which lay Rebecca's final resting place. The appearance of the little bird, and the gift of this beautiful day, gave him the much-needed courage to turn away.

He stopped midturn when he realized he wasn't alone.

"Miss Handland! Shouldn't you be in church?"

She'd put on a blue bonnet, the same blue as the bird's feathers. From beneath the brim of her hat, she watched him. He didn't know if he should be angry or relieved to find her there.

"I grew worried when you didn't return," she said, retying the ribbons of her bonnet.

He looked into her eyes, expecting pity or sympathy. Instead, he saw only concern. "How did you know where to find me?"

Owen found it curious that now she looked everywhere except at him. She shuffled her feet and toyed with those ribbons again. He might have walked over to the creek that ran along the east side of the village, or into the field behind the church. So how had she known to look for him at the cemetery?

"Miss Handland?" He clasped his hands behind his back, rocking on his heels.

"I used to rent a room at the boardinghouse over there," she answered, pointing to a spot across the street. "I was up on the second floor, in the front. My room had a view of the street and the cemetery." She finally swung her gaze back to him. "I thought perhaps you might be here."

He pondered this for a moment, remembering the last time he'd visited his wife's grave. It had been a very difficult day for him. He'd been missing Rebecca with a fierceness he'd never experienced before. He swallowed.

"You were watching me from that room?"

"No—I mean to say—it's not what you think. I happened to see you when I was looking out the window." She took a step toward him, laying a hand on his arm.

He shook off her touch. "Miss Handland, those times were very personal to me."

"I understand that."

"Do you?" He wanted to know what kind of a person would spy on someone during a time of sorrow.

"Owen, please know that I felt horrible for what you were going through. What you're still going through."

"I'm trying to rebuild my life."

"I know you are. And you're doing a fine job." She gave him a kind smile.

He turned away from her, thinking she probably wasn't the only person in the village who'd seen him in the throes of grief. He looked out over the village. Everything looked the same—the bakery, the bank, the schoolhouse all in their places. This little village was his home. He missed coming here.

He turned back to Miss Handland. "Would you care to go for a walk?"

"Shouldn't we be getting back to the church?"

"I imagine the service is about halfway finished by now. I don't want to interrupt the sermon."

"He was getting ready to start when I left."

"Well then, I think we should go for a walk." He waited for her to step alongside him and headed toward the village center.

"All right. But I think your aunt and uncle will expect you to be there."

He winked at her. "Don't worry. I promise we'll return before the last hymn."

They headed in the direction of the boardinghouse, and Owen felt his tension begin to melt. Most of the townsfolk were at the church service, except for a few loggers milling about outside the saloon, so Main Street was empty.

Beside him Miss Handland remained unusually quiet. He didn't mind the silence. Holed up in his house for so long, he'd grown accustomed to silence, going for days without speaking to anyone other than his housekeeper. But ever since the arrival of Miss Handland, Owen had to admit that he looked forward to their chats—perhaps even their sparring over budgets and plans.

"Tell me, Miss Handland. How long were you in residence at the boardinghouse?"

"Not long."

For someone who liked to expound on subjects, he was surprised by her terse answer. "How long is 'not long'?"

He didn't know why he was pushing her. Maybe it was because their conversation from yesterday had been interrupted, and she still owed him a few confidences about her life—three, to be exact.

She pursed her lips and once again looked at everything except him. Now he really wanted to know what she was so reluctant to share.

"Miss Handland, did you have a bad experience here?" They'd stopped walking as soon as they'd reached the white clapboard boardinghouse.

She shook her head. "No. The room was quite nice."

"Still, you don't want to talk about it."

"That's not it at all. If you must know, I was here for a short while. A few months," she said, moving away from the structure.

He tipped his head back, looking up at the second-floor window where she'd told him she'd rented a room. Then he glanced back at the cemetery. She might not have seen all that much from this vantage point. In three long strides, he caught up to her.

"How did you come to be here, in Heartston?"

"If you must know, I came by train."

"I didn't mean literally."

She grinned. "I was in Albany when I heard about this wonderful little village. I decided to see for myself."

"You're from Albany?"

Her grin quickly turned to a curious frown. "Owen, why are you asking me all these questions?"

"I'm simply finishing our conversation from last night . . . before the interruption. I told you three things about myself, and you were going to reciprocate."

He saw the dawning comprehension in her eyes and couldn't help smiling in satisfaction. "Two more bits of information and I'll stop asking . . . for now," he said in a teasing voice.

She narrowed her eyes and, with her mouth drawn, stared at him as if deciding what little nugget of information she would give up.

"All right, two more things, and that's it for today." She held up one finger. "Number one. I'm originally from New York City. Number two, and this is technically number three"—she smiled in triumph, holding up a second and third finger—"I find that I'm happy here in Heartston."

He wanted to tell her that the last declaration didn't count, but her face softened and the sun peeked around the treetops, showering her in a light that made her glow. Owen thought she looked serene, but then he saw the spark in her eye as she grinned. Lily Handland, he was discovering, had many layers to her.

They walked again in silence, and soon they came to the building that housed the saloon. Owen had never set foot inside and often wondered why Heartston needed such a business. A man wearing a dusty chambray shirt and pants tucked into knee boots stumbled out through the swinging double doors, teetering in front of them. The tall, broad-shouldered man lurched toward Miss Handland.

Owen jumped in front of her and grabbed the man's shirt, surprised at the bulk of the man. Still, Owen managed to set him straight on the walkway.

The stranger squinted down at Miss Handland, raised his arm, and pointed a shaky finger at her. "Hey! Don't I know you?"

Lily blinked in surprise when she recognized the lumberjack. "No. I don't believe we've ever met," she lied. Panic swelled inside of her, and her heart began to race.

He squinted, taking a closer look at her. The drunk spit a stream of tobacco juice out one side of his mouth and said in a slur of words, "I *neeever* furget a purty face."

Taking hold of Owen's arm, she turned him away from the saloon. "They must be about ready to sing the last hymn," she said in a hurried voice. "We'd better be getting back."

Even though they were walking away from the man, she felt his gaze on her back. She focused on putting as much distance as she could between them and the lumberjack. By the time they made their way past the cemetery and up a knoll, the strains of "Amazing Grace" were filtering out through the open door.

Lily couldn't remember the last time she'd heard her favorite hymn. She pushed the incident at the saloon to the back of her mind as she hurried toward the steps.

"Do you think we should go back inside?" she asked.

"We were in the last pew, so I don't think anyone saw us leave. Let's wait here," he said, leaning against the railing.

After readjusting her bonnet, Lily rolled her shoulders. Closing her eyes, she let the music wash over her, cleansing her, calming her spirit. Her pulse returned to normal. She couldn't help but think what a timeless gift the English clergyman John Newton had given the world when he wrote those lyrics. A person could easily find redemption in his message.

The music ended. Lily opened her eyes to find Owen watching her, his dark eyes taking in every detail. Something about the way he looked at her sent a shiver of anticipation down her spine. The feeling was one Lily hadn't experienced before, and she didn't know what to make of it.

The vagabond lifestyle of being a Pinkerton had never allowed for friendships, let alone a relationship with a man. She raised her head a bit, waiting to see what he was going to do next. The expression on his face remained serious and intense, reminding her of the old Owen, the one she'd first met a few weeks ago when they first became partners. She'd thought they'd been making good headway. Perhaps she'd been mistaken.

The congregation began to filter out of the sanctuary. Lily moved away from the steps to allow people to pass. Owen chatted with a few men who stopped to shake his hand or pat him on the back. From her perspective, he looked as if he was enjoying the greetings.

Out of the corner of her eye, she saw Desdemona and Rudolph at the top of the church steps. Desdemona stopped briefly, shielding her eyes with her hand. The woman's hawklike gaze swept the crowd until she spotted Owen. Nudging a few people out of her way, she rushed down the steps to be with him. Rudolph followed at a much slower pace.

"Owen! There you are!" She looped her arm around his. "That was such a lovely service. Didn't you think?"

Owen nodded as he looked over the top of his aunt's head at Lily and gave her a slight smile. She caught the glint in his eyes, and Lily's palms grew moist. Again, an unfamiliar feeling simmered low in her belly. She was saved from further assessment of these feelings by a young woman she recognized as a guest from the tea.

"Miss Handland, I had a lovely time at the Murphy Camp," the petite woman said, her words bubbling with enthusiasm. "I was hoping you'd have a Saturday free next month. I'd like to host my own celebration tea, just like Miss Mitchell's."

"I'll check our date book when I get back," Lily said.

"That would be wonderful." Reaching into her reticule, she pulled out a linen card and handed it to Lily. "Here is my name and address. Perhaps you could send a message to me listing the free dates."

Lily took the card, her earlier worries forgotten. "I'd be happy to send someone around."

Before long, three others came over and asked for information on hosting events at the camp. Lily was beyond thrilled by this turn of events, but after dealing with the tea yesterday and the overnight guests, it had become abundantly clear that they needed to hire additional help. Lily and Mrs. Cuddieback were no match for the amount of work it took to host events and keep the guest rooms at the ready.

Lily had the ride home to come up with a plan, one that Owen would agree to. But as soon as they were on the road, she found her mind drifting back to that man at the saloon. She still couldn't believe he'd recognized her.

As they neared the camp, she hadn't shaken the image of the lumberjack's face from her mind. How long did she have before someone else from her past came along?

Chapter Fourteen

Two days later, Lily found herself in the office, wishing Desdemona Murphy hadn't come for a visit. She'd set aside this morning's time to work on the reservations that had been coming in since the tea. She'd promised a few people they'd be hearing from her this week. Furthermore, she needed to talk to Owen about hiring staff. She'd already discussed the matter with Mrs. Cuddieback, who'd been relieved to learn she'd be getting some extra help. Thinking about the guest rooms reminded Lily she needed to tell Owen her plans to freshen them up. And she needed to add an inspection of the roof to Owen's list.

There was so much to be done, and here she stood, biting her tongue and fuming.

From the minute she'd entered the office, she'd known things had been moved. The tintype image of Owen's wife was back on the mantel, and the desk had been rearranged. All the papers Lily had spent hours sorting had been moved to a single disorganized stack on the far corner of the desk.

She knew this had not been Owen's doing. Folding her arms across her chest, she glared at the top of the desk, trying to figure out a way to tell Desdemona that she had to mind her own affairs.

From the moment the woman had set foot in the house, she'd been meddling, and Lily wasn't going to stand for it anymore. Turning away from the desk, she headed for the door, dead set on speaking with Owen and his aunt.

Her headlong motion was stopped by the sudden appearance of the woman in question. Desdemona made her usual grand entrance, sweeping into the room, her presence filling the space immediately.

"Ah. Miss Handland, I see you've been admiring my handiwork," the woman declared with a flourish as she stepped behind the desk.

"I wouldn't say I admire your changes," Lily said, deciding it best to not dance around the matter.

The woman's head snapped up, and she speared Lily with a piercing stare. "Really? I daresay this room looks set to right once again. Owen has always kept the lovely image of Rebecca on the mantel. As for the desk, well, it was in disarray."

"Be that as it may, Mrs. Murphy, it is not your place to change things around," Lily volleyed back. "Owen and I have a system that works for us and our business." A system they were still working on, but that wasn't the point.

"*Owen*, you say? Don't you think you're being a tad bit familiar by using his given name, Miss Handland?"

"We are business partners."

"Yes, well. I'm still not clear on how that came to be," the woman said, the disdain in her voice palpable.

"You don't need to be clear on that," Lily countered, hating that this woman was bringing out the worst in her. She'd promised herself she would not be baited into an argument, no matter what Desdemona tossed at her.

Making herself at home, Desdemona planted herself in the chair behind the desk. Lily didn't have time to continue to parley with the woman.

"Mrs. Murphy, don't you have other things to tend to? Perhaps I could have Mrs. Cuddieback prepare you some refreshment. The view from the back porch is stunning this time of year."

"I'm having my tea and scones delivered here."

Lily fought back a nasty retort and turned around, intending to head Mrs. Cuddieback off. She stopped when she saw Owen's uncle standing in the doorway. He had dressed that morning in a lightweight cotton shirt and a pair of woolen slacks tucked into sturdy-looking boots. In his hand he carried a walking stick.

Lily gave him a look that begged for his help, and Rudolph gave her a conspiratorial wink. Happy to have reinforcements, Lily bit back a grin. Unless she missed her mark, she had a fan in Rudolph Murphy.

"Good morning, ladies. Desdemona, I've been looking all over for you. It's time for our walk." He crossed the room in three easy strides, coming to stand by his wife's side. "Darling, before you start with your objections, remember what the doctor said about my needing a daily walk to improve my constitution." He dropped a kiss onto his wife's forehead. "My walk would be so much better if you were to accompany me."

To Lily's delight, Desdemona rose to join her husband. Before exiting the room, she sent a poisonous look over her shoulder. "We are not finished."

Rudolph put his arm around his wife. "Come along, my dear. I'm sure Miss Handland has a lot of work to get done, and she doesn't need any more interruptions."

Lily wanted to hug the man. Instead, she gave him a discreet wave as he escorted his wife from the room. She heard the front door open and then close. As the quiet settled around her, she sat in the chair so recently vacated by Desdemona. Within a few minutes she had the papers re-sorted.

Taking a blank sheet and a straight pen off the desk, she began to make a list of topics she wanted to discuss with Owen. She was writing out her last thought on hiring help when she heard Mrs. Cuddieback's voice in the hall.

"I won't abide by that woman telling me how to run my own kitchen," she said.

Heavy footsteps came closer to the office. "I understand," Owen said. "I'll speak to her."

"And she's been hounding our Lily, too. Saying all sorts of nasty things to her." Even though she lowered her voice, Lily heard her next words clearly. "Miss Lily doesn't know it, but I overheard a bit of their conversation the other morning. She accused Lily of coming here to steal this place away from you. That woman thinks Miss Lily is here to replace Rebecca in your life."

While it was nice to know she had someone else in her corner where Desdemona was concerned, she didn't want to be the cause of another problem between Owen and his aunt. She waited patiently for the two of them to enter the room, curious to know how Owen would respond to this bit of news.

Mrs. Cuddieback entered the room first, carrying the tray intended for Desdemona. She stopped when she found Lily instead. "Has Mrs. Murphy gone off?"

"Yes, she and her husband went out for a walk."

The housekeeper made a humph sound, looking relieved. "Good. Would you care for this tea and one of my fresh baked scones?"

"I'd be happy to take those from you." Moving a pile of paper, Lily made room for the tray.

Mrs. Cuddieback set the tray on the spot, taking the opportunity to lean in and whisper a few words in her ear.

"I'm going to make sure that woman leaves here soon."

Flattered as she was by the remark, Lily knew better than to get any deeper into the mix where these two women were concerned.

Owen made his way into the room, giving a nod to Mrs. Cuddieback as she exited. Dressed in a blue chambray shirt and dark denim pants, he looked well rested. It seemed sleeping on the cot out in the cabin was doing him some good. His dark hair was brushed back off his face, and his cheeks had a bit of healthy color in them.

He gave her a curious expression. Lily could only imagine what he was thinking.

"Good morning, Owen."

"Good morning to you, too, Miss Handland." He wandered over to the tall window at the back of the office. Clasping his hands behind him, he looked out over the back of the property. His expression grew relaxed as he gazed at the lake.

Lily nibbled her lower lip, wondering what he was thinking. She decided to let him take the lead on the issue Mrs. Cuddieback had brought up in the hallway. She had a feeling the discussion of hiring help would have to wait.

"Has my aunt been bothering you?"

"Let's just say she's made her opinions about my presence here known. Owen, it's nothing I can't handle on my own. The last thing I want is to cause trouble."

He turned to face her. "You're not. But my aunt, though well meaning, tends to be very outspoken. I suppose I've grown used to her outbursts. And I know that is no excuse for allowing her behavior." He turned back to the window. "Aunt Desdemona has been particularly protective of me ever since Rebecca died. These past years have not been easy ones. Losing my wife"—he paused, swallowing—"almost killed me. You can be stubborn in your ways, and I'm not inclined to agree with all your highfalutin ideas, but there's no denying you've brought a bit of life back to the Murphy Camp, Miss Handland. I think my wife would have liked that."

"I understand," Lily said, blinking in surprise. He rarely spoke about Rebecca or his feelings. Lily felt a bit of relief—and perhaps some pride—that he thought his wife would be pleased with the changes.

"I can speak to my aunt if you'd like."

"That won't be necessary. I can handle this. After all, it's only for a few more days." Indeed, only moments before, she'd been ready to let Owen know exactly what had been going on behind his back. Now that she'd had a chance to calm down, Lily realized no good would come of her speaking poorly of his aunt.

"Yes. Their ship will be leaving New York Harbor in less than two weeks. If they want to be on it, they need to leave here by the end of the week."

He walked away from the window, coming to stand beside the desk. "So, what's on your agenda for us today?"

Lily's heart gave an unexpected leap. He referred to them as "us." Knowing that Owen was beginning to think of them as a team lifted her spirits. With the two of them banding together, there was no telling to what heights they could take the new Murphy Camp.

"We need to talk about hiring some extra help," she said, hardly able to keep the excitement out of her voice. "And before you toss the notion aside, let me explain my reasons. Since the tea last week, I've had three requests to host more of them. And Mrs. Cuddieback cannot keep up her normal duties in addition to preparing refreshments for these events."

His silence almost killed her patience. She couldn't tell if he was keen on the idea of hiring help or not. But she decided that if she was in for a penny, she was in for a pound.

"The second issue is one of maintenance. I'd like to go through the guest rooms upstairs and make a list of what needs to be done in each one. If I remember correctly, two of them need a simple cleaning. The others had some water damage. I think you should do a roof inspection as soon as possible."

Owen began to pace. The dark expression on his face put a bit of a damper on her enthusiasm. And she felt as if any headway she'd just made had somehow slipped away. If they were going to make this business a success, then he'd have to put up with some spring-cleaning and a few new hired hands around the camp.

He rubbed his hand along his jawline and paused in front of the fireplace. Reaching out his hand, he took down the image of Rebecca.

"Did you put this back here?"

"I'm afraid your aunt saw to that."

"Hmm." He put the frame back in its spot. "I don't want to move too quickly when it comes to taking on these projects. If there's still no money coming in, where do you propose we get the funds?"

They'd been through this before. Lily stood, placing her hands on the top of the desk. "Owen. I know how you feel about the financial situation, but as I've mentioned before, you need to spend money to make money. These improvements are a necessary investment."

He rubbed his hand over his face. Then he narrowed his eyes, meeting her gaze. "All right. But how are you going to pay for this extra help?"

"We have enough money in the business account if we hire help only on the days we have events. I can figure in their pay with the fee." She saw the flicker of doubt in his dark eyes.

He walked back to the windows, looking out over the lawn. Having learned that pushing him wouldn't do her any good, Lily left him to mull over her ideas. But as the seconds turned into minutes of his brooding silence, Lily's patience frittered away.

"Owen, I guarantee you we will make enough money to pay the help."

He held up his hand, silencing her. "Enough. Your reasoning sounds fair. Now, what about your plans for the rooms?"

Lily knew she was about to risk their newfound harmony, but that couldn't be helped. "We'll have to use the money I put into the business."

Disapproval flashed in his eyes, and her first instinct was to argue with him. She could remind him this plan would bring them closer to setting an actual grand reopening date. She could also bring up the fact that the tea party she'd given Elsie had garnered a lot of attention, which meant Lily could now hold teas every Saturday at four o'clock and expect a steady stream of guests. And she hadn't even mentioned her newest idea—placing an advertisement not only in the weekly Heartston paper but also in the Albany newspaper. If her calculations were correct, they'd make the money back quickly.

All these arguments were on the tip of her tongue, but one look at his stony expression told her now might not be the best time to share some of her bigger plans, at least not until Owen came around to her way of thinking.

"You know how I feel about using your funds," Owen said, interrupting her thoughts.

Lily came around from behind the desk, deciding to try a bold tactic instead of arguing with the man. "I do. But you know what, Owen? If we continue to debate these business decisions, we'll never see any progress. My ideas make good sense, and you know it. I'm going upstairs to work on the list of repairs. I'd like it very much if you would join me."

She grabbed a ledger and straight pen from the desk and strode out the door into the hallway. Once again, he'd managed to frustrate her to the point of her not caring whether he followed her.

Chapter Fifteen

As Owen followed her up the staircase, he fought the urge to continue to parley with the woman. These changes were a necessity, but knowing that didn't make doing them any easier. To say it rankled his pride to take money from her would be an understatement. He wished he'd never let things get so out of hand.

At the top of the stairs, Miss Handland turned to the left, her heels tapping along the wide-board flooring as she hurried along, intent on her mission. She disappeared into the farthest room on the right. He took his time walking down the hall, not eager to jump to her latest request.

A thumping sound, as if Miss Handland was beating her hands against something solid, floated into the hallway. What on earth was she doing?

As he entered the room, his nose twitched at the musty scent. The original contents were still in their places: a pine bed, a single nightstand, and a dresser. The door to the outer porch had been blocked by the dresser. He remembered moving it away from the wall after the first roof leak. From the looks of the warped wood on the top, it seemed those efforts had been useless.

His swung his gaze to where Miss Handland stood pressed up against the window frame, trying to open it. She turned to him, spearing him with a stubborn gaze. He knew better than to say anything about how she looked. A pretty flush spread over her forehead and cheekbones. Her hair had loosened out of the bun at the nape of her neck, the strawberry-blonde strands curling from the humidity.

He hurried to her side, chuckling as she continued to struggle with the window, her hands pushing up against the sash. Coming up beside her, he placed his hands on her waist, gently moving her aside.

Time seemed to stand still as she turned to face him. He forgot about the window. His hands lingered on her trim waist, and he felt a catch in her breath.

A fine sheen of perspiration above her brow caught in the sunlight, and her long eyelashes swept up as she met his gaze. There was a softness in her eyes that he hadn't seen before. He took in her pert nose and rosy cheeks. But when his gaze finally settled on her mouth, it was his breath that caught in his chest. Her soft lips parted. He felt the lightness of her breath on his face as she exhaled.

He closed his eyes, battling the emotions rolling through him. Owen couldn't be attracted to this woman. He would never betray the memory of Rebecca in that way. He released his hold on Miss Handland.

Turning, he banged his fists along the sides of the window frame. When he finally spoke, his voice came out gravelly. "Sometimes the only way to get these darned things open is to take out your frustrations on them."

He let out a grunt when the window finally moved. He managed to push it up a few inches, letting in the fresh pine-scented air. Turning, he surveyed the room. Miss Handland was correct; the room needed fixing.

He tipped his head back to examine the water damage. "It looks to me like this section has been leaking for a while." He pointed to the crack that ran across the ceiling and down the plaster wall on the opposite side of the room. "I'll get Theodore to go up on the roof with me this afternoon. I think there might be some broken shingles. The last big storm we had carried a lot of high winds."

Owen realized she hadn't said anything about his observations. He lowered his head, finding her standing at the foot of the bed with a dusty white sheet in her hand. He could see that the exposed mattress would need replacing. Miss Handland seemed intent on scribbling notations on her paper while he inspected the walls, thankful that only one needed repair work. As for the other three, sprucing them up would require nothing more than a good washing with some soap and water.

"So how long do you think it will be before this room will be ready for guests?" he asked her.

"I'd say a week or two at the most." She spun around and left the room.

Feeling like she was in command, Owen followed her. They entered the room to the left. Miss Handland seemed to be working her way back toward the staircase. Owen was pleasantly surprised when he saw that this room only needed fresh linens and a good cleaning.

"What would you say to putting new draperies on the windows and porch doors of all the guest rooms?" she asked.

He shrugged. "I'm not sure. My first thought is—"

"What will it cost." She filled in his sentence with ease, twisting her mouth into a wry smile.

Owen grimaced, wondering when he'd become that predictable. "In my defense, someone has to keep the bank balance in check."

"I'll see if I can find some fabric remnants at the mercantile. That should help keep the cost down." She jotted down some more notes. As her brow furrowed in concentration, she said, "I'd like for us to set a grand reopening date. Doing so will give us a goal for completing these improvements."

His mouth dropped open. Today must be her day for declarations. "Don't you think we have enough goals already?" Folding his arms across his chest, he rocked back on his heels. The reason he'd taken her on as a partner had been to fix up the place and make it viable once more, but she was moving along too quickly. "When did you want to officially reopen the Murphy Camp?"

"I think we could have everything fixed in three weeks," she said confidently.

He dropped his arms to his sides. "Three weeks!" Owen's shout echoed off the empty walls. Her only response was to press her lips together. Lowering his voice, he said, "We can't possibly be ready to open in that short amount of time."

"You and Mr. Cuddieback can get started on the roof and anything else that needs to be tended to on the outside. Alice can help me work inside the house."

"That's not going to be enough time to do things properly."

Sometimes you need to jump off the ledge.

He blinked, hearing his wife's voice as clearly as if she were standing next to him. He swallowed, feeling the familiar twist in his stomach as he remembered the day she'd declared they would need to rebuild the front porch. Even back then he'd been afraid to take a chance . . . to make a change.

If he really wanted to bring this camp back to life, then he was going to have to let go and trust that Miss Handland knew what would work.

She'd been standing in front of him, her forehead wrinkling. He could almost see her thoughts churning.

Just as she opened her mouth in another attempt to convince him, he cut her off. "Looks like I'll need to come up with my own supply list. Tell you what: you finish up yours, and I'll head outside and see what

I'll be needing. Then we'll meet back in the office in, say, two hours to compare notes."

Her face lit up as she smiled. "I have a better idea. I'll make us up a picnic basket and meet you down at the edge of the pond. The spot behind the flower garden."

He hesitated.

"Come on, Owen. When was the last time you went on a picnic?" The minute the question left her mouth, she looked as if she regretted her words. He knew she must be thinking the last time he'd done anything like that had been with Rebecca. And she'd be correct in that assumption.

"I'm sorry. I shouldn't have—"

"You shouldn't have what, Miss Handland?"

"I shouldn't have been so eager," she finished, laying a hand across the hollow of her neck.

The sunlight slanted in through the porch door, catching her form in a very flattering light. Owen froze as a realization dawned on him: he *wanted* to spend some more time with her. He'd never met a woman as smart and determined as Lily Handland. A pang of guilt hit him square in the chest. It wasn't that Rebecca hadn't been smart. Miss Handland was just so self-assured, and she had an uncanny knack at being perceptive.

Shoving his hands into his pockets, he spoke. "All right. I'll meet you at the pond."

The edges of her mouth turned up, revealing just a hint of dimples on either side. He'd never noticed those before.

Owen didn't know what to make of any of this. Perhaps he should tell her he needed to work through the midday meal. Clearing his throat, he was about to say that he'd changed his mind about the picnic when she came close to him, smelling like roses and all things good.

"I'll see you in a few hours. Bring your list." She patted his arm on her way past, her step light as she practically bounced out of the room.

He stared after her as an old, almost forgotten feeling began to thrum through his veins . . . that of anticipation.

Lily made short work of her list, avoiding the room Owen had shared with his wife and the room Desdemona and Rudolph were using. She ended her inventory with her own bedroom. Hugging her notes against her chest, Lily looked over the place she'd been calling home for the past month. She'd added some of her own touches to the space, like the vase of flowers on the nightstand, which she refreshed every few days with new blooms. There were so many beautiful species growing out here, not only in the garden but along the edge of the woods, where she'd found the delicate buttercups in the vase now.

Her ivory-handled hairbrush, the one that had belonged to her mother, sat next to a matching handheld mirror on the dressing table. The white porcelain washbasin and water pitcher she'd found in the hall closet sat on a stand nearby.

As she patted her hair into place, Lily realized that for the first time in her life, she felt safe and—*dare she even think it*—at home. She knew things with Owen were still tenuous, but at least they were moving forward.

She sat on the bed and put her notes aside, thinking about what had happened earlier when he'd helped her with the window. She ran a hand down the side of her dress, stopping at the exact spot on her waistline where he'd touched her. Though she'd never been in love, Lily knew in her heart there was something more than business going on between them.

The way he'd looked at her, never letting his gaze waver, still sent tingles down her arms. Then his gaze had fallen to her lips. Closing her eyes, she imagined what it might have felt like if he had kissed her. His lips might have felt warm against the tender flesh of her mouth. Her eyes snapped open. *What am I thinking?* Giving herself a mental shake, she rose from the bed and went out onto the back porch.

Lily gazed out over the railing, past the smattering of oak trees. From here she had a view of one of the meandering pathways. A small herd of deer poked their heads out of the bushes. Twin speckled fawns ran out, wobbling on their newborn legs. The sight made Lily wistful. The creatures were so beautiful, a part of the fabric of the landscape that was the Adirondack Mountains.

She turned her attention back to the porch, which needed a bit of sprucing up, too. Right now, the second-story porch area had only one rocking chair outside her door. They could eventually add a sitting area for each of the rooms, or maybe even a row of chairs. She imagined their guests lounging outside, whiling away their time by learning about one another. She liked that idea the best.

For larger gatherings they'd have the great room where they'd held Elsie's tea. After a long day's hike, guests would relax by a roaring fire while listening to a pianist or harpist. Maybe they could invite in some poets to do readings. Lily's mind tripped from one idea to another as she daydreamed about how popular the Murphy Camp would be with the city people. Focusing on the tall pines stretching almost to the sky, she reined in her musings.

First things first. She and Owen had to deal with the cosmetics of the camp. Returning to her bedroom, Lily picked up the paper she'd been writing on. She added the bit about needing more chairs for the second-floor porch. Looking down the page of notes, Lily realized the best way to tackle the items would be to divide and conquer. Of course, she'd wait to see what Owen had come up with for his tasks before finalizing their plan. Right this moment she needed to get to the kitchen to pack up their picnic basket.

Lily made haste going downstairs and into the kitchen, where she found Mrs. Cuddieback at the stove, stirring a pot on the back burner. Pausing inside the doorway, she let the delectable aromas wafting from the pot wash over her. In all her travels, she'd never encountered such culinary talent.

"You've done it again, Mrs. Cuddieback. Whatever you have cooking in that pot smells like heaven!"

Mrs. Cuddieback smiled and offered a half-filled spoon. Lily walked over to take a taste. Putting the spoon into her mouth, Lily felt her taste buds come to life as the sensations of a delicate spice she couldn't identify danced over her tongue.

"What *is* this?"

"That, my dear, is my version of duck stew. The mister brought down a few of the birds a couple of days ago."

"But the flavoring . . . tell me, what is the flavoring you used?"

The woman beamed. "I'm afraid that ingredient is this cook's secret."

Lily handed her the empty spoon. "I have some big news for you!"

The spoon clattered onto the stove as Alice clapped her hands. "You and Mr. Owen are going to begin a courtship?"

Lily's mouth dropped open.

Her mind spun in a hundred different directions. What had Mrs. Cuddieback seen or heard?

"Um . . . no. And why on earth would you think such a thing?" she stuttered.

"The two of you seem to have come to a truce." She grinned as she wiped her hands on the towel hanging from her apron ties. Then she leaned in close to Lily, giving her a conspiratorial wink. "I haven't seen Mr. Owen this relaxed in a very long time."

Lily furrowed her brow. She thought Owen seemed relaxed? She shook her head. No, none of what this woman was saying made sense. Had the two of them been getting along better? Why, of course, but that was because they were working in concert to bring the camp back to life. Sucking in her lower lip, she paused those thoughts. Hadn't she just been daydreaming about this very matter? *Oh dear.*

"Mrs. Cuddieback," she said, using a soft but stern tone, "I was not about to declare what you're thinking about myself and Owen. I wanted to tell you that he has agreed to let us hire extra help."

"I sure could use the help." She looked at Lily with a twinkle in her eyes. "But I'm not giving up on the two of you," she said softly.

Lily tried not to think about what Mrs. Cuddieback had said about her and Owen. Instead, she told the housekeeper about her plans to hire staff, explaining how they would begin by focusing on temporary help for special events.

After listening attentively, Mrs. Cuddieback turned back to tend the pot. "That's good enough for now."

Lily's thoughts continued to swirl in confusion. Mrs. Cuddieback was not right in her assumption. Lily and Owen were business partners. What had happened earlier at the window hadn't meant a thing. It was the surprise of the moment that had caught her off guard, nothing more.

Going into the pantry, Lily poked around the shelves until she found a wicker picnic hamper that looked as if it had seen better days. Broken reed ends stuck out along the sides, and the leather-strapped hinges were cracked and worn. Still, she took it from the shelf, thinking it would have to do. Setting it down on the floor, she flipped open the lid. Then she spotted the jars of pickles and canned peaches on the shelf next to her. *These will be perfect!*

Carefully she placed one of each in the basket. Then she found plates, silverware, napkins, and two glasses and added them to the stash. Taking what she had so far out into the kitchen, she put the basket on the work counter.

"Owen and I are meeting down by the pond to share a midday meal."

The housekeeper spun around to look at Lily, tipping her head to one side when she saw the basket. Her mouth opened and then snapped shut. There was no doubt in Lily's mind that the woman had been about to tell her that this could be construed as something two people in a courtship would do.

"There's some leftover chicken and a loaf of fresh baked bread. I think a nice jug of lemonade will go well with all of it."

"Thank you. I'll add them."

Bustling over to where the desserts were kept, Mrs. Cuddieback wrapped up two apple turnovers. "Take these. I've never known a man to turn down dessert."

After the basket had been filled with food, Lily topped it off with a red-and-white-checkered tablecloth, perfect to sit on. Then she lowered the lid, pushing a wooden toggle through a leather loop to keep everything in its place.

"Well, I'm off to meet Owen. We have a *business meeting* planned," Lily declared, stressing the words "business" and "meeting."

Mrs. Cuddieback laughed. "You can call it that if you like." But the look she sent Lily said otherwise.

Rolling her eyes, Lily left the house, heading toward the agreed-upon spot. She saw Owen standing at the edge of the pond. He had his back to her, but he turned when a twig snapped under her foot. A flock of geese alighted from their feeding spot in the middle of the pond. The tall pines swayed, their branches creaking as a warm wind rippled across the water.

The breeze ruffled Owen's dark hair. He gave her a half smile. Lily ignored the jittery feeling in her stomach. Moving forward to join him, she let him take the basket from her. When he reached for the handle, his knuckles brushed hers, sending a frisson of awareness up her arm.

"What a beautiful place this is," she said, looking out over the water to distract herself from what she was feeling. "Have you ever thought about building a gazebo here? It would be lovely for picnics or bird-watching."

He laughed. "You never give up, do you?"

"Not when I think something has merit. Maybe we can put it on our goal list for next year."

He raised his eyebrows as if surprised to think that they would still be working together a year from now. Perhaps he thought this arrangement was temporary. She felt a catch in her throat.

After opening the basket, Owen took the tablecloth and shook it out, and Lily grabbed the opposite ends. They made short work of settling it on a flat grassy area a good ten feet from the shoreline. Then Owen began handing her the plates and food. She arranged them so they both could easily reach everything.

Owen surveyed the bounty. "Looks like you thought of everything."

"Mrs. Cuddieback added the apple turnovers. She said no man could resist dessert."

"A wise woman."

Joining him on the picnic cloth, Lily sat with her knees curled to one side. Owen had stretched his long legs out, crossing them at the ankles. For a few minutes they both concentrated on filling their plates.

"Should we say a short blessing?" Lily asked softly.

He nodded.

Lily closed her eyes. "Dear Lord, thank you for giving us your bounty to share," she said. "Thank you for this beautiful day. May you continue to bless us. Amen."

"Short and sweet. My maternal grandmother was known for her rather lengthy blessings. I can remember many a holiday gathering where she would expound for a minimum of five minutes."

Lily laughed.

"She had to bless everyone at the table," he said with a smile. Then the smile faded, as if a memory had risen from years past. He turned to look at the water, his face settling into a pensive expression.

Lost in his memories, Lily supposed.

"I didn't have a big family," she offered. "It was only my mother and myself. And then after she died, it was just me."

She took a small bite of the chicken leg, wondering why she'd told him that. Of course, she'd wanted to make him feel better, except now he would want to know how she had survived. Lily wished she could take the words back. Chewing the meat, she waited for him to say something. Instead, he appeared to be studying her, much like he had the other night.

"It must have been very difficult for you," he finally said. "Did you at least have a distant relative or friend to help you out?"

"Yes. I did have a friend who took me in." And that was the truth of the matter. John Oliver could be considered a friend.

"I can't even imagine being alone, without any family."

Lily's mind flashed back to the lonely nights when she'd hidden in alleyways to avoid being caught by the metropolitan police. John Oliver had saved her from a horrible fate. Still, the Pinkertons were no substitute for a real family.

"I was one of the lucky ones." Hoping to divert the attention away from her past, she asked him, "How did you make out with your inspections?"

Wiping his mouth with one of the napkins, he grimaced. "There is a lot to be done. I should have taken better care of the place." Wagging a finger at her, he added, "And you're changing the subject. You said you were from the big city. I imagine being out here in the wilderness must come as a shock to your senses."

"There certainly aren't a lot of people here in the Adirondacks. The streets in both Albany and New York are bustling with activity. But I don't mind the quiet here." She looked beyond him at the whirls and ripples on the lake, thinking how tumultuous her life had been up until this point. Moving from town to town, assignment to assignment, had not been an easy way to live.

"You came all this way for a fresh start. That takes a lot of courage." He paused, and then said softly, "I'm sorry you don't have any family to share this experience with."

"I can't change the past. And we never know what the Lord has in store for us."

"Amen to that." He uncrossed his ankles. "I never thought I'd find myself a widower at the age of twenty-eight. But here I am trying to piece my life back together. You know, I was always afraid of being alone. Growing up, I was surrounded by family, and then I traveled here, and well, you know the rest of it . . ." His voice trailed off.

Lily hadn't meant to dredge up those painful memories for him. "I think everyone must be afraid of something. Ever since I can remember, I've been afraid of thunderstorms."

He looked surprised by her declaration. "I love storms. Wait until you see the ones we get here in the late summertime. The way the streaks of lightning flash over the high peaks. The sight is magnificent."

She shivered at the thought, remembering the first storm she'd been alone in. It had been a week after her mother had died. She'd hidden under the thin blanket in their one-room apartment. The violent storm had seemed to last forever, and she'd had no one to keep her safe. That had been the first time she'd prayed for someone to come take her away.

She shook off the dark memory. "I don't think I'll ever learn to like storms."

Owen studied her for a long moment. "All right, then. Tell me something else about you. What is your favorite thing?"

"Hmm." She tapped her index finger against her lower lip. Their eyes locked, and she saw his warmth and kindness and something else she couldn't put her finger on. Lily felt a shift in her world. *My favorite thing might just be sitting here with him.*

She dropped her gaze. The picnic had taken an unexpected turn. It hadn't been her intention to share so much of herself with Owen. "My favorite things are Alice's apple turnovers." Picking out one of the turnovers, she took off the paper wrapper. She bit into the delicate pastry crust, enjoying the taste of the tart apples with just the right amount of sweetness.

After washing it down with some lemonade, she commented, "We need to get back to our renovations. We should take our ideas with us to Heartston. I can see what bargains I can find at the mercantile, while you can take care of buying replacement shingles for the roof."

"Divide and conquer. I like the way you think, Miss Handland." He began to help her with the cleanup. "I think we should head off to town tomorrow. That way we'll have an entire day to tend to our tasks."

"What's this about a trip into town?"

Desdemona's shrill voice shattered their peaceful moment. Rudolph and Desdemona burst through the underbrush into the clearing. Rudolph wore hiking clothes, and his dark pants were tucked into knee-high boots. He leaned heavily on his carved walking stick as he gave Owen and Lily's picnic an appraising look. His wife's cheeks were flushed, and she seemed overheated in her long-sleeved blouse and midcalf vest.

Desdemona puffed out a breath. "I do need to purchase a few more necessities for my trip abroad."

Rudolph groaned. "Desdemona, what more could you possibly need? Our trunks are overflowing as it is."

Owen stood, brushing the crumbs off his pants. Lily started to rise, but looked up in surprise as he cupped a hand under her elbow, pulling her to stand beside him on the blanket.

"I hope you enjoyed your hike," Lily said in a cheerful voice.

Lily could feel the disapproval—finding her here, alone with her nephew—rolling off Desdemona.

Owen's aunt looked down her nose at Lily. "The walk did wonders for my constitution. You should try it sometime, Miss Handland."

Lily's mouth fell open.

Desdemona clapped her hands together. "Now then, shall we leave at nine sharp?" The woman positively beamed as she looked expectantly from Owen and back to Lily.

Lily closed her mouth, amazed at how quickly the woman's mood changed. She kept a tight smile on her face, even though she knew all her plans for an uneventful trip into town had just evaporated.

Chapter Sixteen

Owen was up before the crack of dawn, preparing for the trip into Heartston. By the time the sun had hit the horizon, he'd already had his breakfast and was in the barn, cleaning out the horse stalls. He was quite content to have a few extra hours to set the stable to right. After he finished mucking out the stalls, he worked at cleaning the tack. When he was satisfied with his efforts, Owen started getting the wagon ready. The horse shied away from him when he tried to put the harness on.

"Not up for a trip to town? If you behave, I promise I'll give you some oats when we get back," he whispered softly as he looped the harness around the mare's neck.

Hitching the horse up, Owen wondered how this morning would turn out. He didn't relish the idea of sharing the trip with his aunt and uncle. Certainly, this hadn't been in Lily's—*Miss Handland's,* he reminded himself—plans when she'd suggested the idea. His aunt had been making her opinions of his partner known throughout the household. Owen knew he needed to talk to his aunt about her attitude toward Lily, but then again, maybe everything would blow over. After all, they would be leaving for their vacation in a short while.

He suspected that Aunt Desdemona didn't need anything else for her journey and was only using a need for more things as an excuse to stir up trouble. As he tightened the harness, he decided to put an end to her interference today. He loved his aunt, but she could be strong-willed and vocal with her opinions. Lily—*Miss Handland*—seemed to have no trouble handling herself where Aunt Desdemona was concerned; still, she didn't deserve the treatment she'd been getting. Having witnessed his aunt's clipped responses to Lily's polite questions, Owen decided he would find the time to speak with her.

He walked the horse and wagon around to the front of the house, enjoying the moment of solitude, thinking about how much his life had changed over the past weeks. Where he'd once dreaded the morning, now he actually looked forward to each day.

The image of Miss Handland sitting on the picnic blanket by the lake flashed in his mind . . . the sunlight caught in her hair. He pushed the thought away. *No.* Hard work and seeing the fruits of his labor had brought him this new peace. He'd been idle for so long. He remembered how Rebecca had once told him idle hands were the devil's playground. As he tried to remember her exact words, he realized that somehow his wife's voice was growing fainter in his mind.

He didn't want to ponder that, so he shifted his mind back to the camp improvements and how they were beginning to take shape. He'd met with Theodore yesterday and decided that between the two of them, they could fix the roof repairs. His groundskeeper had mentioned that since the missus would be getting extra help, he wouldn't mind some of his own. Owen had added to his list the possibility of finding a young lad or two to help out during the remainder of the summer months and then on Saturdays. A few hours here and there would make all the difference if they were going to make the grand reopening date.

Thinking of this reminded him that he needed to get an exact date from Lily—*Miss Handland*, he reminded himself again—so they could post the news around the village.

Beyond opening the doors for visitors, Owen had no idea what her plans were for opening day, but he figured they could discuss it on the way to town. He tied the reins off at the rail in front of the steps. Then he bounded up them with an exuberance he hadn't felt in a very long time. Much to his surprise, his uncle greeted him at the door.

"Uncle Rudolph, I'm surprised to find you up and"—he took in the outfit he wore, a pristine white shirt and dark slacks—"looking like you're off to a soirée. The trail to the village can be dusty this time of year. You might want to change into something that won't show the dirt as much."

"Trust me when I tell you it's easier for me to wear the outfits my wife sets out for me than to argue with her," Rudolph said, clapping him on the back.

"Did you get breakfast?" Owen asked as they entered the hallway.

"Yes. Had some of the scones and a fried egg. I tell you, you have a gem with that cook of yours."

Owen let out a laugh, thinking about how many times Miss Handland had mentioned that very thing. "That's what I've been hearing. I intend to keep her on as long as she'll stay." Truth be told, he couldn't imagine this place without either of the Cuddiebacks. They'd held him up through his darkest days, and for that, he owed them.

"Listen, I hope Aunt Desdemona wasn't planning on a big shopping spree. I only hitched up the small wagon," Owen said.

"As far as I know, she doesn't need another thing." His uncle nudged him in the side. "Between you and me, I think she wants to keep an eye on your Miss Handland."

Owen knew it would do no good to tell his uncle that other than being his business partner, Miss Handland wasn't his anything.

"I can tell from the look on your face that you're in denial. Well, let me tell you, Owen. You're actually smiling, and there's color on your face that wasn't there the last time we visited."

"Perhaps my face has color in it because I've been working out in the sunshine." He didn't want to consider his uncle's words to be true, yet if he really thought about it, he had been feeling better, both physically and emotionally. Gone were the days when he'd hidden away in the office with the curtains drawn. With each passing day, the light had begun to return to his life. He turned from his uncle, walking into the office, where beams of the morning sunshine poured through the tall windows behind the desk.

He looked up in surprise to find none other than the woman of their conversation sitting behind the desk. "Miss Handland, you're up and about early."

She set the paper she'd been writing on aside. "I needed to finish our list. We have a lot to accomplish today, and I don't want to waste one minute."

Wandering around to the back of the desk, he stood behind her. He rested his hand on the desk along her right side and leaned in to look over her shoulder to see what she'd been working on. Her sweet scent of lemon verbena collided with his nose, sending his senses reeling. Owen tried to focus on her neat handwriting.

But all was lost the moment she turned to look up at him. Her blue eyes sparkled like gemstones. He noticed how smooth her skin looked in the morning light, and how she had woven her long hair into a single braid today and tied it off in a pretty yellow ribbon that matched the color of her gown.

"Owen? Is something the matter?" She rested her hand on top of his, repeating his name. "Owen?"

He pulled his hand from beneath hers, standing tall. "No. No, I'm fine. I . . . um . . . I wanted to see what you added to our list." He cleared his throat, moving away from her.

Where Owen seemed to be a bit flummoxed, his uncle appeared to be taking great delight in his discomfort. The man, who had witnessed their exchange, was chuckling. Then he gave a nod in their direction, as if to say, *I told you so.*

Narrowing his eyes at his uncle, Owen walked from behind the desk. "Finish up your list, Miss Handland. I want to be leaving here by nine sharp."

"Owen! What's gotten into you?" She pulled out her pocket watch and looked at the face. "According to my timepiece, we've half an hour."

Owen strode from the room. He'd almost cleared the doorway when he heard his uncle's voice.

"It appears what's gotten into my nephew . . . is you, Miss Handland."

The sound of her shocked gasp forced him back outside where he spent the next half hour pacing along the walkway. He stopped when Miss Handland came out of the house. She paused at the top of the staircase with her hand on her hip, the other holding a black leather satchel, watching him rather intently, he thought.

"Owen. I want you to know that I've decided to add one more thing to my list." Her movement toward him was slow and deliberate as she came down the steps to meet him on the walkway.

"And what might that be?" he asked with a feeling of dread. If she was going to address his uncle's comment, he wasn't prepared to give her any answers, not when his feelings were confusing him. No, he hoped she was about to bring up yet another one of her "ideas." As he dug his toe in the dirt, waiting for her response, it occurred to him they couldn't possibly fit one more thing in the already lengthy list.

They walked over to the wagon. "I think we should consider hiring a guide."

He exhaled. "Where did that thought come from?" he asked, relieved to learn they would not be talking about what his uncle had blurted out earlier.

She tossed her satchel onto the front seat of the wagon. "I read an article in the local paper about this man who acts as a guide for guests over at the Sagamore Camp. He takes the men on game hunts. They bring supplies and tents and stay out in the wilderness for days. Sometimes the women accompany them."

He let out a groan. "I know what a guide does. You do realize that a good guide can cost a small fortune, one that we don't have." Owen offered his hand to help her into the seat.

She accepted with a smile, placing her hand in his. He ignored the feeling that skittered up his arm. With her free hand, she took hold of the small railing on the edge of the wagon and hiked herself up onto the seat. The conveyance jostled under her. After adjusting her skirts, she finally rested her hands in her lap.

"We could work the cost into the stay for anyone who is interested in the service," she said in the sweetest of tones.

"*Lily.*" He watched her eyes widen as her first name sprang from his mouth. "You are going to get us in over our heads," he said in his sternest of voices, wagging a finger at her. "Let's just start with the renovations. And then after we open, we'll see how things go. I can't keep agreeing to the addition of new services, not until we know how successful we are going to be."

She tipped her head to one side, and the look she gave him told him she was on to his conservative ways. "And how long do you think it will be before you know this, Owen?" she asked in a patient tone.

He ignored her question. The woman's enthusiasm exasperated him. He was also amazed by how perceptive she was. How had she learned to read people so well?

He pulled his timepiece out of his pants pocket and flipped open the lid. It was five after the hour. He wondered what could be keeping his aunt and uncle—Desdemona was never late for an outing. Snapping the watch closed and putting it back in his pocket, he headed back into the lodge.

Owen took the steps two at a time, hitting the landing just as his uncle appeared in the doorway. He noticed right away that he'd changed clothing and was now wearing a dark shirt and pants that looked a bit worn at the knees.

"I'm afraid Desdemona has asked me to tell you we won't be accompanying you to Heartston," Uncle Rudolph said, giving him a broad smile. "She is suffering from a headache."

"I hope it's nothing serious, Uncle Rudolph."

He shook his head. "No, no. She gets them every now and again. Usually when she's been meddling too much in another's affairs." He winked at Owen.

Owen laughed. "Uncle Rudolph, did you have something to do with her decision?"

Uncle Rudolph shrugged. "Now go on and have a good outing with your lady friend." Puffing out his chest, he declared, "I am going to try my hand at rowing across that pond of yours."

If he'd thought it would do any good, Owen would have told his uncle to be careful. Instead, he said, "Enjoy your day. And if Mrs. Cuddieback asks, tell her we'll be back in time for dinner."

"Will do." With a salute, his uncle closed the door.

Owen went light-footed down the steps, joining Miss Handland. *Lily.* He untied the reins and hopped up next to her. "My aunt and uncle won't be joining us."

"I hope everything is all right."

"Aunt Desdemona has a headache."

"I see. Does she need us to bring back anything? Perhaps some headache powders?"

"I'm sure Mrs. Cuddieback will see to her needs. Besides, I'm not really sure she has a headache. I think my uncle might have talked her out of coming with us." They set off as Owen slapped the reins against the backside of the mare.

"Why would he do something like that?" she asked.

Owen debated about telling her what he thought, and finally decided on the truth. "I'm pretty sure he thinks we need to spend more time together."

Lily didn't know if she should be thanking Owen's uncle or not. Time alone with her partner was nice, but then again, she'd been feeling jittery around him for the past few days. She began to worry. He'd been asking more and more personal questions, and while she'd been able to deal with most of them by giving him simple yet honest answers, she knew one day soon she would have to tell him about the things she'd done.

Her only hope was that he'd be able to accept the truth.

They arrived in the village about an hour after they'd left the Murphy Camp. Anxious to get the poster done up for the opening, she knew her first stop was the printer's office. She wanted to surprise Owen. He let her off in front of the mercantile and let her know he'd be down at Oliver's lumberyard, getting the supplies for the roof repair.

"I'll catch up with you in an hour or so." She gave him a wave as she hurried along the boardwalk, turning left at the end of the short block.

The print shop was in the second building, across from the back of the saloon. The minute she opened the door, the acrid smell of the printing ink hit her. Lily rubbed her nose. Walking up to a low counter, she looked around for someone to help her. The sound of the press clanking away drifted from the back of the shop. Then the noise stopped. Lily took that as a sign she should let her presence be known.

"Hello!" she called out.

Within seconds the oilskin curtains dividing the two rooms parted and a short balding man came through, covered from head to toe in inky smudges. The dark leather apron he wore hung loosely from a string tied around his neck. Lily felt a jolt of panic. He looked familiar. She dug around in her mind, trying to remember if the man had been someone she'd served while incognito in the saloon. If that was the case, would he recognize her as the lumberjack had?

"May I help you?" he asked, wiping his hands on a rag.

"Yes." She put the satchel she'd brought with her on the counter and unclasped the latch holding the sides together. She reached in, pulled out a piece of parchment paper, and slid her rendition of the advertisement in front of the man. Not wanting to be caught off guard again, she asked, "Have we met before? You look so familiar."

"I'm Benjamin Goodwin. You might know my brother, the banker."

Relief flooded through her. Lily nodded, seeing the family resemblance. "That's it, then."

He pulled a pair of spectacles out of his shirt pocket. Putting them on, he studied her sketch. "This looks fine. When do you need this by?"

"As soon as possible. As you can see, we're holding our grand reopening on the twentieth of this month."

The printer took a wadded-up handkerchief from his apron pocket and wiped it over his bald head. "A mighty hot one today. I'd say the way this humidity is climbing, we could be in for a thunderstorm."

Looking over the paperwork for her poster one last time, he added, "August is a busy month for the camps in these parts. Those city-folk fill the trains and stagecoaches, scrambling to escape the heat. Some days it's hard for a body to move about. They leave their luggage piled on the sidewalks while they wait around for the wagons to take them up into the mountains."

Lily wasn't quite sure the man liked the idea of the Great Camps. That didn't matter to her, though. She needed to get them done.

"I'm happy to get this typeset and printed by the end of the week," he said. "How many copies do you think you'll be wanting?"

"I think two dozen should do it." That would give her enough to put up around the village. They agreed upon the pickup time, and she left to continue her errands.

Her next stop was the mercantile. Since she would need an entire bolt to get the new curtains made, Lily anticipated making a good deal on the fabric. Hopefully, Patricia would be in the store today and could help her make a choice. Since she'd figured out that Owen didn't have a strong preference about the way the rooms were decorated, Lily decided she'd make those decisions.

The bell above the door rang as she pushed it open and entered the mercantile. She made her way down a narrow aisle packed with sturdy work boots and tall piles of heavy denim pants. Patricia's cheerful voice drifted from the back of the store. Lily wandered through two more aisles, these containing household goods, until she came to the counter where Patricia was finishing up a gentleman's order.

He turned and Lily swallowed. Her knees went weak. She reached out to grip the edge of the shelf.

It was him, the same man she'd seen last week out in front of the saloon. She didn't want to believe it, yet there he stood. Today his eyes looked clear, though his outfit could stand a good washing. His pants and shirt were smudged with dirt and grass stains. He gave her person a slow perusal, and she almost cringed. But Lily stood tall, deciding she wasn't going to be forced to back away. If he remembered her, he'd say so, and then she would once again deny his memory of her.

He turned back to Patricia to thank her, as if he didn't recognize Lily. He tipped his worn felt hat to both of them and walked by Lily. Once he was halfway down the narrow opening between the dry goods and clothing, he paused. Her fingers went numb. She held her breath, sending up a fervent prayer that the man wasn't going to call out to her. With dirt-smudged fingers, he opened the bag and peered inside, looking for something. Eventually, he pulled out a tobacco pouch, shoved it in his pants pocket, and continued.

Lily blew out a relieved breath.

Patricia came around from behind the counter, smiling warmly. "Miss Handland! I'm so happy to see you. I've been hearing a lot of good things about the Murphy Camp. Miss Mitchell was in here the other day, buying some baking supplies, and I overheard her telling the banker's wife all about how lovely the celebration tea was."

"Thank you." Lily paused to take a breath, still trying to calm herself after seeing that man. When she was sure her voice would be steady, she continued. "I'm wondering if you could help me make some fabric choices? I need to have curtains made for six bedrooms in the main house. I have the measurements." Lily rummaged around in her satchel until she found the piece of paper.

Her hands shook. She couldn't keep going on like this, looking over her shoulder every time she came into town. Lily had been so naive to think that she could simply start her life over again. She handed the paper to Patricia, hoping the woman hadn't noticed how nervous she had become.

"Let's look at what we have," Patricia said, leading the way to the sewing section of the mercantile. She stopped in front of a colorful selection of bolts and scanned Lily's notations. "This project will require a good deal of fabric. Would you be amenable to using different patterns and colors?"

"I had hoped we could do the same fabric in all the rooms, but if we can't, I'd be happy with whatever choices you have that will fit my budget."

Patricia picked up several bolts of material from the stack on the table, setting them aside until she uncovered the loveliest fabric Lily had ever seen. The mauve color seemed to shimmer and change as the light hit it.

Lily couldn't resist touching the shiny material. It felt cool and rich beneath her fingertips. She knew it wasn't right to want to give in to vanity, but she'd not had occasion for a new dress in so long. Her mind wandered as she daydreamed about wearing a gown made of the satiny fabric to the grand reopening.

Patricia must have seen the dreamy look on her face. "That fabric arrived last week. I know it seems like a risk to put it on the table, but every woman should have one dress in her wardrobe for that special occasion."

Lily couldn't resist running her hand down the satiny folds once again. "Yes. However, I imagine living so far away from the city, there would be few excuses to wear a dress made from this."

Patricia's smile fell to a frown. "That's what Mr. Moore said."

"I wish my budget could allow for an expenditure like this." Feeling horrible that she'd upset the girl, Lily said, "We can put the fabric purchase on my wish list."

Patricia's face brightened once again with a beautiful smile. "I like that idea."

Having settled one issue, Lily continued to look over the bolts until she spotted one containing a simple white muslin. "This might be a little too thin for curtains," she said, fingering the fabric. "It would be lovely in the warm months, but then I'd have to change them out for the fall and winter. I don't think Owen would appreciate the extra cost."

"How about this one?" Patricia pulled out a bolt that was also white, but had a heavier weight.

Lily was about to agree to the choice when she spotted a pretty blue one that reminded her of the morning sky.

"Let's go with that one," she said, pointing to the blue bolt that was third from the bottom.

While she and Patricia were wrestling it free, the bell above the front door rang.

"Patricia? Are you in here?" a woman's voice called out.

"I'm over here, Mrs. Fenton," Patricia shouted back as she and Lily finally freed the material. She moved it to a clear spot on the table. "This one's heavy."

A woman wearing a gray bonnet over her black hair and a matching nipped-at-the-waist gray day gown came over to join them. Lily didn't recognize her.

"This is Mary Jane Fenton, our seamstress. Might I introduce Lily Handland. She's working up at the Murphy Camp," Patricia said.

Lily shook Mrs. Fenton's hand, once again admiring the cut of the dress she was wearing. "That is a lovely gown."

"Thank you. I made it."

"You are so talented! I wish I could sew. At the moment, I don't have either the time or patience to learn."

"I find it calming." Mrs. Fenton turned her attention to Patricia. "Did my thread order come in yet?"

"I'm afraid it hasn't. I'm glad you came in, though. I think Miss Handland might have a big project for you." Patricia gave Lily a nudge of encouragement.

Lily went on to explain what she needed done.

"Curtains are simply straight sewing and require nothing more than running a seam down the sides of each panel," Mrs. Fenton said. "And I could make a basic rod pocket for the tops. Show me the fabric you picked out."

"The heavy blue cotton."

"A good choice," she said, rubbing a piece of the fabric between her fingers. "These could stay up year-round."

"What do you think a project like this might cost?"

Mrs. Fenton took a look at the window measurements and, after a few moments, gave Lily her estimate. "That's not figuring in the cost of several spools of thread."

While Lily did not doubt the woman's talents and her promise to deliver the curtains next week, she knew the price was above her budget. And then an idea came to her.

"Mrs. Fenton, have you heard of the Murphy Camp?"

The woman nodded. "Isn't that the place once owned by Owen and Rebecca Murphy?"

Lily nodded.

"Such a terrible thing, his wife dying so young. I heard he's been in seclusion, although I could have sworn I saw him in church recently."

"Yes, his wife's dying was a tragedy, one that he's working through." So as not to appear uncaring, she chose her next words carefully. "You see, I'm in a partnership with Mr. Murphy to reopen the camp, which is why I need these curtains. I was wondering if you'd be interested in bartering your services in exchange for a full weekend stay?"

The woman shifted her weight from one foot to the other. Sensing her trepidation, Lily added some incentives to the offer. "I promise you won't be disappointed. Our cook is the best in the entire upstate region. And our rooms all have views and come with individual outdoor seating areas."

Lily knew half of that last statement was true—the outdoor seating hadn't been purchased yet. She'd make sure it would be ready by the time Mrs. Fenton picked her date.

"Can I bring my husband?"

"You may. I can arrange a guided day hike for him while you relax in your outdoor seating area."

The time the woman took to deliberate the offer nearly sent Lily over the edge. She had to make this work; otherwise, she'd be stuck with bare windows. When the woman stuck out her hand, Lily let out a relieved breath.

"All right, then. You have yourself a deal, Miss Handland."

"Thank you, thank you so very much!"

"I'll see you in a week. I'll have my husband bring me so he can take a look around."

Happy with the surprising turn of events, Lily left the mercantile and walked to the lumberyard to meet Owen. She'd been so caught up in picking out the fabric that she hadn't realized nearly an hour had passed. If there was one thing she'd learned about the man in the past weeks, it was that he didn't care much for tardiness.

Chapter Seventeen

She could hardly wait to tell Owen about the deal she'd struck with the seamstress. With a spring in her step, Lily hurried along Main Street. Her steps faltered when she saw John Oliver standing with Owen outside the Oliver Lumber Company building. The man looked at her with an intensity that reminded her of her early days with the Pinkertons.

She reminded herself that John Oliver had always been there to protect her. He'd also agreed to set her free. And now she wondered what he was thinking as he watched her make her way across the street to meet them. Pasting a bright smile on her face, Lily greeted them.

"Gentlemen!"

"Lily, I was getting ready to leave without you." Owen made a great show of looking at his watch. Putting it back in his pocket, he winked at her.

Her heartbeat tripped. "I know I'm here with five minutes to spare, Owen."

He came to her, put his hand on her arm, and drew her toward John Oliver. His movement caught her by surprise, causing her to lose her footing. Her foot slid on the soft earth. Owen pressed his hand against her elbow, steadying her.

"Thank you," she said, as her gaze slid to John. Her mind raced as she tried to imagine what, if anything, he'd told Owen about her.

"I'm not sure if you know the owner of our lumberyard. This is John Oliver." Owen nodded in the man's direction.

Lily glanced at John, hoping for a sign or coded look, but his face remained stony. The man towered over her, eclipsing even Owen in height. Lily knew better than to feel intimidated—John Oliver had a kind heart. He folded his arms across his chest, his gaze on her intense. At that moment, the only emotion she sensed from him was disapproval.

"Owen tells me you've partnered with him."

"Yes."

"I hear there's a grand reopening in the works."

"Yes, there is. You should come out."

"I will try to be there. This is a busy time of the year for my crews, and I like to stop by the lumber camps to make sure things are running as they should be."

Lily put a smile on her face, trying to decide if John was sending her a covert message with his choice of words. Worry began to gnaw inside her stomach. Pushing her shoulders back, she turned to Owen.

"I wanted you to know that I made a deal for our curtains."

One eyebrow quirked upward. "What sort of deal?"

"I bartered the sewing services of the local seamstress, a Mrs. Fenton. She will do them all, and deliver them within the week, in exchange for a weekend stay at the camp for her and her husband."

Owen threw his head back with a laugh. "That's wonderful, Lily! Your ingenuity never ceases to amaze me."

Her breath caught in her throat. That was the second time today he'd called her by her first name. She'd written the first time off to the heat of the moment, but he'd clearly just meant to say her name.

"Thank you."

"Wait here. I need to go back to the warehouse and check the order." Owen left her with John and ran off to the back of the building.

Lily nibbled her lip and readjusted the satchel in her hand. John gave her the slightest shake of his head. This time there was no mistaking his disapproval.

The minute Owen was out of earshot, John looked around as if to make sure no one could hear what he was about to say.

"I need to meet you. Right after dusk. I'll come to you. I'll be waiting behind the barn on Owen's property."

Lily's heart rate picked up. She had no idea what John could want with her. The lighthearted feeling she'd been enjoying left her, replaced with a sense of foreboding. One thing was for certain; she would not return to the Pinkertons.

The wagon bounced through a rut, jostling Owen up against Lily. He cast a worried glance at her. She'd been silent ever since she'd met up with him at the lumber company. He wondered what had happened. She'd been so happy to let him know about her clever arrangement with the seamstress. Even he had to admit her thinking had been genius.

The wind kicked up, sending a small pile of dried pine needles across the road. Dark clouds formed above the high peaks. Up ahead he saw a pale flash of light, and the air thickened with moisture and heat. He grew concerned that they wouldn't make it back to the camp before the thunderstorm reached them.

Slowing the horse, he turned to Lily. "I think we need to find shelter before the storm hits."

The sound of thunder rolled down the mountain. Beside him, he felt her give a start. "Lily? Are you going to be all right?"

She gave him the tiniest nod, but her lips were drawn into a pale thin line. He could tell she was trying to be brave, but she held on to the side rail with a white-knuckled grip. He snapped the reins against the backside of the mare. Careful not to spook the animal, he pulled the leather straps to the right, urging the horse off the trail. They moved along at what seemed like a snail's pace until Owen saw a dilapidated shed with an attached lean-to structure.

In the short amount of time it had taken him to move off the trail, the rain had arrived, falling in big drops from the dark rolling clouds, splashing against the dry earth. Owen knew they had mere minutes to seek shelter. Jumping from the wagon, he ordered Lily to stay put on the seat as he led the horse and wagon under the low-hanging roof of the lean-to.

A bold flash of lightning followed by a long rumble of thunder sent Lily from her perch and straight into his arms. Owen let out an oomph as he caught hold of her.

"Hey. It's just a storm," he said softly. Gently moving her aside, he found a place to tie off the reins, securing both the horse and the wagon.

She rubbed shaky hands up and down her arms. Owen felt for her, and for anyone else who feared what was to him Mother Nature's delight. For as long as he could remember, he'd loved to sit outside on the porch to watch summer storms roll through. The walls of the lean-to shook as the next round of thunder hit. When Lily jumped, he couldn't help chuckling sympathetically.

He reached out to her. "Come here."

She hesitated, giving the heavens just enough time to open, unleashing a torrent of rain. Taking one giant step, she fell against him. He felt her body tremble and rubbed his hands up and down her back. The rain continued to fall from the dark sky, creating tiny streams of water that ran under the walls of the lean-to and puddled around their feet.

The horse let out a soft nicker, one hoof pawing at the mud. Owen took a half step backward where he bumped into the hard side of the wagon. Lily had worked her hands up around his neck, and she continued to hold on for dear life, her arms flexing around him in a tight hold. He felt the rapid beat of her heart against his chest and heard her quick intake of breath at every flash of lightning. He became aware of her warmth, surrounding him like a worn patchwork quilt.

He moved his hands to the small of her back, working his fingers in a circular motion, hoping to ease her fear. He could smell the freshness of the rain and the sweet lemony scent of Lily.

Owen stilled.

Lily shifted in his arms, raising her head to meet his gaze. Her trembling subsided. Owen brought a hand to her face, and her soft lips parted. Running his fingers slowly down the side of her cheek, he felt the smoothness of her skin beneath the hard pad of his thumb. He let his hand slide lower until his fingers grazed her tender lips.

Owen looked into her eyes, needing to know if she was feeling the same powerful emotion he felt. Some of the tension had dropped from her arms, which were still wrapped around his neck. He heard her breath expel as he lowered his head, touching his mouth to hers.

Owen expected her to pull away. Instead, she returned his kiss, tentatively at first. Then slowly, her mouth began to move beneath his. Time ceased to exist.

He pulled away. She lowered her arms, wrapped them around his waist, and laid her head against his chest.

Outside the thin walls of their shelter, the rain continued to fall, making it impossible for them to continue their journey. The rolling thunder and flashes of lightning began to fade. Lily's breathing evened out. A cool summer breeze replaced the harsh wind. The air smelled of sweet piney earth. Closing his eyes, Owen rested his hand on the small of her back, wondering what he'd just done.

He felt Lily raise her head and opened his eyes to find her looking up at him.

"Owen?" Her voice came out in a whisper.

He started to pull away from her, but his movement only caused her to hold him tighter.

"I'm sorry." His voice sounded raspy.

"Please don't regret kissing me."

"Lily . . . I . . ."

Lily kissed him again, silencing his words, soothing his soul.

He broke away, resting his head against her forehead. "I don't regret kissing you." *Because he was falling in love with Lily Handland.*

"Owen."

He placed his hands on her arms and moved them to her sides. He took her soft, warm hands in his and brought them to his mouth, kissing the backs. "You make me feel things I haven't felt for a very long time."

Her mouth tilted upward.

He gave her hands a gentle squeeze. "Sometimes your actions infuriate me. But other times, like now, you make me feel like I can live again."

"Oh, Owen."

He saw the dawning wonder in her beautiful eyes . . . "I never imagined that there would come a time when I looked forward to a new day."

She looked at him as if surprised to hear him say those words. "I make you feel that way?"

"You came upon me in my darkest hour, at a time when I thought my life was over. Lily, can't you see how your presence in my home, in my life, has changed me?"

She nodded. "Owen, I don't know what to say."

"Say you feel the same way."

"I do."

Another round of thunder shook the shed.

Lily let out a yelp and covered both ears with her hands. "I'm sorry, I'm sorry. I hate storms."

He caught hold of her hands, pulling them away from her ears. Owen grinned at her. "And that, my lovely Lily, surprises me. For someone who is so brave and so stubborn and so strong . . . I would never have expected to find you shivering in fear over a tiny storm."

"It's not tiny, Owen." She admonished him. "And don't tease me."

"I only want you to see that there is nothing to be afraid of. When did this fear start?"

"Ever since my mother died." She had a wistful expression on her face. "Those first days I was alone." She turned away from him. "A few nights after she'd died, I was by myself in our one-room apartment. The storm came on without any warning. I had nothing except those four walls and a thin blanket to keep me safe."

"I thought you told me a friend took you in."

"Oh yes. But not in those first days." She walked to the front of the wagon to pet the mare's nose. "Owen, please understand, I don't want to ruin this moment . . . our moment . . . with those memories."

He wanted her to share even those darkest of times with him. "How did you survive?"

"I managed."

Owen cocked his head to one side. He didn't like that Lily seemed to be pulling away from him. Perhaps the storm had dredged up the memories of her mother's death, and with it, her sudden melancholy. Still, he wished she'd tell him about her life before they'd met. He wanted to know everything about her.

Stepping away from the mare, she peered out from the safety of the shed. "It looks like the rain is stopping."

"Storms in these parts can circle back around. It's best if we wait a bit longer before attempting to go home." His boots made a squishing sound as he walked over to join her. Laying a hand on her shoulder, he turned her to face him. "Lily, have I done something wrong?"

Some of the light had gone from her eyes. "No. Why do you ask?"

"You seem sad."

"I was thinking about my mother."

"Would it help if you talked about her?"

"I'm not sure." She shivered and wrapped her arms about her waist before she stepped away from him, looking out at the remnants of the storm. "It just seems like our time together was so short. She'd been ill for a very long time before she died. Thinking about it now, I know she's better off in heaven than here on earth."

Owen completely understood her feelings. Even though Rebecca's death had been quick, he would not have wanted her to suffer. He realized it was the first time he'd thought about Rebecca in a while. He hadn't spoken of her death to anyone other than Alice and Theodore Cuddieback. They'd been there by his side throughout the ordeal, and now he wanted to share this with Lily.

"Rebecca and I had gone for a hike, on a day a lot like this one. We'd had a storm in the morning, and when the sun came out, she wanted to go for a hike. We walked the trail that my aunt and uncle came off the day of our picnic. I wasn't being careful enough. She was bitten by a timber rattlesnake."

Lily gasped.

He swallowed, wishing he hadn't started down this road. "Her death was horrible. And for a long time, I blamed myself . . . I still blame myself."

"Oh. Owen, that's so terrible. But you couldn't have known about the snake."

He rubbed his hand over his face. "No. But I knew enough to be on the lookout for them."

He waited for the rush of pain that these memories usually brought on. They arrived, as they always did, but they weren't as strong this time. Perhaps it was because of the woman standing beside him.

He realized he was ready to move forward with his life, to leave behind the dark trench he'd dug for himself.

Lily's voice penetrated his thoughts. "Being at the Murphy Camp is the first time I've ever felt like I belonged somewhere."

Her words gave him pause. He couldn't imagine not having a place to call home.

She stood with her back to him, still looking out at the horizon. He closed the distance between them in two easy steps. Taking hold of her shoulders, he turned her around gently, drawing her into his arms.

"I hope one day you will be able to call Murphy Camp your home."

"Owen. There's so much you don't know about me." She put her hands against his chest, putting distance between them.

He tucked his hand underneath her chin, tipping her head so he could look fully into her eyes. And when he did, the only thing he saw was her pain and her eyes filling with tears.

"Lily. You can tell me anything."

The sun picked that moment to burst through the clouds, showering them in warmth and light. Owen took that as a sign from above that he needed to be with her. More of his guilt fell away as he realized there was room in his heart to love again.

She stepped out of the circle of his arms. "We should head out." Her breath hitched. "I'm sure Mrs. Cuddieback is wondering where we got off to."

Owen untied the horse and wagon, led them outside, and waited for Lily to join them. Once there, she grabbed hold of the railing and started to pull herself up onto the wagon seat. Owen rushed to her side. "Here, let me help you." He offered his hand.

"I'm fine, Owen."

"Lily, why are you pulling away from me?"

"I'm sorry."

He had the strangest feeling that he was losing her. He had to do something to convince her to trust him . . . to trust herself. Granted, he was more experienced than she when it came to matters of the heart. Maybe that's what was bothering her.

Owen decided to get right to the point. "Lily, I'm not going to lie to you. I want there to be something more between us than just a business partnership."

She cast him a cautious glance and then smiled. "I know. I'd like that, too."

He thought his heart was going to burst from his chest. "Then please don't shut me out."

When she didn't say anything, he took the reins and joined her on the wagon seat. They left the clearing and headed out on the roadway. As they were cresting the rise before the camp, a double rainbow appeared in the sky. It seemed to originate from somewhere behind them, stretching over their heads, ending near his property.

Pulling on the reins, he stopped the forward motion of the mare so they could admire God's handiwork. "Now that's what I call one of God's miracles."

Lily tipped her head back and looked up at the sky, her mouth dropping open. "I've never seen anything quite so lovely. I wish I could memorize each of those colors."

"When I consider your heavens, the work of your fingers, the moon and the stars, which you have set in place, what is mankind that you are mindful of them . . ." Owen quoted what he remembered from part of Psalms 8:3–4.

He crooked a grin at her. "I think rainbows should be considered as part of that verse."

"I agree."

Since the mare knew the way from there, Owen relaxed his hold on the reins, letting the horse take the lead. He turned to Lily. "Just like this rainbow has appeared like a gift, I feel that you came into my life for a reason. Maybe it was to heal my wounded soul. I don't know. But whatever the reason, I'm glad you came."

She reached out to lay a hand on the side of his face. "Owen, that is the sweetest thing anyone has ever said to me."

Again, he saw the tears forming in her eyes and wondered why.

Chapter Eighteen

Lily let Owen drop her at the front steps, taking her satchel and jumping from the wagon before he could help her down. She knew her actions were confusing to him. Heck, they were confusing to her. She'd been so happy when he'd taken her in his arms, making her feel safe and needed. And then her past intruded on her contentment. Yes, she'd done a lot of good, but to the outsider, the things she'd done would look questionable.

Knowing Owen might never understand, Lily began to regret allowing him to kiss her. She ran up the steps, which were still wet from the rain. They glistened in the sunlight. Lily wished she could take the time to admire how pretty the flowers flanking the stairs looked, with their dewy petals. Instead, she felt the need to be alone.

"There you are!" Desdemona's loud voice shattered Lily's thoughts. Owen's aunt stood at the top of the steps, blocking her path to the entryway.

"Good afternoon, Mrs. Murphy."

"Afternoon? It's near supper time. We expected you and Owen to be back long before this."

"I apologize for our tardiness. We got caught in the rain."

The older woman narrowed her eyes, scrutinizing Lily, who wanted nothing more than to be allowed to pass so she could go to her room and freshen up before supper.

"We were worried."

"I appreciate your caring, but as you can see, we're fine."

She peered around Lily, no doubt expecting to see Owen. "I don't see my nephew. How do I know he's fine?"

"Trust me, he's fine." *More than fine,* Lily thought. Hoping to avoid any more conversing with the woman, she added, "He took the wagon and horse to the barn. I'm sure he'll be in soon."

Satisfied that no harm had come to her nephew, the woman finally stepped aside. Lily walked by, hurrying up to the quiet of her room. Once inside, she shut the door. Sitting on the edge of the bed, she bent down to unlace her shoes. They were covered in mud. She sighed when she realized she'd tracked mud across her bedroom floor, which meant she'd tracked it through the hall and up the stairs. If she hadn't let Desdemona get to her, Lily would have taken her shoes off before entering the house.

Rising, she picked up the muddy shoes and placed them outside the porch door, where they could dry out in the warm sunshine. Once inside again, she took a cloth from her dressing table and brushed it along the front of her gown, doing her best to release some of the dried mud. When she was satisfied she'd gotten most of it, she repinned her hair. Seeing her reflection in the oval-shaped mirror gave her pause. Lily touched her fingers to her lips—lips that not so long ago had been soundly kissed.

Hope filled her heart. A moment later, that same hope turned to sadness. She wanted to believe she wasn't falling in love with Owen Murphy, and yet that's exactly what had been happening. She was falling hard for a man who knew nothing about her. And then there was the fact that John Oliver wanted to meet with her under the cover of darkness. Lily fought back her growing panic.

What was she going to do? She couldn't very well go downstairs, join Owen and his family at the dinner table, and act as if nothing had transpired between the two of them. And what about her clandestine meeting with John? Yet one more deception to pile on with the rest. Owen deserved someone better than her.

Fighting to keep the tears at bay, Lily sank down onto the edge of the bed. One thing was certain; she would not go back to the life she had before. No matter what John asked of her tonight, she would tell him no. For now, she decided, she would stay in her room until the appointed time. If anyone came upstairs inquiring about her absence at dinner, she would simply say she was fatigued from the outing.

Having made her decision, she laid her head down on the bed pillow. Staring up at the ceiling, she wondered why God insisted on putting another barrier before her. Lily's faith had carried her through many a dark hour. Over the course of the past few months, she'd finally—*finally*—seen a clear path to the future she wanted.

Her thoughts were interrupted by a light tapping on her bedroom door.

"Lily? Are you all right?" Mrs. Cuddieback sounded concerned.

Lily pushed herself up off the bed and opened the door. Mrs. Cuddieback wore a pretty yellow dress, under one of her white aprons. The woman looked at her with nothing but kindness and concern, making Lily feel terrible about feigning fatigue. Mrs. Cuddieback reached out to lay a hand on Lily's arm, her brown eyes crinkling at the edges when she smiled at her.

"Your seat at the table is empty. Are you coming down for dinner?"

"I'm sorry. I'm so tired from the day and getting caught in the rain." Unable to bear seeing the concern in the older woman's eyes, Lily cast her gaze down. "I think I ruined my gown."

Following Lily's gaze, Mrs. Cuddieback made a tsking sound with her tongue. "I might be able to get most of that dirt out. We can raise the hemlines on your day gowns so this doesn't happen again."

"Oh. I hadn't thought of doing that."

Lily almost added that when she'd lived in the city, she hadn't worried so much about these sorts of inconveniences. Of course, thoughts being what they are, one led to another, which brought her current dilemma full circle. The sun was beginning to set, leaving her only a short time until her meeting with John Oliver. Trying not to show her worry, she smiled.

"I can bring you a tray if you'd like."

"No. Please don't go to any trouble on my behalf. I'll come down to the kitchen later."

"It's no trouble." Mrs. Cuddieback turned to leave and then came back to the door. "Lily, you know I've come to think of you as a granddaughter. As such, I want you to know that you can come to me with anything, and I mean *anything at all* that is troubling you. After what you've done for our Owen . . ." Her eyes welled with tears.

Lily managed to choke out a thank-you.

Mrs. Cuddieback leaned in. "I can tell he's worried about your absence," she whispered. "He can't seem to take his eyes from your empty seat. Did something happen today?"

Lily's pulse jumped. Had Owen told her about their kiss? *No.* He would never confide such a thing. She hated the thought that he was downstairs worrying about her. But she couldn't face any of them, not when she could very well be about to betray Owen and the Cuddiebacks. There was no guessing why John wanted to see her and why their meeting had to be so clandestine. If she had to hazard a guess, she thought he might want to try to bring her back into the service.

"Please tell everyone I appreciate their concern, but I'm simply done in."

Mrs. Cuddieback's eyes crinkled at the corners once more as she gave Lily a comforting smile. "All right, dear. I will pass that along and leave you a covered dish for later."

"Thank you."

Lily closed the hall door. She walked to the porch door and opened it, letting in a delicious cool breeze. Standing at the edge of the room with her arms spread wide, the crisp air on her skin, she tipped her head back and closed her eyes in prayer.

"Dear Lord, please guide me in my choices. Help me to find the strength to make the right ones. If it is your desire, show Owen and me the way together. And thank you for opening my heart. Amen."

Opening her eyes, she saw a monarch butterfly land on the railing. Its wings fluttered, the deep variant orange hues segregated by thin black veins, coming in and out of focus. Lily couldn't help but think of butterflies as nature's stained-glass windows. The sight of that one tiny creature gave her renewed strength and hope.

Bending down, she picked up her shoes and clapped the soles together to knock the rest of the dried mud off. Then she closed the doors, brought her boots over to the bed, and put them on, lacing them tight. Below her was the main dining room, and she stopped moving to listen for voices, trying to ascertain if anyone was still in there. Desdemona's booming laughter rose through the floorboards like the sound of rolling thunder. Cocking her head to the left, she listened for the other people in the room. Instincts she'd thought long buried came to the surface as she waited.

Rudolph's voice came, sounding muffled. "Remember . . . the . . ." followed by the scraping sound of a chair being pushed back. Then Rudolph's voice again. "Would you care for sherry?"

Desdemona accepted his offer, and Lily heard Owen decline. If she were to sneak out of the house unnoticed, she'd need to be sure they'd left the dining room. She heard a door shut . . . downstairs . . . the sound coming from behind her. That had to be Owen going into the office. An uncomfortable tingle settled along the hairline at the nape of her neck. Lily brought her hand up to rub it away.

In front of her, the sun dropped like a rock, lining the horizon in a sea of red.

It was time.

Getting out of the house proved to be much easier than she'd antici-pated. With Owen still busy in the office and his aunt and uncle in the dining room enjoying their nightcap, Lily slipped out the front door with ease. She held on to the railing as she quickly descended the steps. Ducking around the shrubbery, she stayed along the edge of the lawn. Halfway to the barn, she heard a twig snap.

She froze. Listening. The twig snapped again. She'd been followed. Her palms began to sweat. She swallowed down the panic. Boldly, she turned her head, looking behind her. She gasped as a deer ran off into the woods. Laying her hand over her chest, she willed her heartbeat to settle. Panic had been the downfall of many an inexperienced agent. In that regard, Lily knew better.

She waited for the quiet to settle and, deeming it safe, continued. She crept along the edge of the woods until the outline of the barn came into focus. Looking behind her to make sure she was alone, Lily stepped out of the shadows. Light-footed, she followed a narrow path-way around to the back of the building. There she found John Oliver waiting, his tall, lean form resting against the side of the barn. He might have looked casual and relaxed, but Lily knew he stood at the ready.

"I didn't think you were going to come." His deep voice resonated in the darkness.

"You gave me little choice."

"I'm sorry for that. For this."

"What exactly is this?"

None of this made any sense. He'd signed the paper releasing her from her Pinkerton duties. She'd bartered for her freedom once before, and she wasn't about to do it again.

"I needed you to take one last assignment."

"That's not going to happen. I fulfilled my duties. I don't owe the agency or you anything else." Lily stiffened her shoulders. Wait, did he say "needed" her, as in the past tense?

"You're correct, you don't owe me anything."

"Then why are you here?"

"Something came across my desk recently, and I thought you would be a good fit for the job. That was before I saw Owen today." He pushed away from the building. "I wanted to give you this opportunity in case things here were not what you'd hoped for."

A knot formed in the pit of her stomach. "Did Owen say something that seemed odd to you?"

"Quite the contrary; the man couldn't stop talking about you." John paused and then said, "Lily, he's falling in love with you."

There was a catch in her throat as she thought about what had transpired between them on the way home. Owen had kissed her and she'd kissed him back. John didn't know about any of that. He couldn't know of the growing feelings that Lily had for Owen.

"I didn't come here to find love. I came here to find a home."

"And I'm here to tell you if you haven't told Owen about your past already—and I'm guessing from my conversation with him earlier that you haven't—you need to tell him before someone else does."

"Who else is there besides yourself, Will, and Elsie that knows the truth?"

John gave her an exasperated look. "Lily. These things have a way of getting out," he said in a firm tone, "especially when you live in a small town."

She started to tell him he didn't know what he was talking about, and then she remembered the man from the saloon. How long would it be before his memory became clear? The next time he saw her, would he call her out? Lily felt as if she were being sucked into a deep hole. She couldn't risk Owen finding out in that way. Their relationship was too fragile.

"I don't know if now is a good time to tell him about what brought me to Heartston."

"What have you told him so far?"

"That I'm from the city. I was orphaned from a young age and eventually a friend took me in." She looked at him. "That friend would be you, John."

He shook his head. "Lily. A secret much like the one you are keeping almost tore Will and Elsie apart."

"I'm doing the best that I can." She rolled her shoulders.

"You need to have faith that whatever is going on between you and Owen will withstand the test of time. If you are falling in love with the man—and I think you are—then you have to be honest with him, or it will never work."

When she didn't respond, he urged her, "Lily, let me make myself clear: Owen is my friend. His wife's death nearly did him in. I haven't seen him this happy in a very long time. I won't have you ruin him again."

The fear that she'd kept at bay for so long came back with a vengeance. *She wasn't good enough to be loved by Owen.* She'd looked to John for guidance for so many years, and now he was abandoning her. "I cannot believe you're choosing sides," she said, raising her voice.

His gaze softened, and he shook his head. "I'm not. You are a part of Owen's life. You need to consider all that comes with being there for him. You might not want to believe this, but you've healed his broken heart, and I can see that he's opened yours up to the possibility of love." He put his hands on her shoulders. "Let him in, Lily."

She stepped away, biting back a sob. Leaving John standing in the growing darkness, she retraced her steps along the edge of the woods. Just as she was almost free and clear, the sight of a familiar figure in the distance stopped her dead in her tracks.

Owen stood in the shadows on the front porch.

"Lily, is that you?" he asked, stepping into the open.

Gathering her skirts, she met him at the top of the steps. "Yes. It's me."

"I went upstairs to bring you a dinner tray. But you weren't in your room. What are you doing out here?"

"I just needed a bit of fresh air before I settled in for the night."

"I thought I heard voices out by the barn. Was someone with you?"

She gave him a shaky smile and denied John's presence. "Looks like you caught me talking to myself. I was working on the grand reopening. I know, a silly thing to be doing." Lily didn't know if he believed her or not.

He caught her hand in his, giving it a comforting squeeze. His touch warmed her, the feeling spreading up her arm and into her heart. Time to heed John's advice and tell Owen about her past before it was too late. But then she saw the way Owen looked at her, his expression filled with the trust and the love that John had told her about. She didn't have the courage to tell him who she'd been before she met him. Her confession would ruin everything they'd worked so hard to build together.

He kissed her on the forehead and then lowered his head to drop a kiss on her lips.

Her breath caught in the back of her throat. Gently, she placed her hands between them, resting them lightly on the hard wall of his chest. She felt the steady beat of his heart beneath her fingertips. She didn't deserve this man.

"Thank you for worrying about me."

"Lily, of course I was worried when I couldn't find you in the house. But I did leave the tray up in your room."

"That was very thoughtful of you." She stepped away from him. "I'm afraid I'm done in."

"I can walk you up to your room if you'd like."

"That won't be necessary, Owen."

Holding the front door open, he gave her a gallant bow from the waist as he waved her in. She laughed at his antics. It felt so good to laugh after the day she'd had. Leaving him in front of his office, Lily went up the stairs to her bedroom where she found not only the dinner tray but a lovely freshly cut rose.

Her heart swelled as she touched the tender petals. "Oh, Owen," she whispered.

A rapid knocking sounded at her door. Thinking it was Owen, she held the rose between her fingers and rushed to the door. She swung it open. "Thank you for the . . ." Her words trailed off when she saw Desdemona standing there in her nightclothes.

"I don't know what excuse you gave my nephew, but I saw you sneaking out." She wagged a finger. "Miss Handland, I know you are up to no good."

Rudolph's muffled voice bled through the open door. "Desdemona! Get yourself back over here and leave that poor girl to her sleep." He appeared in the doorway and took his wife by the shoulders, spinning her around to face their room.

The woman glared over her shoulder at Lily. "I'm coming! I'm coming!"

"You need your sleep, too, darling. We've got to be up at the crack of dawn if we're to catch the stagecoach."

Frozen in a fear she'd never known before, Lily stood in the open doorway. Desdemona Murphy wanted to ruin her life, and now she had the power to do it. Lily had to confess her love to Owen and tell him the truth before it was too late.

Chapter Nineteen

Owen sank back on his heels. Using his sleeve, he wiped the sweat from his brow. Good thing he'd gotten to the roof repair early.

He took in the view from the rooftop of the house. God was certainly in all his glory today. Off in the distance the tall peaks that made up the Adirondack mountain range jutted into a sky dotted with fluffy white clouds. Closer to him lay the sparkling pond and woods of his own property.

It had been a very long time since he'd felt this untroubled. And he had one Lily Handland to thank for that.

Turning his attention back to the job, he searched the grounds below for his newly hired helper. "Bobby, can you grab that pile of shingles over by the foot of the ladder and bring them up here?"

"Sure thing, Mr. Murphy."

Waiting for the redheaded lad to make his way up the ladder, Owen thought that maybe he'd been too hard on Lily when she'd suggested the idea of hiring extra help. Having the boy here now certainly made this task easier. It also allowed Theodore time to do other, less dangerous work, like helping his wife rearrange the furniture in the great room.

For the past week, Lily had been keeping everyone on their toes with her assignments, so much so that he'd hardly had a moment alone with her. That was the reason he'd planned a surprise for her today. Picking up one of the cedar shingles, he overlapped it onto the previous one and pounded a nail through the top of it. Even Owen had to admit that the main house was looking better than it had in a very long time.

All the guest rooms had been cleaned and freshened. The curtains that Lily had insisted on ordering were set to arrive today, along with her surprise. Once the curtains were in place, the rooms would be complete. Sitting back on his heels again, he admired his handiwork.

"I'd say we're about done up here, Bobby."

"Looks like you got that hole all covered up," he replied.

"Yup. And we're ready for the next storm." He tossed the unused shingles to the ground. Gathering his tools, he stepped onto the top rung of the ladder.

"What's next, Mr. Murphy?" Bobby asked.

Owen took his time going down the ladder. Once on firm footing, he answered the young man. "I'd say it's time for a break. If you head on into the kitchen, I'm sure Mrs. Cuddieback will have some fresh-baked cookies for you."

"Gee, thanks, Mr. Murphy."

Bobby trotted off, leaving Owen to laugh at his enthusiasm. All in all he'd say the youngster had been a great help. Having him here had saved Owen repeated trips up and down the ladder. Once again Lily had been correct with her advice. After cleaning up the work area, he joined Bobby in the kitchen.

"Oh, Mr. Owen, we are getting closer to our big day!" Mrs. Cuddieback proclaimed as she took another pan of what looked like chocolate chip cookies out of the oven.

He reached out to take a hot one off the pan, only to get his hand slapped.

"Yours are over there on that plate," she said, indicating the spot where Bobby stood shoveling cookies into his mouth.

"Hey, save me some." Owen laughed as the boy chewed on a mouthful of cookie.

After Mrs. Cuddieback set the baking sheet off to one side of the stove, she brought a pitcher of milk along with two glasses to the table. "This might help those cookies go down."

Owen thanked her. Bobby took the first full glass, downing the contents in one gulp. The woman poured the second glass and handed it to Owen with a bright expression on her face. Her brown eyes twinkled, as if she were keeping some delightful secret.

He looked at her over the rim of his glass. "Mrs. Cuddieback, is there something you'd like to share with me?"

She patted him on the arm. "Just that I'm happy to see you so . . . happy."

"All right."

"Bobby, Mr. Cuddieback needs your help," she said. "He's down by the pond. Follow the pathway and you'll meet up with him." She nodded her head toward the back door.

Grabbing a handful of cookies, the boy shot out of the kitchen as if he were being chased.

"He sure can eat," Owen observed, watching him go.

"He's still growing." Mrs. Cuddieback made a great show of rearranging the cookies on the plate. Then she took the near-empty pitcher of milk back to the sink. She picked up a cleaning cloth and came back to wipe up the table.

Owen was beginning to think she might have something she needed to get off her mind. He couldn't decide if he should help her out or wait until she was ready. Biting into another cookie, he savored the sweetness of the chocolate chips, letting the tiny, delicate morsels melt in his mouth. He took another swig from the glass, washed it down, and set it on the table.

"I think I'll get back to work."

"Wait."

Owen raised an eyebrow again, wondering what she had going inside that head of hers. He saw her fidgeting with her apron strings. "Mrs. Cuddieback, if you've something to say to me, now's the time. I have a lot of projects to finish today." And one surprise to set up for Lily.

"I know that things haven't been easy for you these past years." She wadded one end of the apron in her hands. "Oh, I'll just come out with it! I'm so happy that you and Lily seem to be . . ."

"We seem to be what?"

"Getting along better," she said softly, and then her eyes filled with tears. "I believe you're falling in love with her."

Owen already knew how he felt about Lily, but hearing the words from this woman who had taken care of him ever since Rebecca's death made his feelings seem even more of a reality. Swallowing down his emotions, he gathered Alice Cuddieback in his arms. She smelled like vanilla and sugar and comfort. "I believe you are right. I am falling in love with Lily."

He heard what sounded like a soft sob come from her, and then she gave him a grandmotherly squeeze and released him. Using the end of her apron, she dabbed at the corners of her eyes.

"You know when she first came here," she said in a wobbly voice, "I wasn't so sure you were going to give in and let her become your partner. I certainly didn't think you'd let her stay. But you did. She's brought life to this place. She's brought life to you, Owen."

Owen took in a deep, freeing breath of air. "She's changed me."

"You wouldn't have changed if you didn't want to. I think the good Lord has had a hand in some of this."

"Maybe."

She tilted her head to one side, smiling. "No maybes about it. I've prayed for you to find your way out of the darkness every night for the past two years. I don't know if you can see it, but those deep lines of worry are gone from your face."

He knew what she was talking about. The tension he'd carried inside and out had disappeared. From the moment he'd accepted his feelings for Lily, he'd changed. But after kissing her during the thunderstorm and nearly declaring his love for her, Owen felt deep in his gut that Lily was holding something back. He had seen the hope in her eyes turn to despair, and he didn't know how to get her to open up to him.

He needed to let her know that no matter what, he would be there for her because he loved her.

He thought about Rebecca and the short time they'd had together. The pain and guilt over her death had consumed him. "It hasn't been easy to let go of the past."

"I understand. Can't imagine my life without my mister." Her eyes filled with tears. She quickly blinked them away. "Is there something else you're not telling me?"

Perhaps Mrs. Cuddieback could offer some more advice where Lily was concerned. He delayed admitting his fears by pushing some of the leftover crumbs around the plate. "I'm not sure Lily shares my feelings."

Mrs. Cuddieback waved her hands in front of her face as if swatting away a troublesome fly. "Nonsense. That woman is head over heels for you. I can tell by the way she looks at you. Listen to me: this is all new for both of you. You just need a little more time, that's all." She waved her hands at his back, shooing him out of the kitchen. "Now get on with yourself. I've got plenty left to do here before dinnertime."

Owen left her to her baking and headed upstairs. The supply wagon would be arriving soon, and he wanted to be ready to unload the special order he'd placed with John earlier this week. Lily had been so adamant about wanting to add some seating near the pond. While he didn't have time to put up her gazebo, he'd come pretty close with his idea. There was just enough time for one more inspection of the ceilings in the bedrooms. He wanted to be sure he didn't miss any other repairs.

He headed off to the right, opening the door to the bedroom his aunt and uncle had shared. The bed looked freshly made, and there wasn't a thing out of place. He walked around looking up at the ceiling, checking for water stains and cracks. Everything appeared to be in place. Leaving the room, he thought it a shame that his aunt hadn't taken to Lily. The woman could be hard on people. He hoped that eventually she'd come around.

He stepped across the narrow hall, standing in front of the door to Lily's room. This was the last room that needed his inspection. He hadn't seen Lily all day and thought perhaps she might have been hiding out in there.

He rapped his knuckles against the door. "Lily?"

Leaning his ear against the wood, he listened for sounds of her moving about. Silence greeted him. He turned the handle, opening the door just enough to stick his head inside.

"Lily. Are you in here?"

There was no sign of her. Owen stepped over the threshold, surprised at the way she'd decorated the room. He recognized the buttercup-colored quilt covering her bed, one of the first ones Rebecca had sewn when they'd first moved out here. Odd that Lily would have chosen this one for her use. It felt strange to be in here. All around him was her lemony scent.

Over the back of a rocking chair she'd draped a shawl. The wardrobe on the opposite side of the room was closed. An ivory-handled hairbrush and matching mirror sat on the washstand. To the right of that sat a rather dilapidated trunk, the leather on the top worn and frayed around the edges. Even the latch looked broken. Owen decided that the next time he was in Heartston, he would go over to the mercantile to see about purchasing a new one for her. Reminding himself of the reason he'd entered her room without permission, he began the ceiling inspection.

Starting by the doorway, he worked from his right, sidestepping around the bed and washstand. Satisfied that there was no sign of water damage in this side of the room, he moved by the outside door and around the wardrobe. His neck began to ache, so he stopped to roll his shoulders and rub the crick out of his neck.

"That's better."

Again he tipped his head back and stepped to one side. His momentum came to an abrupt halt when his boot thunked against the corner of the trunk. Bending down, he grabbed hold of one of the leather handles and was giving it a tug when it broke off in his hand, sending the lid of the trunk sideways. Owen knelt, setting the strap on the floor, and started to close the lid. His hand froze on the edge.

"What on earth?" His eyes widened at the sight of black lace and bright red fabric. He didn't understand what he was looking at.

Unable to stop himself, he pulled the garment out. The red dress had a black lace skirt underneath. Owen's senses were sent into a tailspin as the smell of heavy perfume and stale cigar smoke filled the air around him. He let out a groan as his confusion grew. The Lily he knew smelled like lemons and roses and goodness . . . not this. He held the dress in one hand. And then, lifting the lid to let in more light, he saw more clothing like this, along with black stockings and a pair of high-heeled shoes.

His pulse pounded in his ears. He didn't understand. "Lily, what have you done?"

"Owen?"

He heard the question in her voice, and he turned to look at her in the doorway.

"Owen! What are you doing in my room?" Lily's face paled when she saw him kneeling in front of the trunk.

She gasped and covered her mouth. Then she ran to him, yanking the dress from him. "It's not what you think," she cried. "It's not what you think. I can explain."

All the words of warning from his aunt flooded through his mind. All the times she'd told him Lily wasn't who she said she was . . . that she was hiding something. Owen couldn't believe that Lily would have anything to do with whatever these garments represented. And yet . . . his thoughts stumbled.

"Please . . . ," she pleaded. "Let me explain."

She dropped to the floor and shoved the garment back inside the trunk. Her entire body shook as she tried to force the lid closed. When the edges of the fabric refused to stay inside, she continued to push at them, forcing the folds into the crevice.

"I should have left this behind." She was wringing her hands together and sucking in deep breaths. Her gaze darted around the room, until she looked at him.

Owen stood with his hands hanging at his sides. His stomach churned. His heart raced. He couldn't speak.

He saw her lips tremble. He pulled his shoulders back, straightening his spine. There was only one type of woman who wore dresses like that.

His voice shook when he finally asked, "Do those dresses belong to you?"

Chapter Twenty

She nodded, feeling her entire world fall way. "Owen. Please, let's go outside onto the back porch."

"I don't want to go onto the porch."

He clenched and unclenched his fists. Even though she stood a few feet away from him, she could feel his anger. He paled, staring at her as if she were a stranger. She bit back a sob. This couldn't be happening. None of this would be happening if she'd been honest about her past from the very beginning. John and Will and Elsie—they had all been right when they'd told her that secrets like hers always had a way of coming out. She knew he was thinking the very worst of her, and yet she didn't know if she could tell him what he needed to hear.

He hadn't moved from his spot on the floor, but she could see the dark fury building in his eyes. His held his mouth in a tight line. And he waited. She caught a glimpse of movement outside her window and heard voices. She thought she heard someone mention her name and then ask where Owen was. Mrs. Cuddieback called out their names, and Lily opened her mouth to answer.

Owen held up his hand as if to silence her response. Together they waited until the voices faded away.

Lily didn't know what he wanted her to say, so she just started talking. "After my mother died, I found myself in desperate circumstances. I didn't know what to do. I had no relatives, and the area we lived in was less than desirable. For days, I wandered around the few blocks near our one-room apartment, looking for food, taking any handout I could get." Owen's face hardened into an unreadable expression. Her words weren't reaching him. She kept talking.

She laid a hand in the soft hollow of her neck. "I was so alone. Desperate. I began watching the boys who lived in the alleyway next to my building. They were very clever with their hands, picking pockets for billfolds. Eventually I . . ." She hesitated, thinking how she'd broken one of the commandments.

"Eventually, you what?" Owen's voice broke through her dark thoughts.

"I learned how to steal from people without them knowing."

"Is that all you did?" He glared at her, sweeping his hand in the direction of the trunk.

She started to shake her head. Her hands trembled. "It's not what you think. I promise you."

"I don't want your promises. I want you to tell me the truth." He ground his teeth together.

"Owen, please can't we sit down?" She dared to step forward, hoping he'd let her pass, so she could at least sit in the rocking chair.

He didn't stop her, and Lily lowered herself into the chair. Her mouth was so dry, which made little sense, because her palms were sweating. She wiped her hands on her dress. And that one tiny motion sent her mind tumbling into the past when the only thing she had to wear was one dress that she washed over and over again until it became threadbare.

One tear slipped from beneath her eyelids and then another fell and another, until she couldn't stem the flow. Closing her eyes, she willed herself to stop crying. Finally, the tears subsided.

She started talking again, her voice sounding flat to her ears. "I learned how to steal, and one day I got caught."

Lily could have sworn she'd heard his quick intake of breath, but when she looked up, his mouth was drawn tight. "I was given a choice: I could go to the state penitentiary for young girls, or I could go into service for the Pinkerton Agency. I chose the latter."

The bed frame creaked as Owen lowered himself down to sit on the foot of the mattress. His face had turned ashen. "My God, Lily. What did they make you do?"

"Owen, it's not what you think."

"Those clothes tell me otherwise." His gaze met hers. "You told me you had a friend who helped you. I don't understand why they didn't take you in and keep you safe."

"They—he," she corrected, "did take me in."

He dropped his head into his hands. Then he looked up over the tips of his fingers. "Oh, Lily, I don't like the sound of this."

"John Oliver was the one who found me stealing. I worked with him and William Benton," she blurted out.

Owen's mouth dropped open and then snapped shut. He stood and began pacing in front of her. "None of this makes any sense to me."

"I came to Heartston last year. I was working in concert with Will and John to solve Will's last case."

She saw something dawn in him. Owen turned and pointed an accusing finger at her. "That drunkard, the one who bumped into you on the street the other day, he said he recognized you."

"He did."

He raked a hand through his hair, and when that didn't seem to help, he scrubbed both hands over his face. Lily thought he might be trying to rid himself of her. "You were a saloon girl?"

Her lower lip trembled. "No—yes, but only as part of my cover."

"Did you . . ." He stopped, sucking in a pained breath.

"No."

"My God." He spun to face her. "How could you keep this from me? Why, Lily, why?"

"I came here to start a new life. I wanted someplace to call home. Then I met you, and your pain . . . it was everywhere, Owen. You were a broken man. You didn't need to know who I was before."

The corners of his mouth sagged. "Lily. When things between us started to change, you should have told me."

"I knew I could never compete with Rebecca!" Lily stood. Splaying her hands outward, she continued, "Owen, you put her on a pedestal. How could anyone be expected to compete with that?"

His eyes widened. Red blotches appeared high on his cheekbones. "Don't you utter her name!" he shouted.

The breath whooshed out of her lungs. *What had she done?*

"Owen!" She sobbed. "I'm sorry. I'm sorry," she pleaded. "I never meant to hurt you. Please forgive me."

Her body trembled, her shoulders heaving as the tears flowed down her face. She couldn't believe her life was being dealt another cruel blow. Lily didn't want to let Owen go. She couldn't. She needed him to make her life whole.

The look he gave her was so full of loathing that Lily stumbled back against the chair. She watched him leave. The slamming of the bedroom door echoed in her ears.

Lily stood there, stunned by what had just happened. Eventually the sounds of the day came back. A bluebird flew in, landing on the porch rail and chirping. Lily rubbed a hand across her neck, feeling her pulse beneath her fingertips. Dropping her hand, she pushed open the porch door and walked out onto the wooden deck.

The bird flew away.

Looking down at the clearing, Lily saw a pair of chairs nestled in front of a fire ring. If she sat there, she would be able to take in the view of the wildlife near the pond. She wondered where they'd come from. Mr. Cuddieback dropped an armful of wood next to the spot. He must have sensed her watching, because he looked up and gave her a wave.

"Nice of Owen to get these chairs for you!" the man hollered.

Lily waved back, forcing a smile that didn't even come close to what she was feeling. And then his words sunk in; Owen had gotten those chairs for her. Her heart broke all over again. Turning away, she went back into her bedroom, shut the door, and sank down onto her bed.

For the next week, the days became routine. Lily would rise each morning, go downstairs to the kitchen before anyone else had risen, and eat her breakfast. Then she'd pick up where she left off the day before, preparing for the grand opening. Today she planned on hanging the curtains that the seamstress had delivered. Lily hadn't even opened the boxes. They'd been sitting on a long table in the hallway since . . . she paused in her thoughts . . . since the last time she'd seen Owen.

Heading off to the hall, she found two large boxes and one small one. She picked up the top two and took them upstairs, leaving them in the hallway outside the last guest room to the left. Then she went back down for the last box. Once she had them together, Lily opened the larger boxes. She'd save the small one for later. Maybe Mrs. Fenton had done up an extra curtain panel. Pulling out the first curtain and seeing how pretty it looked lifted her spirits for the first time in days.

They were going to look so beautiful on the windows. It didn't matter that all the guest rooms would look the same. What mattered was that Lily would leave her mark here. Her heart caught at the thought. This might be the last time she'd be allowed to do anything at the Murphy Camp.

Owen hadn't sought her out since their argument. He didn't know, but she'd watched him putting the finishing touches on the new outdoor sitting area. He'd added some large pots with flowering shrubs that he'd transplanted from the edge of the woods. Pushing those thoughts aside, Lily got to work hanging the curtains.

With two sets of curtains in hand, she entered the bedroom. As soon as she realized she wasn't tall enough to install them, she spread them on the freshly made bed and headed back downstairs.

She found Mrs. Cuddieback washing the windows in the kitchen.

"Do you know where I can find a stepladder?"

"Lily!" The woman spun around to look at Lily, nearly toppling over from the effort. "Where have you been keeping yourself? I feel like I haven't seen you all week."

"I've been busy. There's so much to be done before Saturday." She put her hands on her hips. "Like hanging the curtains Mrs. Fenton delivered."

Her brow furrowed, Mrs. Cuddieback set her cleaning supplies on the counter and wiped her hands on her apron. "She came all the way out here. Rode in that big uncomfortable wagon right beside those big chairs Mr. Owen had made special for you, and you didn't even come out when I called for you. And Mr. Owen has been grumbling like he got into a hornet's nest. And I think he's sleeping on the sofa in his office again."

She knew the woman deserved to know what had happened, but Lily didn't think she could bear it if this woman, who had become like a grandmother to her, thought as poorly of her as Owen did right now. She wished Owen hadn't gotten the chairs after all since she wouldn't be here to enjoy them.

"Did you and Owen have some sort of falling-out?"

"You could say that," Lily replied glumly. "Mrs. Cuddieback, I know you want what's best for Owen, but I can't tell you what's going on. You'll need to discuss this with him."

The woman's bosom heaved with a big sigh. "You'll find a short stepladder next to the keg of root beer in the pantry. And be careful. I don't need you taking a spill this close to the party."

Lily found the short, three-rung ladder right where Mrs. Cuddieback said it would be. While she was there, she found a hammer and some nails. Since she didn't have the heart to ask any of the men to make her some rods out of branches, she planned on temporarily tacking up the curtains. Going back up to the guest room, Lily made short work of getting the first room done. Gathering the ladder, curtains, and tools, she headed down the hall to the next room.

She followed the same steps installing them until she came to the room that Desdemona and Rudolph had shared. Standing in the middle of the room, she looked up at the window and realized it was a bit taller than the others. Even with the ladder, Lily knew she would never be able to reach the top of the window.

She scanned the room until she saw a chair behind the door. She brought it over to the window and, juggling the fabric in one hand and the hammer and nails in the other, hiked herself up onto the seat of the chair. Standing on tiptoe, she had just begun to tack the curtains in place when she felt the chair teetering. The hammer and nails dropped from her hand as she tried to grab onto something to stop her fall. Letting out a yelp, she toppled backward.

Closing her eyes, she braced herself for a hard landing and was surprised when she found herself caught in midair.

"Lily! What on earth are you doing?"

Owen set her down on her feet. Pushing herself free, she turned to look up at him. "I'm hanging these curtains."

"You should have asked for help."

Lily's heart thumped against her rib cage. She felt the warmth from where Owen's hands had touched her. She pulled at her blouse and pushed a lock of hair off her forehead. "In case you haven't noticed, everyone is busy getting ready for Saturday." Folding her arms across her chest, she stared at him.

One thing was certain—Mrs. Cuddieback was right to be worried about him. He looked tired, and Lily thought it might have been a few days since he'd taken the time to shave. His appearance reminded her of that first day she'd met him, sitting behind his desk in that dark and dreary office. She felt a sharp pang in her chest. There was a lifelessness in him that scared her.

This was all her fault. And she had to fix what she'd done.

"Owen, can we talk?"

He gave a shake of his head. "I'll finish up here." He walked past her, picking the hammer and nails up off the floor. "Go on to your next project, Lily." He dismissed her.

Her heart sank. She knew trying to spar with him wouldn't do either of them any good. Still, she needed to find a way to prove to him that she was worthy of his love. She had to find a way to make things right.

He stood at the window, his back rigid. Lily could think of only one thing to say.

"No matter what you think, I'm not a bad person."

His only response was more silence. Lily hung her head and left him there.

Back in the hallway, she collected the last box and brought it into her bedroom. Placing it on the bed, she noticed that it looked different from the other two. This one had a thin ribbon wrapped around the outside. Curious, she untied it and lifted the lid to find a folded piece of stationery sitting on top of a layer of tissue paper.

Miss Handland, I saw you admiring the bolt of mauve silk. While this isn't exactly the same, I made this gown for a customer who decided not to take it. I think it might be a good fit for you.

The note was signed by Mrs. Fenton.

Anxious to see what lay beneath the paper, she carefully moved it aside, revealing a lovely lavender gown.

"Gracious me!"

Pulling it from the box, she admired the simple cut of the lined bodice. The small puff sleeves would be perfect for the warm weather. The bodice and waistline were trimmed with black velvet ribbon and white lace. Lily realized the material was indeed similar to the one she'd been admiring at the mercantile. She didn't deserve this kindness. As soon as she was able, she'd pay the seamstress for the gown.

Bringing the gown with her, she went to stand in front of the mirror and held the dress against herself. Sighing, she thought it might be a perfect fit. This dress was the one bright spot in what had been an otherwise dreary week. She wished she'd be able to fully enjoy the festivities, but the pall of the situation between her and Owen hung over her like a dark cloud.

Still holding the gown close, she twirled around in front of the mirror. The single moment of anticipation was lost when her gaze collided with Owen's.

Chapter Twenty-One

She'd left her bedroom door ajar. Owen thought he could simply walk past and not look in, but then he caught sight of her reflection in the mirror. She looked so pensive as she admired the dress she was holding in front of herself. The light-colored gown suited her. And then her face softened and there was a bit of a spark in her eyes, the same look that had first attracted him to her. He watched Lily turn in a circle, her motion drawing to an abrupt halt when she saw him standing in the doorway.

Whatever spark he'd seen in her eyes left her. She lowered the gown, gathering the folds loosely in her arms. She tipped her chin up a mere fraction of an inch. He couldn't decide what he saw in her at that moment. Defiance? Stubborn resolve? He felt a tug of regret at what might have been. But it was too soon to forgive and forget.

He spun on his heel, leaving her alone. Once downstairs, he locked himself in the office. He strode across the room to the windows, yanked the heavy draperies closed, pulled out the chair behind the desk, and sank into it.

Owen stayed there for some time, brooding. Mulling over what had happened between Lily and himself. Wondering how he could have misjudged her. Wondering how he could have fallen in love with a woman he knew absolutely nothing about. His head ached. His heart ached. Owen folded his arms on the desk and laid his head down.

He stayed in that position for a while, trying not to think. The doorknob rattled.

"Owen, are you in there?" Mrs. Cuddieback called out. "If you are, you best get over here and unlock this door."

"Go away!"

"I will not."

Owen grumbled. That woman could be infuriating. Pushing back the chair, he stood and let her in. She took one look at the darkened room and flew by him to open the drapes.

"I thought your brooding days were over."

He put a hand over his eyes to shield them from the blinding light. "Don't you have things you need to be doing?" he groused at her.

"What's gotten into you?" she demanded. "You *and* Miss Lily, for that matter. The both of you have been in foul moods, and I want to know why."

Owen didn't know what to say, mainly because he didn't know where to begin. He watched Mrs. Cuddieback lower herself into the chair. She looked tired. Even though they'd brought in extra help for the event, everyone had been doing double the work. He felt bad that he'd upset her. This woman had stayed by his side during his darkest time. Perhaps she did deserve to know the truth.

"I don't even know where to begin. You see, I've learned something about Lily that I never expected. She's not the woman I thought she was."

"What does that mean, exactly?"

"It means that my aunt was correct in her assessment of the woman."

"Owen, I know you love your aunt, but she has a way of making a mountain out of a molehill."

"Not this time." He wandered over to the sofa and sat. Stretching his legs out in front of him, he thrummed his fingers on the sofa arm.

"Well, be that as it may, you need to fix whatever has gone on between you and Lily."

"I'm not sure I can do that."

Lily had claimed to have told him the truth about her time as a saloon girl, but how did he know that for sure? What had her assignments been like before she'd arrived in Heartston? Perhaps what she'd done couldn't be undone.

"She's changed you, Owen. She brought you out of that darkness. You know what I think?"

He gave her a crooked smile. "I'm sure I don't, but I bet you're going to tell me."

The woman rose from the chair, wagging her finger at him. "I think the good Lord saw your need and sent Lily Handland to bring light back into your life." Then she surprised him by walking over to him and dropping a kiss on his forehead. "I know I'll find out soon enough about what's going on between the two of you. In the meantime, take my advice and think about how her being here has changed you."

The woman went back to her work and left Owen to stew in silence. She was right, of course. Lily had made him feel something, and it had felt so good after living in a dormant state for so many months. But the fact was he couldn't get past what she had done . . . he might never be able to forgive her deception.

He looked out over the room, thinking what a mess his life had become. Seeing Rebecca's framed image on the mantel had him remembering how sweet and innocent she'd been. He knew it would be dangerous to compare the two women, and yet he couldn't seem to help himself. Rebecca had been quiet and reserved. Lily was stubborn and outspoken. *And,* he thought, *brave.*

He closed his eyes, trying to remember the sound of Rebecca's voice. All he heard were Lily's confident tones. His wife's memories were fading, as if she were leaving him all over again. Owen rubbed his chest, trying to soothe the ache. He wished Lily hadn't come to the Murphy Camp.

Two days later the Murphy Camp prepared to open its doors to visitors. From the rafters to the floorboards, the house had been scrubbed. The great room had been set up with long tables laden with stacks of dishes and rows of silverware, and three punch bowls sat filled with tea and lemonade. The entire house smelled of scents both savory and sweet. Alice Cuddieback and her staff of three had been working before dawn to prepare the food.

Lily sat at her dressing table, signing her name to the note she'd finished writing in the early hours of the morning. She'd been up all night making sure the words were right, although she doubted there would ever be enough words to make up for what she'd done. She folded the paper and slid it into the envelope. With a shaky breath, she steadied her hand as she wrote Owen's name on the outside. Then she put the straight pen back in the tiny porcelain inkwell, leaned the envelope against the mirror, and tipped it just so, to be sure he would find it after she'd gone.

Bracing her hands against the top of the table, she stood. Her packed satchel sat at the foot of the bed. She'd put in only the necessities; she would send someone to fetch her trunk after she'd settled back at the boardinghouse.

Lily sniffled. *This is the only way.* Casting a longing glance around the room she'd come to think of as hers, Lily realized she was far from ready to leave. But Owen's actions over the past week had made it clear that he did not want her here. Lily tried not to think about what her future would be. She knew John would find a way to get her back into the Pinkertons.

A tremble ran along her spine. She didn't want to go back to that life, not after being here and feeling what a real home could be like. Brushing a tear from her eye, she left the bedchamber, pulling the door shut behind her.

All the entrances inside and out had been opened to allow the guests to move freely throughout the house and property. Lily wanted everyone to feel as if they belonged there. Standing at the top of the staircase, she felt proud of all that had been accomplished.

For her last day at the Murphy Camp, she'd decided to wear the lavender gown that Mrs. Fenton had been kind enough to deliver to her. And as predicted, it was a near-perfect fit. If anything needed to be fixed, she would have liked to have had the hem taken up a mere half an inch.

Careful not to trip on the hem, she lifted the skirts and descended the stairs. She looked around for Owen. He should have been here to help her greet their guests.

Just as she was about to head off to the kitchen, he walked out of the office, and her breath caught at the sight of him. He looked as handsome as ever, maybe even more so dressed in gray striped pants and a white shirt, over which he wore a walnut-colored canvas double-breasted vest.

"Good afternoon, Owen."

"Lily." He nodded.

As much as she'd hoped the tension between them would have lessened, if only for this special day, she could tell from the set of his jaw that Owen's anger toward her had not dissipated. One look at his face told her leaving was the right decision. Even so, she didn't want their problem clouding the grand opening.

"Owen, might I have a word with you in the office?"

He stepped aside to let her enter and then closed the door softly behind them.

"I'm not clear on how to proceed." She could see his confusion. "What I mean to say is, how am I supposed to act around you?"

"Lily. We will act as business partners do."

"All right. I'm to go back to calling you Mr. Murphy and you will call me Miss Handland. Is that what you truly want?"

"What I want is for this day to be a success."

Lily didn't think her heart could sink any deeper into the depths of despair, but his words sent a chill through her.

Any further discussion was cut off by the arrival of the first wagonload of people.

"I believe we need to get to work," Owen said.

He let her exit the room first and followed her to the door. Standing by her side, he smiled broadly. Cupping her elbow in his hand, he leaned in and said in her ear, "Try to look happy, Lily."

She managed a smile even though her heart was breaking. The day went by faster than any other. She concentrated on remembering every single moment; they would have to carry her a lifetime.

The first wagon carried the banker, Mr. Goodwin, along with Mrs. Fenton and her husband and several couples Lily recognized from church. For the next hour people continued to arrive. And before long, the house was filled with the sound of conversations and merriment.

Elsie Mitchell arrived in a carriage accompanied by Will Benton, John Oliver, and Amy. Lily was touched that she'd taken a day off from running the bakery.

As Elsie entered the house, Lily reached out to draw her into a hug.

"Lily! Look what you've done. This place is stunning." Elsie turned to take hold of Will's arm. "Will, don't you agree?"

"I do." He tipped his hat to Lily. "Lily, you've outdone yourself."

"Thank you." Lily wanted nothing more than to take Elsie aside and tell her what had happened. She needed a friend now more than ever. Elsie, more than anyone else, would be able to advise her on how to proceed with Owen.

The grand reopening of the Murphy Camp was soon in full swing. From the great room came the sound of piano music. Lily had hired the same young lady who'd played for Elsie's tea. People wandered from room to room, and Lily even took several groups upstairs to show off the newly renovated guest rooms. Everyone seemed impressed with the views from both the top and bottom porches.

Except for the fact that she hadn't seen Owen in a few hours, the afternoon was looking to be a success, although without him by her side, their accomplishment seemed hollow. Finally, she spotted Elsie standing off by herself in the great room with a cup of lemonade in her hand. Lily made her way through the crowd to her friend.

"Elsie, might I have a word with you?"

Elsie looked up from her cup and frowned. "Is something the matter?"

Looping her arm through Elsie's, Lily led her outside away from the throng of people, hoping that they appeared to be nothing more than two friends walking along one of the garden paths having a casual conversation. But Lily so needed someone to talk to that she'd blurted out the truth before they'd gotten far from the house. "Owen knows about my past."

Elsie pulled her to a stop. "When did this happen?"

"A week ago. I discovered him in my bedroom. He'd found my trunk, the one I used to store all my disguises in."

Elsie's violet eyes darkened with concern. "Goodness! Tell me everything."

Lily proceeded to recount the day, pausing every few minutes to regain her composure. "I'm afraid I've ruined his life, my life, and any hope we have of a future together." She stopped and took in a breath. "I've decided it would be best if I left here and moved back to Heartston."

Elsie's eyes widened. She put a hand on Lily's forearm, giving it a gentle squeeze. "I'm so sorry. You know what happened between Will and me. But we found our way back to one another. Eventually I forgave him. I hope you'll reconsider leaving here."

Lily wanted to cry, but she had a houseful of guests who were probably wondering where she'd gotten off to. "I'm not sure Owen will ever forgive me. You know, I am nothing like Rebecca. I came here with a sullied past, and even without my service to the Pinkertons, my past was less than desirable. I told him how John found me practically living in the streets of the city. I honestly thought I'd redeemed myself through the service."

Elsie embraced her, holding her firm. "You need to pray for strength and guidance. I believe the Lord sent you here for a reason. I'm not sure how my life would have ended up if you hadn't come into it."

Lily sniffled. "That is quite possibly the sweetest thing anyone has ever said to me."

"Lily, stop comparing yourself to Rebecca. Yes, she was wonderful in many ways, but so are you."

It didn't matter what Elsie told her—Lily had made up her mind. She couldn't be here with Owen, seeing him every day. She couldn't bear the pain.

Lily heard the piano music stop, and the sound of a fiddle replaced it. "Did someone bring instruments?"

"Oh. That would be the Goodwin brothers. They are wonderful fiddlers. Come back to the house with me. I know there will be dancing."

"I suppose it would appear impolite if I didn't go back."

"Yes, it would. Come on, my friend, I'll show you how to dance the jig."

Lily burst out laughing at the thought of the schoolteacher throwing her feet about in those crazy steps. It felt good to laugh. The moment of joy faded as she followed her friend into the house, knowing the memory of this celebration would have to last her forever.

From the doorway of the great room, Owen watched the couples dancing. At some point during the afternoon, the tables and furniture had been moved against the walls, creating an impromptu dance floor. He remembered how Rebecca had wanted to do this exact thing. He enjoyed seeing his friends and neighbors having such a good time. He only wished he felt like joining in.

He looked over the tops of the dancers' heads, trying to see if Lily was in the room. Eventually he spotted her standing just inside one of the doors leading to the porch. She swayed to the beat of the fiddles. Owen wished he felt like appreciating the talents of the Goodwin brothers; he hadn't danced the Virginia reel in some time.

A tap on his shoulder caught his attention, and he turned to find John Oliver standing behind him.

"I think we need to have a word."

Owen couldn't take that as a request, not when John's stern tone clearly commanded that he join him.

"Is there a place where we can talk in private?" John asked.

"We can go out to the barn," Owen replied, and John motioned for Will to follow.

The trio slipped out through the kitchen. Owen didn't have to wonder why John had summoned him. He did wonder what sort of excuse he would be offering for Lily's behavior. They walked along the dirt path that led around the back of the house, trailing along the edge of the lawn, until they reached the barn.

Owen let the two former Pinkertons enter ahead of him. Dust motes danced in the shafts of light coming through the slats of siding. The mare in a nearby stall pawed a hoof along the bedding in her paddock. No doubt, she wanted a treat. He took a sugar cube from a box on the shelf. Laying his hand flat, he let the mare take it from him.

John broke their silence. "I understand that you know about Lily."

"I do."

Will leaned his back against an empty stall door, eyeing him with interest. "You should know that without that woman, there is a possibility that Elsie would be dead."

His comment gave Owen pause.

"I found Lily acting as a sneak thief on the streets of New York," John said. "It was a dangerous way for her to survive, but that was a long time ago. She's done a lot of good, Owen."

Owen blew out a breath. "I understand all of that, I really do. But what I don't understand is how the two of you let her come out here under false pretenses."

"If it makes you feel any better, I did warn her that something like this might happen," Will said.

"One of you should have come to me with this information," Owen argued. "Then I wouldn't have . . ." His voice trailed off. He didn't even think he could say the words.

Will pushed away from the wall, finishing his sentence for him. "You wouldn't have fallen in love with her?" He gave Owen a lopsided grin. "I'm afraid we have no control over who we fall for. I couldn't live without Elsie. And if not for being a Pinkerton here on an assignment, I would never have found her."

Owen couldn't help scoffing at that. "Now you're being overly dramatic."

"I'm telling you—don't let Lily go. You need to find a way to forgive her. She had my back the entire time I was working. Can you say such a thing about anyone else you know, Owen?"

He shook his head. He'd never considered what Lily had done. He suspected that line of work could be dangerous. Still, he couldn't get past her time in the saloon. "I'm afraid I can't get over the fact that she masqueraded as a saloon girl."

"You think she did something other than serve drinks?" Will descended on Owen, pulling himself to his full height and poking a finger in his chest.

"Aside from Elsie, Lily Handland is the most virtuous woman I know. And my word on the matter should be enough to settle your worry, Owen."

Owen pushed Will's hand away, his emotions in turmoil. He did love her, and he couldn't imagine what his life would be like right now if she hadn't appeared on his doorstep. He couldn't forget that. Hearing the things these men said about her, how loyal they were to her, how quick they were to defend her honor . . . well . . . that did account for something.

Deep down, Owen realized Lily's past wasn't the only thing keeping him from moving forward.

Owen blinked and rolled to his side. Slowly, he opened his eyes, sensing a change in the air. He pushed himself up to a sitting position, listening to the sounds of the house waking up—Mrs. Cuddieback's mumbling on her way by the office, the stair tread creaking as she made her way up the stairs. After all she and Theodore had done for them this week, he was going to send them on a much-needed vacation. But first he had to make things right with Lily.

Scrubbing a hand over his face, he tossed the thin blanket aside, getting up from the sofa. Not caring that his hair was disheveled and that he'd slept in the same shirt and pants he wore yesterday, Owen ran from the room. Taking the steps two at a time, he bounded upstairs and stopped in front of Lily's room.

Strange that the door stood open.

"Mr. Owen! Come quickly!"

He crossed the threshold with long strides, stepping around the bed topped with the buttercup-colored quilt, and realized the bed hadn't been slept in.

"*No!*"

He joined Mrs. Cuddieback at Lily's dressing table, taking an envelope that bore his name out of her trembling hand.

"This can't be good." The woman's voice shook with emotion.

He tore open the envelope and pulled the folded paper out. Letting the envelope fall from his fingers, Owen started to read what Lily had written.

My dearest Owen . . .

"Out loud!" Mrs. Cuddieback urged him. "Please, Owen, I need to know where she's gotten to."

He cleared his throat. "My dearest Owen. It is with a heavy heart that I must tell you of my decision to leave and to return to the village of Heartston. I fear that my actions, that of keeping my life as a Pinkerton agent from you . . ."

A gasp came from Mrs. Cuddieback. "I *knew* she was braver than any other woman I'd ever met. She took *you* on, didn't she?"

Owen sent her a look over the top of the paper. "May I continue?" After she nodded, he read, "I fear that my actions, that of keeping my life as a Pinkerton agent from you, may have been too much for our relationship to bear. Please know it was never my intent to bring you more pain. Being here at the Murphy Camp provided me with the best days of my life. You not only gave me a sense of hope, but you also gave me a sense of home. I shall miss you. I wish you all the happiness you truly deserve. I will continue to be a business partner at the Murphy Camp, but I think it best we conduct our business from a distance. I only ask one thing of you, Owen . . ." His voice cracked.

Clenching the paper between his thumb and index finger, he read the rest in silence. *I only ask one thing of you, Owen. When you are ready, I ask for your forgiveness.*

She had signed the note simply, *Wishing you all of life's blessings, Lily.*

He crumpled the paper in his hand and tossed it onto the floor. Then he spun on his heel and ran out the door.

Chapter Twenty-Two

The bluebird sat on the wrought iron fence, singing its little heart out. Above the creature, the cloudless blue sky beckoned. A gentle breeze carried the luscious sweet scent of the pink honeysuckle that grew along the edge of the cemetery.

Lily set the satchel on the ground alongside her feet. Putting her hand on the latch, she slid the bolt open and swung the gate wide.

A bee buzzed by her ear. Though she'd seen the grave from a distance, this would be her first visit inside the fence. Her hands trembled, and she prayed she was doing the right thing.

"Dear Lord, please give me guidance and strength. You know it's been a perilous time for both Owen and me. I pray that I'm doing the right thing by coming here, and by returning to live in Heartston. Please show me the way . . ." Lily's voice trailed off as her steps faltered.

The branches of the large oak tree shaded Rebecca's grave site. Lily welcomed the coolness. She knelt, laying her hand on the headstone. She let her fingers trail over the carved letters. She'd never done anything like this before. Being here on Owen's sacred ground was her last hope.

"Rebecca." She spoke the woman's name in a whisper. "I need to know what to do. Owen loved you so much that when you died, a part of him died, too. I used to watch him visit you from the window of the room I once rented here." Lily knew it made no difference; still, she pointed over her shoulder as if Rebecca were here with her.

She looked back at the headstone. Her voice growing weaker, she said, "You see, I love your husband with all my heart." A tear fell from her eye. "And I'm afraid I've done something . . . unforgivable. I wish you could tell me what to do to make this right."

Covering her face with her hands, Lily sobbed. She cried for her lost childhood, she cried for Rebecca, she cried until she didn't think she could shed another tear.

She heard the snap of a twig and the rolling of a pebble out from underneath the sole of a shoe. She didn't need to turn around to know that he'd come.

But when a hand gripped her upper arm, pulling her off the ground, she let out a surprised yelp.

She looked up at the tall, burly man and gasped. The lumberjack from the saloon.

He smelled of stale cigar smoke and sour beer. Her stomach heaved. She swallowed down the bile.

"I know who you are. You're that serving girl."

She tried to tug her arm free, but he pressed his fingers into her flesh, causing her to cry out again in pain. She swatted at him with her free hand, but her attempt at escape only made him laugh.

"You are a feisty one."

"Let me go!" She attempted to kick him in the shins, but her foot got caught up in her skirts. "Oof!" she grunted in frustration, then elbowed him hard in the ribs.

He let out a laugh. "Is that the best you got?"

Doing the one thing she knew would help, she began to shout.

"Let me go! Help! Help! Someone help!"

In the next instant, the man was lying facedown at her feet. And in his place stood the only man she'd ever loved.

"Owen! Oh, thank God." She flung herself into his arms.

He took her face in his warm hands and kissed her soundly on the mouth. "Are you all right?"

She nodded, tears flowing down her face once more.

"I thought I'd lost you." He pulled her close to his chest. "After I'd read your note—I thought I'd lost you forever."

The lumberjack moaned and rolled over.

Over Owen's shoulder Lily saw John running across the street. He hurried into the cemetery. "Owen, Lily! Are you two all right?" He stopped when he got to them and looked down at the man lying on the ground. "I thought I told you to hightail it out of town!"

The man rolled to his knees and stood. His eyes widened when he realized he was outnumbered. John tried to grab for him, but the man took off running.

"I don't think we'll be seeing him again," John said.

Lily let out a nervous laugh.

"I'll leave you to Owen's care." John winked at them and then left them alone.

Owen took her hands in his. The warmth of his touch spread through her, making her whole.

"Lily, please don't leave me," Owen said in a husky voice. He rubbed the pad of his thumb over the tender spot on the palm of her hand. "These past few days have been hard on both of us," he acknowledged.

He cupped her cheek and turned her head so she was looking straight into his eyes. When she saw his pain, she gasped.

"Oh, Owen. I'm so sorry for what I've done. I thought I could leave my past behind and start fresh." She nodded toward the disappearing figure of the lumberjack. "It seems I was mistaken." Her voice cracked. "I've been wrong about so many things."

"You were right about one thing," he said.

"What's that?"

"You were right to stay here in Heartston." He paused and then said, "Lily, I'm sorry, too, for the way I hurt you."

He brought his mouth to hers and kissed her. "I can't do this"—he gestured to Rebecca's grave—"I can't keep looking for something that's no longer here. I need to let her go, so I can let you into my life."

"Owen, I don't want you to ever forget Rebecca. I understand how important she was to you."

"The Lord sent you to me for a reason."

She nodded. "And because of the decisions I made, I nearly lost you. I really made a mess of things, didn't I?"

"No. It wasn't all you. I haven't been the easiest man to get along with."

"Owen. My life . . . before I met you . . . I didn't have any other choice. I need you to understand that."

"I do now. John and Will set me straight last night."

"You talked to them about us?"

"They didn't give me much choice in the matter." He grinned.

"If you're not ready for us, I'll understand."

"Lily, I've been ready since the day you came into my life." Gathering her in his arms, he pulled her close to him.

Laying her head against his chest, she listened to his heart, feeling his love in each beat.

"I've been carrying the guilt over Rebecca's death around like some sort of shield. It kept me from moving on with my life. I was holed up in my dark office for a very long time."

She tilted her head back so she could see him.

He gave her a wry smile. "If not for you, I'd still be there."

Lily swallowed. "I never had a home. All I wanted was to find a place to call home. When I came to Heartston and saw how beautiful it was, I knew I wanted to stay. After the last assignment with Will, I went to John and told him I had fulfilled my duty. He let me sign my discharge papers. Then I went to the bank, and Mr. Goodwin told me about your plight. The minute I saw you and your Murphy Camp . . ." Her voice broke.

"You found your home." Owen kissed her. "I love you, Lily."

"Oh, Owen, I love you, too."

He released her, took her hand in his, and as he led her out of the cemetery, he said, "Let's go home."

Chapter Twenty-Three

Two months later . . .

Lily sat behind the desk in the office, looking at the registration ledger. When she saw they were booked all the way through the following fall, she gave herself a little round of applause. Then she turned the chair to face the window. The green leaves on the oak and maple trees were just beginning to change color. The afternoon sunlight filtered through the branches, dusting the tips of the leaves where the tinge of orange and yellow was just starting to show up. Along the back edge of the property, she caught sight of the magnificent maple tree with the branches spread out over the gazebo. That spot had already proven to be a popular resting place for their guests. In a few weeks the leaves would be ablaze with a vibrant red.

She nibbled on her lower lip. Behind the gazebo was a project she'd been working on for the past few months—a surprise for her husband. She and Owen had gotten married two weeks ago. They'd enjoyed a very quiet ceremony, right here in front of the fireplace. Elsie, Will,

Amy, John, and the Cuddiebacks had been in attendance. It had been the most glorious day of her life.

The office door opened, and Lily turned to see her husband approaching her. His dark hair skimmed along the edge of his blue chambray shirt collar. Owen's eyes glinted as he gave her a sly grin.

"Good afternoon, Wife."

She gave him a wide smile. "Good afternoon, Husband."

"I have a surprise for you." Owen had his hands behind his back, hiding her gift.

Lily sprang from the chair, going to him. "What is it?"

"A wedding present." He kissed her on the tip of her nose. Taking his arms from behind his back, he presented her with a box. There was a lovely red ribbon wrapped around it, neatly tied off in a bow.

Lily took the box from him. "I love presents!" Returning to the desk, she set it down and yanked at the ribbon, freeing it from the box. Lifting the lid, she gasped. Inside the box lay their new stationery.

Centered on the top of the cream-colored paper was an image of their Great Camp, and underneath that three lines were inscribed:

MURPHY CAMP, HEARTSTON, NY
LILY AND OWEN MURPHY, PROPRIETORS
YOU ARE ALWAYS AT HOME HERE.

"Owen! This is beautiful." She spun around to kiss him soundly on the lips. "I have something for you, too." Her stomach fluttered again, only this time she felt a bit nervous, wondering how Owen would receive her gift. She took hold of his hand. "Come on. We have to go outside."

Hand in hand they made their way through the kitchen, exiting into the backyard. Lily led him down the pathway and stopped in front of the gazebo. The area was surrounded by a new flower garden, one she and Mr. Cuddieback had planted over the summer. Though the blooms on the daisies and Queen Anne's lace were sparse now, next year at this time the soil would fill in with color as the new plants spread out.

"The garden is coming along," Owen said.

"Yes, it is. I have some ideas on how to expand it next year. Mr. Cuddieback has given me some bulbs that need to be planted at the end of this season." Lily squeezed Owen's hand. "I have something for you."

She brought him around to the far side of the gazebo. There on the ground was a raised square block covered with a dark cloth. Turning to her husband, she said, "Would you like to do the honors?"

"What's this all about?" He raised an eyebrow.

"Lift the covering, Owen. Please." Lily's heart started to pound.

Owen bent and picked up the cloth, revealing a bronze plaque. He read the inscription aloud. "Rebecca's Garden. May all who enter here find peace."

Owen's eyes glistened as his gaze found her again. "Lily." His voice came out in a whisper. He gathered her in his arms. "You didn't have to do this."

"Yes. I did."

"Have I told you lately how much I love you?"

She nodded. "But you can tell me over and over again."

Acknowledgments

There is a lot of behind-the-scenes help that goes into making a small idea grow into a great book. I can't thank the crew at Waterfall Press enough. From my editor, Sheryl Zajechowski, the rest of my editorial team, artwork, marketing, and to my author reps, you are the best people to work with!

I owe a tremendous debt of gratitude to my fabulous and patient agent Michelle Grajkowski of 3 Seas Literary Agency. Thank you! Thank you! Thank you!

To my friends and family: I don't how you all put up with my antics when I'm under deadline stress, but I'm glad you do . . . And lastly, I couldn't do any of this without the love and support of my husband, TJ.

If you are interested in learning more about my books, I invite you to visit my Amazon Author Page at www.amazon.com/Tracey-J.-Lyons/e/B001JSC7CQ, or my website, www.traceylyons.com.

Author's Note

When I came up with the idea for Lily and Owen's story, I knew it had to take place at an Adirondack Great Camp. Imagine a time when people would travel from faraway places to hike the many trails or lounge on a porch in one of the famed Adirondack chairs. The intricate, grand structures of the Great Camps are part of the unique landscape and history that make up the Adirondack Mountains of upstate New York.

The Great Camps were built during the latter part of the nineteenth century. One of the most famous ones, still in existence, is the Great Camp Sagamore located in Raquette Lake, New York.

To learn more about these camps visit http://greatcampsagamore. org/ or the Adirondack Museum website at https://www.theadkx.org/.

About the Author

Photo © 2016 Joel Danto, Dano Photography

Tracey J. Lyons is the author of many historical romance novels, including the Women of Surprise series. A 2107 National Excellence in Romance Fiction Award finalist, Tracey is an Amazon Top Ten bestselling historical romance author. She is a member of Romance Writers of America, American Christian Fiction Writers, and Novelists, Inc. Her books have been translated into several languages, and she has appeared on the award-winning Cox cable television show *Page One*. Tracey lives with her family in Orange County, New York. When not busy writing, she enjoys making her husband crazy with renovation projects at their 1860s home. Visit Tracey's website at www.traceylyons.com.